LOVING THE RODEO QUEEN

LOVE OVERSHADOWS
BOOK ONE

REBECCA REED

For my family.

ACKNOWLEDGMENTS

This story is a culmination of over ten years of actively pursuing writing with the desire for publication. It wouldn't exist without the combined encouragement and support of my family and my writing friends, or the slow process God has put me through to prepare me for this moment.

By name, I'd like to acknowledge some of my biggest supporters. My daughter, Sierra, a constant source of inspiration and the one who helped brainstorm, edit, and proofread this novel. My son, Terrance, who supplies me with MacBooks because he believes in my writing and my dreams. My husband, Brad, who defends my work when others tell me it isn't good enough. My Huddle and Novel Academy friends, who pray for and support me daily. My editor, Shyla Wenzel, who made me rethink my motivations and convinced me to rearrange my odd sentence structures. Rebecca Yauger, Suzanne Montgomery, Mary Beth Dolmanet, Susan Misey Anderson, ACFW and especially the members of the Indiana Chapter for their teaching, encouragement, and critiquing of my writing so I could learn and grow my craft. My students and staff at West Central for their belief in my writing and the time off to pursue it. Kyle Whitaker, Montana State University Rodeo Coach, who graciously answered my many questions about his program, facilities, and other things rodeo. I hope I've represented Bobcat Rodeo in a positive light.

Many thanks to Susan May Warren and Sunrise Publishing for introducing me to so many wonderful writers.

Without them, I'd never have met the lovely and talented Kate Angelo who invited me to her Discord channel where I met even more talented writers. Finally, a huge thanks to Lisa Phillips for believing I was worth the risk as a new author.

I'm blessed to have Jesus walking beside me on this journey. All the glory to Him while any mistakes within are solely mine. I trust in his wisdom and timing. I pray each of you, my reader friends, pursues your passion and experiences joy in every sunrise. ¡Que te vaya con Dios!

CHAPTER 1

"I'll bet this place gets loud." Tiago Vargas hooked his thumbs in his front jeans pockets and turned in a circle, head tilted back to view the eight thousand-plus seats of Montana State University's Brick Breeden Fieldhouse.

Coach McCloud chuckled. "You could say that. But if you like an uproar, you should be in Bobcat Stadium when the rodeo team leads the football players in. Talk about a stampede."

Tiago caught the twinkle in the coach's eye as they moved across the arena. Coach's sharp wit reminded Tiago of his father. He liked the man who was maybe double his own twenty-four years. Probably more than he should considering how on-the-fence he was about this hasty road trip to Montana.

"You all set on that application?"

"It's already submitted, but to be honest, Coach McCloud, I've no idea what area I'd study to pursue a graduate degree."

He'd come to Bozeman following his Argentine-immigrant father's insistence he "find his *pasión*" because a certain ebony-haired, gray-eyed rodeo star who'd once called him her hero had lived here two years ago. Tiago scuffed his boot along the smooth surface of the basketball court.

Above, beams and rigging crisscrossed the domed ceiling, suspending darkened scoreboards and shadowed banners. Tiago's skin prickled, and he battled the urge to run. From the arena. From the coach. Maybe from himself. His chest struggled to rise as if his overactive heart clutched his lungs in a tight grip.

A hand clapped him on the back. "Let's get out of here before your ghosts latch on."

McCloud propelled him up a stairway onto the wide apron crowded with closed vendor stalls. Tiago exhaled when they pushed through glass doors to emerge in a land-scaped entrance. Late-morning sunlight touched his skin with calming warmth. He sought the blue expanse overhead populated with stringy clouds and took a full breath for the first time in over a minute.

"You okay?" The coach adjusted his Stetson and met his gaze with an assessing eye.

Tiago nodded. "I am now. Not sure what happened in there."

The man pursed his lips, rippling his blonde moustache. "I imagine you're a bit overwhelmed with the changes you're contemplating. Bozeman's a long way from Nashville."

The rodeo coach moved away from the building, and Tiago fell into step, absorbing the beauty surrounding him. Not only the buildings and green spots on campus, but the ethereal backdrop of mountains in three directions brought him closer to the Creator somehow——something he desperately needed.

"Tiago, I've found it best to get all the unbalancing done at once."

"Sir?"

The man released another throaty chuckle. The warm sound eased Tiago's clenching gut.

"I'd like to offer you a job, providing you're accepted into one of the graduate programs here at MSU."

"A job? Doing what, exactly?"

Coach paused beneath a young tree and faced Tiago. "I need a graduate assistant to help with recruiting and training. Probably a few more responsibilities once the season starts. If you're interested, I'll have a benefit package drawn up. Nothing too fancy, but it'd keep you in grub and boots."

Tiago's mouth hardened into a thin line. "My father called."

"It's not like that, though my dad knows yours. Best Argentinean food in Tennessee. The wife and I eat at Casa Vargas whenever we're in town, which isn't often. 'Bout once or twice a year to visit my uncle's tribe." Coach McCloud shook his head. "I've been looking to hire someone, but no candidate with your qualifications has applied. The business degree's worth a lot, but your rodeo know-how is exactly what this program needs."

The words rocked Tiago, and only years of practice kept his voice steady. "Thank you, sir. I'll keep your offer in mind."

The coach stretched out his hand. Tiago hesitated mid-grasp. "Sir?"

"Call me Chet or Coach."

"All right. Coach, I'd hoped to say hello to Quinn Mulroney. I noticed she wasn't with the team at the CNFR this past week. Know where I might find her?" His chest tightened. What if his whim was only a wild goose chase?

Coach smoothed his mustache in a habitual gesture. "Well, now. She's around but not in rodeo. Took a year off and didn't come back. Never said why. Sold both her horses. If you find her, give her a message from me. There's a spot and scholarship waiting with her name on 'em."

Once more Tiago's facade hid his spinning mind. Quit rodeo? Sold her horses? She'd been badly beaten that day two years ago, but to walk away from her talent and the sport she loved made no sense.

"Why don't I arrange a tour of the boarding facilities most rodeo athletes use for tomorrow? You'll want to bring your horse, right?"

Tiago nodded, still reeling from the news about Quinn.

"Sam Gallagher's the manager. I'll let him know you're coming out sometime in the morning." Coach passed Tiago a card. "This has the address. He'll be there at sunrise, but you go whenever you like. I'll be waiting to hear your thoughts. Pleasure to meet you." With another firm handshake, Coach McCloud left Tiago alone.

Tiago stared at the polished toes of his best boots. He should give up this craziness and go home. What had he been thinking? That he could catch hold of a two-year-old memory? Even if he managed to find the woman who'd hijacked his dreams, she'd likely made more of an impression on him than he'd made on her. After all, except for one meeting when she'd been dazed and bruised, they'd only ever connected across an open arena through air clogged with the dust of her calf-tying or roping prowess.

Maybe he'd imagined their connection. He'd been one face amongst hundreds. Doubtful she'd even seen him—merely looked in his direction.

But he couldn't forget the intensity in her eyes—a mixture of joy and triumph—heady and intoxicating. Alluring. Like her words the night he'd literally stumbled over her in the dark recesses surrounding the stock pens. Then, after he'd driven her to the emergency room, she'd repeated them even as she'd denied his insistence to escort her inside and refused to see him the next day.

"You're my hero."

They haunted him. Mocked him. Captivated him.

His future as his father's business partner may have crumbled to dust, but it wouldn't matter if he could be Quinn's hero. That hope wouldn't let him abandon his search until he found her and proved whether their relationship was a figment of his imagination.

She was still around, so he couldn't leave. Not yet. He turned the card over.

"Logan and Marshond Rodeo Facility: boarding, training, practice areas and stock"

It listed an address south of the city.

Best get some lunch then find a room. He might be here awhile. The thought brought a smile, and Tiago's heart did a little prance.

U

"Giddy-up, giddy-up, giddy-up, whoooa." Quinn's knee bounced to the rhythm of her words. On the "whoooa" she leaned the little girl backward toward her chest and tucked noisy kisses into the toddler's neck to her giggling delight.

"Gin. Gin. Or-sey."

Quinn laughed, but stood, bringing the curly-haired girl with her. "Mommy's already done the horsey too many times. I'll be late for work."

The little mouth puckered into a frown. "A-gin." A fist closed on Quinn's nearly-black braid where it trailed over her shoulder and shook it like a rein. Freckled arms plucked the diaper-clad child from Quinn's chest and suspended her until Quinn freed her locks from the chubby brown fingers and stepped out of reach.

Missy bounced the baby, tossed her into the air, and spun her to fit against a hip, her arm pale in contrast to Reina's honeyed skin. She sent Quinn a pensive look. "I don't know why you let them schedule you to work so much. At least one day should be for family."

They'd never spent a whole day as a family, even when Quinn was little. She wasn't sure Missy knew what family was. Quinn restrained her thoughts with a quiet prayer. She inhaled and counted to five before answering. "Everyone else is away or sick. I'm their only choice."

Her heart softened. She'd never seen her mother so happy as when the baby was in her arms. Maybe Missy was changing. "I'm glad you're here for Reina. It's easier to leave her with family."

Missy's smile radiated warmth toward the child who squirmed to be let down. "She's a joy, and it's your turn to achieve your dreams. Cal and Jesus gave me more than I ever thought I could have. Much more than I deserved."

Quinn bit off her denial. Reina trundled to the ratty recliner, pulled herself onto the seat, and waved her arms up and down, babbling, then saying, "Ma-ma. Or-sey. Go."

Despite Quinn using Missy and Cal rather than Mom and Dad growing up, Missy had taught Reina to say Mama and GeeGee when referring to Quinn and herself. Quinn didn't recall ever having a conversation about this oddity, only that she'd cried the first time she heard the title. Missy had joined her, confusing Quinn even more. Were they celebrating or mourning? She'd never quite made up her mind.

Missy cocked an eyebrow and set a hand on her hip. "Definitely *your* daughter."

A strangled sound escaped Quinn's mouth. *Breathe. It's past. You're in control.*

She stepped away, grabbing her bag off the table. "Barring emergencies, I'll be home by five."

"We'll be here." Missy's voice trailed her out the door.

Cal's truck coughed like an old man before the engine caught and chugged Quinn out of the short drive. Turning toward the highway, she eased down on the gas. When money grew tight following Cal's sudden death last February, selling her newer Ford Fiesta had made sense. In truth, that sale had been much easier than the ones six months later of her beloved horses, especially Delilah. Thinking of the black mare she'd trained was still enough to close her throat around a knot of grief.

If only the money had lasted longer. Missy had shooed her past the landlord's overdue rent notice two days ago.

Her tumultuous thoughts blinded her to the beauty of the fifteen-minute drive south of town to the newer vet clinic where she worked. No sooner had she pulled into the gravel drive when her cell vibrated in her bag. She parked and dug it out, checking the name on the screen.

Polly.

Goose pimples rose on Quinn's bare arms. *Please, not an emergency.* Instead of answering, she rushed from the truck and inside the neat, blue-sided building. "I'm here." She let the door slam, sliding to a halt before the effervescent office manager.

"You're a lifesaver, Quinn."

Polly's blonde ponytail bobbed as she spun to her phone and tapped the blinking red hold button. "Our veterinary assistant will be there in fifteen minutes. Thank you for your understanding. Miss Marshond's mare is in good hands, I assure you."

Minutes later, Quinn exited the office of Two Sister's Veterinary, her violent shiver more from the mention of Genevieve Marshond than the breeze infused with livestock musk and Montana's unique open scent. The mid-June morning promised pleasant dry heat. A few wispy clouds broke up the sky's blue expanse, leveling her emotions. She reached Doc Liza's top-of-the-line Silverado, Two Sister's logo in silver on the midnight blue door, and climbed in, tossing the bag from her truck into the passenger seat.

The roar of power at the turn of the key contrasted with the feeble chug Cal's––her––Ranger managed. At least the compact truck had a backseat for Reina and enough clearance to navigate basic winter snows. Quinn nosed the cab toward the edge of the city. The familiar route roused a stinging ache she clamped down. Her mind couldn't go there because her rodeo days were over.

She focused on the hay fields and green stretching up the leading edges of the nearby Spanish Peaks. Navigating the route required no thought, leaving her mind to swirl through all the reasons she was venturing out here alone instead of with either of the twin vets who'd opened Two Sisters a mere three years ago after earning their doctorates of veterinary medicine through the WIMU Regional Program.

They'd both had successful rodeo careers at MSU-Northern in Havre, Montana, but had fallen in love with the Gallatin Valley and decided to found their practice outside Bozeman. At the moment, however, Liza was down with a persistent flu bug, and Macie honeymooned in Italy. Each of the two techs had family gatherings.

That left only Quinn when a frantic Sam Gallagher, the boarding facility's manager, called saying Genevieve Marshond's horse had hurt itself.

Nerves tore at Quinn's stomach as the tires whirred over the pavement, drawing her closer to a situation she wasn't at all sure she could handle on her own. It wasn't only the charged emotions between her and the Marshonds due to their forced purchase of Delilah––the best of Quinn's former mounts––when the board money ran out, but also that she hadn't even completed her undergrad degree, let alone qualifications for any sort of veterinary license.

Rodeo Queen Quinn would have jumped at this chance to

prove herself, but toddler-mom Quinn was more reserved and careful. Not as prone to stampeding off half-cocked with more courage than thought.

The fields parted to reveal a vast complex of barns, pens, and pastures of various sizes, and a smaller white office labeled, "Logan and Marshond Rodeo Facility."

Ahead, near the barn where many of MSU's rodeo team members boarded their horses, a slender figure in a black Stetson cowboy hat waved her forward. Quinn frowned as the truck bumped over the cattle guard spanning the drive between sturdy wooden gates, not recognizing the gorgeous blonde until the truck came to a stop.

They'd met once, but never competed together since the girl had joined the team the year Quinn took off to have Reina. Thanks to Missy's breakfast time rodeo updates, Quinn knew the cowgirl had made an immediate splash, qualifying for the College National Finals Rodeo her first year and winning barrel-racing gold a few days ago as a sophomore.

Quinn flung the Silverado's door wide and jumped out, wincing as it slammed. *Get a grip!*

This wasn't her first emergency call, and it wouldn't be her last. She retrieved the general-purpose bag from the main storage compartment and faced the girl bouncing on her toes.

"What happened?" The name clicked. "Rhiann, right?"

The girl nodded, long hair caught in the breeze. "Delilah spooked after unloading and caught a corner of the barn as she made the turn. Left a pretty big gash in her shoulder."

Quinn had to clench her jaw to keep from accusing Genevieve of foul play. Her horse was high-energy but well-mannered. However, Delilah was no longer Quinn's, and Quinn had no right to question or accuse. "Show me."

Rhiann eyed her before setting off at a quick clip.

Was that recognition or had the girl noticed the controlled set to Quinn's jaw? She followed the petite figure to the entrance where a squat cowboy with a huge cream Stetson blocked the door. If she were a dog, she might have bared her teeth. As it was, the hairs on her nape stood up.

The man looked her up and down, a sneer twisting his sculpted features. "You still hanging around? I thought you'd hightailed it north to Shelby or whatever backwater you rode in from."

"Rude, Blayden." Rhiann turned her back on the steer wrestler to speak to Quinn. "I'm sorry about Delilah. If I'd known the men were unloading her, I'd have stepped in."

"Crazy horse nearly took you out."

Rhiann scowled and patted his shoulder as one might placate a child. "Why don't you get the car?"

With a sniff, he strode toward a low-slung vehicle parked apart from the others.

Rhiann took Quinn's hand. "Genevieve wasn't even here."

With Rhiann's swift rise through the ranks, some team members, despite their comradery, likely resented her quick success. Quinn had experienced the same thing, and the pair would probably have connected had Quinn remained with the team.

"I can guess how hard parting with Delilah was for you. I wanted you to know, it wasn't the mare's fault. Go fix her." Rhiann squeezed Quinn's hand, then jogged after Blayden.

Why would someone as beautiful, talented, and compassionate as Rhiann hang with that loser? Maybe if Quinn hadn't quit . . . *Don't go there.*

She entered the skylighted barn. Several people crowded the entrance to the second stall on the right. The tallest among them glanced her direction.

"Quinn!" The man's frown flipped to a welcoming smile. He broke free of the onlookers and charged toward her like the raging bulls he rode as part of MSU's rodeo team. His movement shifted everyone's attention toward Quinn, and in the group was a face Quinn had never expected to see again. She had no time to acknowledge that haunting smile as her former teammate loomed.

"Morning, Chantz." She sidestepped like a matador, tucking her med bag close to her body as if it could protect her from his enthusiastic lift and swing.

He released her and boomed a laugh, opening the frequently mended hole where she stuffed the dreams from her former life. His large hand gripped her shoulder and squeezed, a comforting gesture, full of comradery and friendship that left a bittersweet taste on her tongue.

A short man burst out of the stall, his bulk scattering the younger onlookers. Orange hair ringed his balding head and matched the fire in his eyes. "Where's that--" He stopped short when he sighted Quinn in her scrub top embroidered with the Two Sister's logo. "Thank God."

Quinn stepped out of Chantz's grip toward the red-faced manager. "Where is she, Sam?"

He eyed her for a fraction of a second before gesturing into the stall behind him. A barn helper held the lead of a sleek, black animal. Froth covered the mare's chest where a gash as long as Quinn's hand fed rivulets of blood pooling on the pine bedding.

Horror froze her in the doorway. *Lord, help!* She breathed the words, her mind shoving them skyward. She couldn't manage more.

In another breath, her training took over. She'd studied basic wound care her freshman year and practiced sutures on suture pads. But first, she needed to soothe the mare. Delilah had always been a handful--high-strung, nervous, considered fractious by the breeder who'd sold Quinn the horse as a yearling.

Taking a few seconds to breathe, Quinn reined in her own heightened emotions until her pulse slowed, then she stepped toward Delilah with an outstretched palm. "Hey girl. It's me. How've you been? I hear you ran into something. Were you being a sassy pants?"

Quinn continued to croon as she inched closer, half of her brain surprised by the easy inclusion of toddler talk in her vocabulary, the other monitoring the mare's eyes. When the white band grew, she paused her approach but not her lulling words. As soon as the eyes softened, she again crept forward.

Sam remained in the doorway, his concern searing a spot between her shoulder blades.

At last, her fingers grazed the velvety muzzle. Quinn allowed Delilah a moment to sniff and remember, then stroked the place where the only spot of white spilled into the left nostril, turning baby-girl pink. Quinn swallowed against the sudden constricting in her throat.

When the words stopped, Delilah's head bobbed upward. The handler yanked on her lead, sending the mare into full rebellion. She snorted and thrashed, fresh blood cascading down the leg. Stepping away, Quinn fished a vial and syringe from her bag. She drew the required dosage and slid closer to the horse, avoiding the pawing hoof on the non-injured leg. With a deft hand, she injected the sedative into the horse's neck, rubbing the spot to alleviate the needle's prick and the sting of the drug, then sent an annoyed glare at the handler.

"Sam, would you mind her head?" Quinn couldn't afford an impatient worker sabotaging Delilah's drug-induced calm.

The men switched places, an unusual amount of disquiet in Sam's normally unflappable expression. Delilah's head drooped nearly to the straw as the sedative took effect.

"You might have to steady her a little, but she shouldn't go down." Quinn placed sterile non-stick pads on the wound and applied pressure to staunch the blood. The mare flinched. "Sorry, girl."

How much blood had she lost? Quinn lifted the mare's lip and pressed on the gums. They were slow to return to pink, indicating dehydration.

"She arrived from Wyoming today, right?"

Chantz answered from behind her. "My horse and Genny's pair rode with Jack's gelding on the way home. The storm last night shook them up a bit. They were a mite jittery when we unloaded this morning."

Quinn nodded rather than say something regrettable, like how everyone on the team, especially Genevieve, knew Delilah was a basket case during storms. She readied supplies to clean and suture the wound. When she turned to hand Chantz the tray, another man stood in his place. A man whose serious, dark eyes rocked her back on her heels and dropped her stomach to the stall floor.

He grasped the tray, removing it from her shaking hands. His touch grazed her fingers, the zing jolting her from her stupor. The tentative upward curl of his lips pulled the breath from her chest. She gasped to regain a flow of oxygen.

Delilah swayed. Her head jerked, then settled, bottom lip dangling.

Quinn blinked to refocus her thoughts, then set to work. An inner timer, much like the one she'd used to target a steer's hind legs, ticked the moments until the sedative wore off. She clipped dried skin and closed the wound with tiny stitches, doing her best to prevent an unsightly scar, but certain a hairless line would forever mark the spot.

Delilah had steadied--eyes regaining their shine and focus--by the time Quinn dressed the wound and administered antibiotics. She hugged the mare who'd been her best friend, stroking her muzzle and scratching her throatlatch.

The horse stretched her head forward, opening to Quinn's fingers.

"I miss you girl." Quinn glanced about, but only Delilah's twitching ears seemed to have heard. A soft whoosh of air--what Quinn had always referred to as a "breath of affection"--ruffled the escaped strands from Quinn's braid and warmed her insides. Delilah shared this gift with Quinn the first day they'd met in the pasture, and regardless of stubbornness or differences of opinion, it remained a bond between them--unbroken, apparently, by Quinn's betrayal.

Quinn returned the breath, then forced her feet to back away. She bent to gather the satchel, but it wasn't there. Everyone had cleared out of the stall once she'd begun tending the wound except Sam and Tiago, Chantz's dark-eyed stand-in, who'd aided her during the entire procedure.

Tiago's presence sent a quiver through Quinn's belly. She hadn't thought about him since Reina was born. Not much anyway. Not like her obsession with him after she'd returned home from the CNFR two years ago. Every time she'd been tempted to search for his contact information, she'd reminded herself he didn't need her problems. The reminders had worked.

But now, here he was, toting her equipment to the truck. She pursed her lips and moved to follow only to be halted by someone clearing his throat behind her.

She spun, worry clouding her mind for the barest moment before Sam's face came into focus. He cocked one eyebrow when she continued to stare. Then it dawned on her. *She* was in charge. Responsible for care instructions, billing, and all the details normally handled by the vet.

Ten minutes later, she hurried toward the Silverado to find Tiago speaking on the radio. Maybe the guy had spent a lot of his time rescuing her, but who did he think he was?

She rushed her steps ready to read him the riot act. There was such a thing as too comfortable.

When he swiveled to face her, the set of his mouth stopped her cold and snuffed all hint of ire from her body.

"What's happened?"

Tiago held out the radio. "She can explain while we drive."

Quinn furrowed her brows but closed the gap and accepted the radio. "You're not going anywhere with me."

He nodded. "Right. I'll follow in my truck." He strode away. Shaking her head, she thumbed the radio. "Polly?"

"Get over to the Dunn's place right away. Speed if you can. Their best mare has been in labor for twenty minutes already with nothing to show for it."

"Labor? But I--"

"You're her only hope, Quinn. Get over there." The fear in Polly's voice bled through the radio and prompted Quinn to slide into the driver's seat and buckle up.

"On my way." She started the engine.

Polly's sigh blasted through the radio, and Quinn could picture the short, curvy woman in her oversized headset, pacing the small office while twisting the wedding band around her finger. "I'm sorry, Quinn. This is a lot to ask, but there's no one else. Besides, despite your lack of formal training, both docs say you have excellent instincts."

Quinn scooped up the praise like water in a drought, turned left out of the drive and motored towards the towering peaks. The Dunns' ranch bordered the rodeo facility, but in Montana, that meant little. Acres of land stood between her and the laboring mare. She gunned the engine, speeding along the two-lane highway. Another truck tailed her, with the cowboy at the wheel posing yet another concern.

His story could wait. She had a foal to save.

How could one woman unravel his emotions and tangle them into unrecognizable knots in less than thirty minutes? Tiago tried without much success to settle the excitement clenching his chest in a vise. He was no giddy schoolboy. He was a college graduate with a business degree. They hadn't seen each other in two years. Even then, they hadn't been close. Once, he'd been in the right place at the right time. Any other guy would have done the same thing.

But would they have involved themselves in an obviously criminal situation?

He had no regrets; other than Queen—*stop using her nick-name*—hadn't let him see her again. Leaving Wyoming without saying goodbye had always bothered him, but they'd been barely acquainted competitors from different rodeo teams before he blundered into her that night near the stock pens. He couldn't blame her for restricting access after the vicious beating she'd suffered.

Had it been more?

His mind pressed into the familiar question. Her clothes had been intact. Dirty and disheveled, but intact. Plus, she'd never hinted at anything more. She'd have told him, wouldn't she?

The truck slowed and careened onto a gravel road, where a red arrow pointed to "Dunn's Dunhorse Ranch". The mare's situation must be urgent for Quinn to make the drive in less than five minutes.

He gunned the motor to keep up with the vet truck, admiring Quinn's handling of the large vehicle on gravel. Having the bed outfitted with all those storage compartments likely made it unresponsive. Two minutes later, she made another quick right, then stopped before an old-fashioned red barn. He parked beside the Silverado and killed the engine.

A girl's frantic voice called, "Quinn! Over here."

She was a bit young to be an employee. Perhaps one of the daughters? Tiago unbuckled and opened his door as Quinn jumped out, flung open a compartment, and grabbed a satchel. She sprinted after the girl toward the smaller, more modern barn that fronted several others spread out behind it along with a panorama of round pens and paddocks. If this was a family operation, they had quite a spread. Beyond the paddocks, numerous horses grazed in pastures that stretched into the foothills of the Spanish Peaks.

Racing to catch up to Quinn, Tiago admired her slim figure clad in boots, work jeans, and a dark blue scrub top. Her sleek hair reminded him of the mare she'd just sewn up. That horse had seemed familiar.

"Hurry up!"

His smile widened. Perhaps Quinn did want him along, after all.

He followed her through a walk-in door. Ahead, the teenager's rigid stance projected anxiety and fear through the bars of one of four large box stalls bracketing the well-lit aisle. An office occupied the farthest corner. Closed overhead doors anchored each end.

Tiago glanced at Quinn, who met his gaze, then jerked away. Had her chin quivered? Odd, his memories painted her as bold--even overly brash. The Arena Queen. This hesitancy was new but not altogether unwelcome. He thought to lend comfort but paused, unsure how she'd interpret his touch. The memory of holding her strong, battered body as she cried into his neck had awakened him more than once over the past two years. He shook it free.

Quinn squared her shoulders, catching his eye and lifting her chin toward the stricken girl. He nodded and together they approached. Twin pony tails jerked with each movement of the girl's hunched shoulders.

Beyond the half-open stall door, a man with graying hair in coveralls and rubber boots squatted in the straw beside a round-bellied mare whose color was only a few shades darker than the bedding. Her legs jutted from her body, each ending in black points, like his mother's Siamese cat. Tiago's heart thumped. Were they too late? Was she already dead?

The mare blew out an enormous breath. The contraction stiffening her limbs released and they thudded to the floor. Her wrapped tail flopped as a spasm wracked her, rippling across her hide from tail to head. A low moan escaped, drawn out and desperate.

Quinn joined the man, murmuring as she approached and laid her hand gently on the mare's abdomen. He consulted a gold wristwatch and grimaced, tilting it so Quinn could see. Her gaze stole toward the tail. She eased closer to view the foal's progress.

Quinn's widened eyes told Tiago what he couldn't see due to the mare's orientation and had him clenching the doorframe.

The man stroked the sweat-dampened neck, his voice

croaking despite the enormous swallow that spasmed his Adam's apple. "You must save her. Lady is the most valuable horse we own. Last of her bloodline."

"I'll do all I can, Mr. Dunn." Quinn's voice emerged breathy and uncertain.

The man gripped the strands of black mane in his fist. "Save her even if you have to sacrifice the foal."

Quinn froze, her stricken expression so unlike the dauntless competitor he'd witnessed in the arena. After a disquieting minute, where the two faced off over the mare's body, Tiago took one step forward and pitched his voice low. "What can I do, Quinn?"

His words focused her eyes. She licked her lips and pulled in a huge breath just as the mare's belly grew taught.

"We've got to get her up and walking. This foal's presenting upside down."

The older man frowned. Nodded.

The girl ran off, returning with a soft rope which she clipped to the mare's halter and tugged gently. She clucked her tongue. "Come on, Lady. You heard the doc. Get up!"

Quinn stared, mouth open. Then her jaw snapped closed. She crossed to Tiago. Her changed attitude charged the air, crackled in her clipped, calm words. "Find the antiseptic scrub and a jar of palpation lubricant. Bring them here with a bucket of water. I have to turn that foal." She paused and eyed him. Her inner fire brought out the green always lurking in her gray irises and nearly melted him. "I may need your muscle. You good with that?"

The Rodeo Queen was back. "Aye-aye, ma'am." He flashed her a grin and strode out of the barn with as much dignity as his wobbly knees would grant him. Two years ago, she'd had the power to steal his strength from across the arena when she found him in the crowd after tying a goat or when she smiled at him after flicking her rope from the heels of a steer.

Tiago stopped short at the truck and scratched his head. Which of the dozens of compartments held the items she needed? He flung open doors.

Perhaps she hadn't been looking for him in the crowd back then, but it had certainly felt like it. And oh, how he'd wanted her to. The belief she'd purposely sought him out seemed foolish when he scrutinized it.

Where was this stuff? He grimaced and kept searching.

At the CNFR, Quinn had been top cowgirl in two events while he barely qualified in one. They attended universities thousands of miles apart that never competed head-to-head. Why would she want anything to do with him? How would she even know he existed?

He wrenched open the next drawer, revealing lubricant and a box of gloves. Then located the scrub and a water hose inside the largest compartment. Filling a small plastic bucket, he gathered up the other items and raced to the barn, considering it a success when only a third of the water sloshed onto his jeans. But would she view it the same way?

If he couldn't meet his own family's expectations, how would he measure up in the eyes of a champion like her?

The large overhead door opened to reveal the pony-tailed girl coaxing the mare outside. Each step seemed to sap the strength of both girl and horse. Sweat dripped from each of them, the horse's umber hide sporting a damp patchwork. Flared nostrils revealed their pink lining, and the pungent odor of fluids almost forced him to retreat.

Trailing the horse, Quinn gestured as she spoke with Mr. Dunn. Tiago marveled at her intensity and confidence. What had initiated the change? She lifted her gaze to him and a lump lodged in his throat. He held up the items she'd requested, and she flashed him a smile, then refocused on Dunn who gave her a grave nod. She returned the gesture.

The day's heat seemed to intensify as she approached

Tiago, relieved him of the antiseptic, then squirted it on her hands and forearms.

She tilted the nozzle towards him. "You too."

He held out his arms then mimicked her rubbing motions. What had he gotten himself into?

She observed with a critical eye. Nodded.

Tiago glanced at the mare and swallowed. Two tiny hooves protruded from her vulva, the bottoms facing the sky. "How do we . . .?"

"I'll show you. Come on."

If Tiago had known what he'd signed up for, he would have balked, but after fifteen minutes of unbelievably-intense maneuvering, the foal stood suckling greedily beside the exhausted mare. Amazement expanded within Tiago. The solid warmth of Quinn beside him ignited another emotion inside. One he hadn't experienced in many years. He wanted to grab Quinn around the waist and celebrate their success, but he held himself in check, sensing the distance he'd create if he acted on his desire.

Mr. Dunn had linked arms with his daughter. Smiles split both their faces.

"Keep an eye on Lady, Mr. Dunn. If she shows any signs of abdominal swelling or colic like pain, call Two Sisters right away. There's always the possibility of complications in a dystocian birth."

Quinn's label cut through Tiago's euphoria, reducing it to gut-wrenching regret. The conversation he'd overheard when he was eight blasted his brain, searing his memories with his mother's pain and his father's accusation.

A touch interrupted Tiago's spiraling thoughts. He flinched, then regretted the involuntary reaction as something flashed across Quinn's expression. She withdrew her hand, motioning him out of the stall. As soon as they'd cleared the barn, he attempted to explain. "Quinn, I'm--"

She snatched the empty bucket and beelined her truck, back straight and head high.

Way to blow it. He hurried to catch up, toting the other supplies. Stopping beside her, he lowered his voice. "It's not what you think."

She cocked her head, hand on a hip. "Oh? Tell me, what do I think?"

He sputtered, brain scrambling for a reply that didn't make him seem like a presumptuous creep. He couldn't very well admit he'd come to Montana to find her, and now that he had, he had no idea what to do next. Or that his own dystocian birth had ruined his parents' dreams for a big family. He grasped at the only thing he could think of. "I met with Coach McCloud today."

Her eyes widened, then narrowed. She busied herself cleaning the supplies and replacing them in their spots. "Oh?" Her nonchalance was overshadowed by the tight set of her jaw and her stiff movements.

It hadn't been the reaction he'd expected, though by now, he should expect her to prove him a fool. Her complexity and bravado might turn others off. Many a cowboy had commented on Quinn's aloofness, writing her off as 'Queen Mu-loner'. But he guessed past her walls he'd find a kindred spirit, someone who might actually understand him. That hope drew him closer.

CHAPTER 3

Why had her cowboy come to Montana? Was it presumptuous to call Tiago hers after a few long-distance connections and one horrific face-to-face encounter? If only wishes became reality.

Quinn squinted into the first rays of the sun, coffee cup in hand as soft sleeping sounds emanated from her daughter's crib. She intended to buy her a big girl bed, but other demands on her money always seemed to take precedence. Like food and rent.

Heaving a sigh, Quinn padded from the living room. Her sleep had been riddled with unsettling dreams, sending her to the predawn kitchen to make coffee. She warmed her brew, then sat at the well-used oakwood table, the only thing Missy had brought from their home in Shelby after Cal's funeral.

She pictured Cal in the chair across from her, showing her how to clean and polish saddles and bridles, walking her through the arm and wrist movements to swing the rope, explaining how to time the steer's strides and toss her loop at the exact moment to ensnare both back legs. Cal was the secret behind her rodeo prowess. Not only because he taught her the technical things, but also because he stayed up at night encouraging her when she failed. Talking her down from teen angst and warning against excessive pride.

Now he was gone. Because of her. An exaggeration, she knew. Cal had made no secret about his weak heart or his missing hand. Rather than hobbling him, his struggles granted humility and an ability to live life fully each day--until he hadn't.

Quinn's chest drew down on her lungs like the loop on a steer's horns. Even after seventeen months, she wasn't used to having only memories of the man who'd been her father in all ways but one. Once she'd asked if her babies might be born like him.

He'd shaken his head. *"Don't let that worry you,"* he'd said and given her the biggest hug. When she pulled away, there'd been a tear in his eye. At seven, she hadn't understood. Missy finally came clean the day of Cal's funeral, though Cal had trusted Quinn with the truth years earlier.

Reina babbled on the edge of waking. Such a good baby.

"You were never content to play with your toes." Missy tip-toed from the room she shared with Reina and crossed to the coffeepot. She poured the dark brew into her favorite smiley face mug, added cream, then sat in her seat and peered past the gauzy kitchen curtains. "You were only happy outdoors--a bit of a problem since we lived in northern Montana." She took a sip, cradling the mug in both hands.

Quinn's lips curved upward. "I know. You had to bundle me up, sit me in the bathtub, and bring snow inside so I would stop screaming." She sent Missy a raised eyebrow. "Sounds like you spoiled me."

Missy laughed, rolling her eyes. "You *were* spoiled. Cal

couldn't deny you anything. I tried to keep a lid on it, but you had him hooked good."

"Remember Bully Bobby Brack?"

"I seem to remember Cal ransoming you from the principal's office."

"Only because Bobby said Cal wasn't my real daddy. I started crying, but he wouldn't stop taunting me."

Missy focused on her coffee as if it held a secret. "Surprised him, though, when you didn't run away."

Quinn huffed. "I marched up to Bobby and punched him in the stomach, then stomped on his foot. I still remember his howls. That's when Cal first called me Queen." She leaned against the counter, thinking. Of the fight, Cal's rescue, and the aftermath when she'd confronted Missy with Bobby's accusations.

Reina's babbling grew louder, the word "out" quite distinct among the nonsense sounds. Missy and Quinn moved at the same moment. Their eyes met.

Quinn deferred with a tilt of her head toward the counter. "I'll make more coffee. It's early."

Missy nodded, but Quinn didn't miss the question edging her features. A similar question dug into Quinn's own heart, but habit shoved it down. "You go. Reina loves her GeeGee." Her Rodeo Queen mask served her well as she crossed to the coffeemaker with confidence that hid her percolating turmoil.

Cal had insisted winning in the arena was only partially due to one's skill. The rest depended on disrupting the mindset of one's competitors while guarding your own.

Quinn's shield was rock-solid due to Cal's coaching and her practice against the various "Bobbys" she'd encountered.

As she measured the coffee and added water, Quinn allowed childhood memories to surface--something she hadn't done since Cal's passing. Cal, not Missy, had come for her whenever she awoke with a nightmare or called out in the mornings for help. Cal had tucked her in at night and read to her, or any number of things moms might generally do for their children.

How much had Missy's less-is-more parenting method affected Quinn's relationship with Reina? The pot gurgled and coffee trickled into the carafe. Quinn stared at the dark liquid wishing it held answers. She needed to be more of a mother to Reina but didn't know how. She felt inadequate, terrified she'd mess up. Being around the toddler meant relinquishing control. Easier to let Missy fill in than take the risk. Especially when her brash arrogance in pushing the boundaries of God's promises had initiated their current path, which at any moment could nosedive.

She loved Reina with a fierceness she hadn't known possible until touching her baby's skin, her nose, her fingers and toes. Her reasons for fighting to keep the child remained murky. Made more so by Cal's death mere moments after holding the newborn for the first time. In the vacuum of his loss, as during the interminable months of her pregnancy, she wished she'd let someone else in.

Often she'd thought of Tiago. The concern and kindness in his dark eyes had comforted her dreams. Many times, she'd relived the feel of his strong arms guiding her to his truck. His outdoor, hardworking aroma in the cab, his calm voice anchoring her while he drove her to the hospital. The moments with him were more real than the events preceding his arrival. She thanked God for that fact every day.

Had God brought him back to her?

Maybe it wasn't true, but she could pray, ask God to help her figure it out. Perhaps, if given the chance, she wouldn't push him away this time. Anticipation pricked her stomach.

Two sets of footsteps neared the kitchen. She inhaled. In a perfect world, she could have her dreams. But this was far from a perfect world, and she was reminded every day in the sweet, innocent face of her daughter whom she'd sworn to protect, regardless of her own heart's longings.

Tiago loved Tennessee's mountains, but Bozeman's views beat those from home. He balanced the chair against white vinyl siding on his tiny second-floor motel balcony. His still-groggy eyes squinted at the pink and yellow streaks advancing above the range. His boots rested on the balcony's railing. Coffee steamed in the morning breeze flowing off the not-too-distant peaks.

The mountains here were more chiseled. They screamed rugged beauty and danger, the iconic idea of the West rather than the softer majesty of the mist-shrouded Smokies. They tugged at a place deep inside––a place he wasn't ready to visit.

He dropped his feet to the concrete, the chair thumping forward. His phone taunted him from the small table, as it had all yesterday while he'd passed a lazy Wednesday driving Bozeman's streets and some scenic routes outside the city. He should call his parents. Discuss his options. Gain their insights. Pride kept him from picking up the device. Hadn't his father already given Tiago his thoughts? The words returned in a rush, tightening his grip on the cup.

"Find your passion, hijito. *Don't settle for my dreams when you haven't explored your own."*

His mother, too, had encouraged him to follow his heart and find the Lord's path. *"He has great works planned for you. Be brave and seek them."*

While his head believed they had his best interests in mind, his heart picked out their dissatisfaction with him as a son. *Leave us to ourselves. Stop being a coward.*

Tiago set down the cooled coffee and swiped up the phone, navigating to Coach McCloud's number. He stared at it until the screen went black.

Words composed themselves in his mind. He hadn't called on God for a long time. The practice of prayer, ingrained from childhood, had slipped away as he'd grown—not from conscious decision but from disuse. Tiago swallowed and raised his eyes to the mountaintops in the distance.

Lord, is this the path for me?

No whispers or sense of an answer came. His mom often said, "*Sometimes God waits on people to step toward Him before he illuminates the way.*" Was God waiting on Tiago's move? It seemed unlikely, but what did he have to lose?

His thumb tapped the screen, and he hit send before he could change his mind. Put it on speaker.

"McCloud here." The voice sounded confident but unassuming. Tiago liked that combination.

"Coach, it's Tiago Vargas."

"Have you considered my offer?"

Down to business. No wonder he and his father got along. "I have."

"And?"

"I'd like to meet. Tell you in person. If you can spare the time, sir." Was he being too presumptuous? His father always advised meeting face-to-face. Had even flown back to Argentina to negotiate contracts for beef with the ranchers who produced it rather than make over-the-phone deals. Tiago's business professors had emphasized the advantage of at minimum screen-to-screen communication.

Coach chuckled. "Perfect. My assistant coach and I are at the rodeo office doing a bit of season's end wrap-up. We could meet with you in an hour."

"I'll be there."

"Park at the Fieldhouse's north entrance and come up to the second floor."

"Thank you."

"Dori and I will see you soon."

Huh. Tiago ended the call and sat tapping his leg for several minutes. He'd watched Dori Walstra win Cowgirl of the Year a year ago. Every performance solid. He was nowhere near her caliber. What had prompted them to consider him as an assistant? Was his name the only reason? The thought sickened his empty stomach.

If they were only hiring him on his family's credentials, he'd drive on down the road. He didn't know where he'd go, but he refused to remain in his father's shadow. He'd spent his entire rodeo career battling that specter. No more.

"I'm trying, here, Lord." Had it been too long?

Tiago's gaze rose from his clasped hands to where the sky brightened. Each star winked out against the onslaught of light, until the sun burst above the rocky crags, banishing the valley's shadow. Was this God's answer? It seemed too simple, likely his imagination mixing with desperation.

Tiago blew out a breath, then pushed to his feet, glancing at the time.

Twenty minutes? Already? He had barely enough time to shower and dress. Quinn's ebony braid came to mind as he laid out his best black shirt. The thin silver striping reminded him of the Two Sisters' Veterinary logo on the truck and scrubs. What had made Quinn quit rodeo? He pondered the question as hot water streamed over his road-weary body.

More than anything he hoped he'd have the opportunity to find out.

CHAPTER 4

Tiago parked beside an SUV and a red, sporty something in the thirty-minute space outside Brick Breeden. This part of MSU's campus appeared deserted. He took one last long inhale, then slid from the truck and clicked the locks.

At one minute early, he knocked on the frame beside the half-opened door marked "Rodeo Office."

"Enter."

Again, the warmth and depth of the coach's voice inspired confidence. Tiago pushed through to find McCloud standing at one of three desks anchoring separate walls. The fourth wall hosted two large windows; blinds raised to let in natural light. Framed photographs of MSU rodeo teams graced the walls along with several plaques denoting team honors.

A woman rose from the desk along the far wall, her dark-blonde hair pulled into a single ponytail. Her Bobcat Rodeo t-shirt, faded jeans, and boots matched McCloud's t-shirt and jeans making Tiago feel overdressed.

"Allow me to introduce my assistant, Coach Walstra."

"Call me Dori."

Tiago stepped forward to accept her outstretched hand and welcoming grin. "I'm not sure we've met, but I watched you annihilate your competition last year at the CNFR."

She nodded. "My final shot. I was determined not to leave anything undone."

"And then, I recruited her as my assistant." Coach McCloud winked conspiratorially at Tiago. "Best move I've made so far. She's as good at teaching as she is at doing. Not everybody is, you know."

Tiago nodded, more to himself than the coaches. "Not sure how good I'd be at teaching. To tell the truth, I wasn't much good at doing, either. Which brings me to one reason I wanted to meet." He found first McCloud's, then Dori's gazes.

"Let's sit down. Coffee or water?" Coach crossed to the corner between his and Dori's desks where a partially-full coffeepot sat with a small covered bowl, a stack of Styrofoam cups and some plastic stirrers atop a mini-fridge.

"Water please."

McCloud grabbed three waters and pushed his assistant's chair to the center of the room.

From behind him, Dori rolled the unused chair toward Tiago. "May as well try it out." She grinned, then accepted a water bottle and flopped into her seat.

Tiago caught the bottle tossed his way and sat, braced as if the padded seat were a throne, and he might be recognized as an imposter at any moment.

Dori chuckled. "'Fraid it'll turn into a rattlesnake?"

"Maybe." Tiago met her laughter with a straight face. Inside, his stomach roiled. He would never fit amidst the confidence and comradery of this pair. He'd been accused of being too serious--intense at times--never companionable.

Dori raised her brows, then slapped her hand down on

her chair arm with such force, Tiago jumped. "I like him. He's perfect."

Tiago sucked in a breath trying to slow his erratic heartbeat. Good thing he'd worn the black shirt to conceal his sweaty armpits.

"I knew you'd think so." Coach turned to Tiago. "You had some concerns?"

"I . . . yes." Tiago stilled his tapping fingers. "Sir, why me? There must be any number of more qualified people out there for this position." He forced his shoulders back, spine straight like Dad had taught him. *"Maintain your machismo,"* his dad would say.

Coach met him with an appraising look. "To be honest, we've never had a graduate assistant in the rodeo program before. We weren't even considering it until your father called mine, and mine called me about you."

Exactly what he'd feared. He steeled himself to turn the position down.

"But when we did a little digging and discovered your business degree plus your rodeo experience, we decided you might be exactly what we need to keep this program at the top."

Tiago cocked his head. "How so?"

Dori leaned forward hands on her knees. "We need someone who can balance us, analyze each competitor's strengths and weaknesses and make quantifiable judgments, both on the recruiting end and during the competition phases."

"We need another hand to help with the greenhorns, too."

Dori wrinkled her nose at Coach's statement. "That's the truth. It seems no matter how much rodeo some of them do before they get here, they spaz out when they hit our practice arena and again at their first competition. Forget all they know."

"Then we've got to talk 'em down from the top rail and get 'em sane enough not to hurt themselves in their events. We contacted some of your former teammates, and every one said you were calm under pressure—in control no matter how tough things got. Even when confronted by bullies."

Tiago's head jerked up. Was this about the meanspirited prank his rodeo friends had pulled on Oddball Elvis, or the time he'd convinced his cousin to back down? Definitely not the time he'd slammed his fist into cousin Phillip's mouth for the lewd things he'd said about Quinn.

Dori tucked one leg under her on the chair. "We need what you've got, but don't think you're getting an easy desk job. You'll be in the thick of it every day. Analyzing, learning, teaching. Plus being responsible for whatever classes and research project you take on."

"Can you handle that, Santiago Vargas? Or should we keep looking?"

Tiago blinked. His mouth opened, then closed. He looked between the two until a smile grew on his lips. "You two are good. You should be coaches or something."

Dori burst into a fit of laughter while Coach guffawed. "Is that a yes? I have financials if you'd like to see them first."

Tiago shook his head. "As long as I can afford to live here on the money you plan to pay me, I'm in."

Coach passed him a folder. "It's not your father's salary, but you won't need to eat ramen."

Tiago took the offer and gave it a quick once-over. "A lot of this is scholarship money."

"Yep. Better get busy on that application." Dori had recovered and lounged in her chair, playing with the end of her ponytail.

"Good thing it's already submitted." Tiago paused, thinking of the email he'd gotten yesterday. "And accepted."

Dori shook her head. "You got me again." But her smirk said she didn't care.

"I've got two jobs for you if you're ready to hit the ground running." Coach shuffled through some folders on his desk and handed Tiago three.

Dori's feet hit the floor, her expression shifting to what Tiago recognized as her "game face." He suppressed the urge to fidget by opening the first folder. In large font "Abelardo Alliegro Ruiz" occupied the top of the first page. Tiago lifted a brow at Coach McCloud, then returned his attention to the information: a long list of high school rodeo achievements followed by a short list of fights Abelardo had initiated and others in which he'd participated.

Tiago closed the folder and shrugged. "What does this have to do with me?"

Dori pointed her chin at the next folder. "Read on. You'll see."

The second folder displayed the name "Yoani Alliegro Ruiz" and a similar list of accomplishments minus the brawling. The next page contained a high school transcript with passing grades. Nothing earthshattering. Then a small note on the back of the transcript––accepted: UT @ Martin. He returned to Abelardo's folder. His transcript showed higher grades, mostly As and Bs, and on the back––rejected: UT @ Martin. Followed by another scrawled message. *Said they'd prefer to be together.*

He closed the files, and tapped the edges on his leg, an absentminded motion that helped him organize his thoughts.

Coach and Dori simply watched and waited without pushing, and he catalogued that fact in the back of his brain for later. "You want me to recruit them?" Tiago sent a skeptical look at each coach.

Coach smoothed his moustache before answering. "I declined at first because of the boy's brawling, but Dori reminded me some of the best cowboys have brought tempers from high school and gone on to learn control both in and out of the arena." He gave Tiago a chagrined look. "I was one. Your father another."

Tiago's spine snapped taut. "No way. My father is one of the most controlled people I've ever met."

"I'd agree. Now. But according to my father, yours wasn't always that way. He got in so many fights his freshman year, they almost kicked him off the rodeo team despite his record wins."

"You're kidding." Maybe the struggle to control himself wasn't as alien as he'd thought.

Dori shook her head. "My research shows during the fall season, he was in a fight or some kind of trouble at every venue." She tipped her head at Coach. "Him too."

Coach nodded. "I only learned to change my ways after I broke three bones in my hand. Anyway, Dori doesn't want to count the cowboy out until we can assess whether he's worth the risk. The cowgirl, Yoani, seems the better gamble as far as rodeo is concerned, but our program is built on kids who not only win us championships but also remain eligible. She's not as strong academically."

"We want you to go to Tennessee and interview them. Evaluate their talent, discover what makes them tick, and analyze the data. Bring us back a recommendation." Dori raised a hand, palm up. "What do you say?"

Tiago's head spun. Nothing like throwing the new guy into the fire. "I'll need more data about your program before I dive into this kind of assignment."

Coach stood and clapped a hand on Tiago's shoulder. "We'll make sure you get properly acquainted before you go. Since I doubt you brought your horse or gear with you on this exploratory venture, you can get paid for a trip you'd be making anyway."

"Sounds reasonable. When would I leave?"

Dori rose and returned her chair to her desk. "A week here should give you the lay of the land and familiarize you well enough with MSU rodeo to tell if the Alliegro twins would fit in."

"In the meantime, we've got another assignment for you. The third folder has all we have on Quinn Mulroney. We need her back in our program, and we want you to try to convince her to return."

"Me?"

"You wanted to find her. Some personal stake?"

Coach's expression didn't seem mocking, only sincere.

"I did. I do." Good thing Tiago had taken after his Argentinean side in skin tone because the heat raging up his neck would have turned his mother the color of a ripe tomato. Something his father's teasing invoked with regularity, and a source of embarrassment growing up. A little of that school boy resurfaced, feelings all jumbled at the mention of one girl's name.

But Quinn was no girl and unlike any other woman he'd met.

If pursuing her on behalf of the rodeo program was his in, Tiago would take it. A plan began to form. He covered his tumultuous thoughts by leafing through Quinn's folder. Stellar performances, top grades, success at her fingertips. What had happened in the moments before he'd found her in the dark recesses of the Casper, Wyoming stock pens that had knocked her so far from her original trajectory?

He tapped a finger on her photo in the MSU team vest and a black Stetson, eyes bright with hope and a future. Could he help return that sparkle to her eyes? He looked up and found curiosity on both coaches' faces.

Grinning, he asked, "What do you think of this idea?"

CHAPTER 5

Quinn drove the vet truck away from the boarding facility after checking on Delilah, swiping at her eyes. She'd chanced bringing the mare's favorite treat, Oreo cookies. Genevieve's smirk and self-important extolling of the health risks of feeding her horse cookies looped in her memory. Before, Quinn could ignore her. Now, she risked her job and family's security.

She'd examined the wound while Delilah lipped every tasty morsel and breathed sweet cookie breath into Quinn's hair. There'd been no signs of infection, but the plaintive look in Delilah's eyes as Quinn exited the stall had nearly done her in.

Quinn's cell rang through the truck's speakers on her way to Dunhorse. She glanced at the display. Thumbing the button to answer, she pushed cheer into her voice. "What's up, Polly?"

"A Tiago Vargas called a few minutes ago. Said he was looking for you. That name ring a bell?"

Breath whooshed out like she'd been punched. Tiago?

Looking for her? She slowed the truck, trying to get a grip on the thoughts rushing through her head.

"Quinn, you still there?"

"Uh huh. Did he say what he wanted?" She had to pull herself together before Polly figured out how much the mention of Tiago's name unraveled her.

"Said he helped you with a couple calls Saturday and wanted to know how they were recovering?"

Polly's tone relayed how lacking she found this explanation, but relief surged through Quinn. He was a caring guy. She'd experienced his compassion firsthand. Of course he'd ask about the horses they'd treated. His interest wasn't in her. The relief grew an edge that didn't seem as welcome as she'd originally hoped. The silence grew until Quinn realized Polly was likely posed with a hand on her hip above a tapping foot.

"I'm heading to the Dunn's now. He could meet me if he wants to check on the foal himself." Quinn palmed her forehead. Was she a glutton for punishment? Why invite him into her proximity? She'd thought Reina's arrival had conquered her propensity to storm ahead without thinking. Apparently, it had merely gone dormant.

Polly was speaking. "--patch him through to your phone and you can tell him yourself."

Before Quinn could argue, Polly had her on hold. Quinn sucked a long breath through her nose. She exhaled through pursed lips, then pulled back onto the road. When had she stopped, anyway? With a shake of her head, she focused forward. Maybe he'd be busy.

Seconds later, an incoming call lit the truck's screen. *Stay calm. Think before you speak.* "Hello?"

"Quinn, glad I got hold of you."

The smooth texture of Tiago's voice melted Quinn like butter over oven-fresh bread, reminding her how safe and cared for she'd been in his arms. The rest of the conversation blurred, but whatever she'd said, five minutes later, the greatest threat to her self-control since the attack stood within touching distance--not that she wanted to touch him.

Liar. The voice feathered upward from the deep well of tamped-down emotions created long ago. Her skin grew clammy. If only she'd told him she'd endured more than a beating. Hadn't let him think he'd scared the men away when they'd left her for dead minutes or even hours before. Told him how she'd awakened and struggled to her feet. How she'd refastened her clothing before he'd arrived. Denied the truth.

"The little guy looks good." Genuine concern colored Tiago's voice and dragged Quinn from the danger lurking within.

Quinn nodded, trying not to look at the handsome cowboy beside her, but failing. His smile turned his eyes an interesting shade of gold she'd never noticed before. It sent a shiver through her middle. "Momma, too."

The foal cavorted around his sedate mother in a small paddock. His fuzzy baby coat hinted he'd carry the dark streaks at the withers and upper forearm of a dun-colored animal, the farm's premier product.

"Do you still have your roping horse?" Quinn remembered Tiago competing in team roping her final year on the circuit. "Header, right?"

An odd look--surprise, maybe--crossed Tiago's face before he answered. "He's hanging around his boarding stable getting fat near my parents' place in Tennessee."

"Good."

"What?"

She hadn't meant to vocalize her bitterness, but the loss of her horses still had the power to take her down. Worse than the incident that had spun her life out of control two years ago. At least she'd had a hero show up and rescue her from that nightmare. His solid presence stood beside her. Rendered her legs insubstantial. What thoughts hid behind those eyes?

She grasped the top rail with both hands to focus her attention elsewhere. "I just meant it's good he had somewhere to go after your career ended." *Please don't let me hyperventilate.*

"Would you like to go see him?"

Had she heard him right?

"Quinn!" Mr. Dunn hurried toward them from the path leading to the house. "Bart said you were here. I hoped I'd catch you." His quick breaths made the words jerky and oddly spaced.

Quinn switched to vet mode. "They're both doing well, Mr. Dunn. I see no signs of infection or damage. Of course, when Doc Liza recovers from the flu, I'd recommend you have her check them."

He faced the paddock, his bald patch reflecting the sun, and mopped his brow. The mare nibbled grass while the colt flopped down for a nap. "Looks like they're enjoying the heat, but it's a bit much for me. Quinn, could I trouble you for a few minutes alone? I have an idea I'd like to run by you."

She gripped the rail tighter, fighting for calm. "Uh, sure." She prayed her limbs would cooperate and pushed off in his wake. As if drawn, she peered over her shoulder. Tiago sent her a smile that might have been reassuring if it had reached his eyes.

Mr. Dunn led her to an office set up in the old-fashioned red barn. Ceiling fans circulated air around the lofted space. Hundreds of photos decorated each wall, ranging from what looked like original daguerreotypes to black-and-white prints to color shots. Printed captions depicted the history of the Dunn family and their horses. Quinn's jaw quivered.

What must it be like to know so much about your ancestors? Quinn knew nothing about hers. From the beginning of her memory, there'd only been her and Missy and Cal.

"Never abandon those you love." Cal's words haunted her from the grave.

"Water or coffee?" Mr. Dunn asked.

She shook her head while her mind accused Cal. *Didn't you?*

Mr. Dunn poured himself coffee and indicated a lounge area with several chairs and a colorful braided rug. A large window let in natural light.

They sat opposite each other, Quinn becoming more unsettled with each moment. Too bad she'd turned down the drink.

"I'm sure you're wondering why you're here." Mr. Dunn chuckled self-consciously. "You see, we recently lost our foaling manager. That's why everything was in such a tither when you came yesterday. I don't normally handle that sort of thing, but with my two eldest off scouting horses to buy and my son more of a car guy, I was up a creek in a leaky rowboat as they say."

Quinn had never heard anyone say that but kept her expression bland. What was he getting at? She could apply another cliché here about beating bushes.

"We need someone like you." Mr. Dunn's lips curved upward, an expectant look on his round face.

"Well, Mr. Dunn, I'll be glad to come whenever you need me. Just call Two Sis––"

"Oh, no. You misunderstand. I mean to hire you to be Dunhorse Ranch's new foaling manager."

"You want to . . . hire me? As a foaling manager?" She

sounded like a parrot. "Sir, I'm still in school. I don't have the qualifications for such a job. It's very generous, but--"

He cut her off a second time. "We'll make it worthwhile. There are online training classes. We'd pay for them, of course." He held out an envelope. "Look over this offer. Take a few days to think. Then, give me a call and let me know your decision. My card's inside."

Quinn accepted the envelope and stood, following the man's example. She hadn't felt this off-kilter since she'd discovered she was pregnant. Again, her rodeo training shored her up. They shook hands, and Mr. Dunn escorted her to the door, opening it for her and sending her off with a wave and a smile. What a strange turn of events.

God, is this my answer? She didn't sense any hint or nudge one way or the other, except Tiago still stood at the paddock rail, eyes glued to the path she'd taken.

He pushed off when she neared, striding toward her. His strong gait brought an odd yearning to feel his arms around her. For pity's sake, why couldn't she get over that? Over him? His scent hit her next, a mixture of sunshine and baby horse. Enough to make her light-headed after the confusion of Mr. Dunn. "He offered me a job."

Tiago's step faltered then corrected itself. "After the miracle you performed, I'm not surprised."

She stood in front of him now, close enough to touch if she reached out her hand. She resisted the urge to do just that. "You're . . . not?"

The curls at his nape jostled with his head shake. "Of course not. You're gifted. You'll make a fabulous vet. You already do."

His praise lifted her like Cal's used to. Reminded her who she was and what she'd set out to do. She tilted her head. "Maybe you're right."

"I am right. No doubts."

"Huh."

"What's that for?"

She didn't recognize the wistful quality in her voice. "I'd almost forgotten." Goals. Dreams. They belonged in her past--her *before*. Even the summer class Missy had insisted she take was extravagant, straining their finances. Oh, she'd loved Missy's lofty declarations, had missed learning. But life was about hard truths. Dollars and cents. And the numbers inside that envelope could go a long way towards covering her obligations.

She slid a nail beneath the flap.

Tiago stilled her motions with a gentle hand. "Before you open that, could we get some lunch? I'm starving, and I'm pretty sure your stomach growled earlier too."

Quinn fought her shifting equilibrium to force a wry smile. "Heard that, did you?" She extracted her hand and dug her phone from her pocket. "Nearly one. Let me check in, then we can head to town."

During the silent walk to her truck, his quiet strength seemed to invade her consciousness. A quick chat with Polly confirmed no emergencies loomed, and her next appointment was a young goat the owner was bringing to the office at three.

"Why don't I follow you to Two Sisters? I've been wanting to try some local food. Maybe you can recommend a good restaurant, and we can ride together?"

"There's a fantastic diner not far away if you like American fare."

"Sounds good." His hesitation had her leaning toward him. "Could you do me a favor?"

She righted herself, teeth catching her lip. "I guess."

"Promise not to open that offer until we get to wherever we're eating?"

"Why?"

"Mr. Dunn beat me to the punch, so to speak."

"He what?"

"I have a proposal too. I'm asking you to hear me out before you see his bottom line. Will you humor me?"

Confusion and worry pushed Quinn to refuse, but the pleading in Tiago's dark eyes dissolved her resistance. "I'll wait, but you have to do something."

Arched eyebrows rose above chiseled cheekbones. "I'm willing."

She swallowed the thrill his words induced, shoving the envelope toward him. "Hold this."

His grin ignited the gold in his eyes, and his fingers brushed fire over hers as he accepted her offering.

Her heart fluttered wildly, but she climbed into the truck and grasped the wheel as he closed her door. She turned the key with trembling fingers. What was happening to her? She couldn't fall for him, though the deliciousness of that idea filled her with a rush of pleasure.

He wouldn't understand. About her choices. About Reina. Quinn had sworn to protect her child. Determined to intercept bad men and bullies. Deflect pity. If she had to move away and start a new life, she would for Reina's sake.

It didn't work for Missy. People still found out.

Her Arena Queen persona would banish the thought with a growl. But Quinn's mind felt weak. And while Quinn had deliberately distanced herself from Queen's brash actions and spontaneous thrill-seeking, sometimes she wished she could meld the two parts of herself.

By the time Quinn pulled into Two Sisters, she'd tamped down the most troubling of her thoughts and emotions. Her heart beat a semi-normal counterpoint to the jet-engine rumble her stomach produced.

Channeling Queen's bravery, she ran to Tiago's open truck window before he could get out. "Let's go to Kelsey's

Diner. They have the best patty melts you've ever had. And malts." She closed her eyes and swallowed as if already tasting the goodness.

He laughed and swung his arm in invitation. "Your chariot awaits, milady."

Quinn slid onto the luxurious leather and buckled up, a buzzing anticipation flowing through her veins. "Take a left, go two miles, then take another left. We're about ten minutes away."

The envelope lay unopened in the center, teasing her. Numbers with zeros behind them nagged her thoughts. Could she afford to turn down a steady income for . . . what exactly? She knew virtually nothing about this man.

"You live in a nice neighborhood."

Tiagos's words hit like snowballs to the face. Fear and anger battled beneath her icy mask. She barely managed to squeeze words between her clenched jaws. "You've been to my house?"

He sent her a slant-browed glance. "I . . . yes." Caution tinged his voice. "I tried calling, but you didn't answer, so I swung by the address Coach McCloud gave me. Your--"

"Coach McCloud? What does he have to do with this?" Her heart restarted at twice it's normal rhythm. Had he spoken with Missy? Seen Reina? Too bad running wasn't an option.

Tiago blew out a breath and tapped the steering wheel, slowing to make the left she'd pointed out. "I'm bungling this."

"Bungling what? What's going on?" Her voice had risen in both volume and pitch. She scrunched against the door and pushed her eyes forward. Forcing calm into her voice, she pointed. "Turn right at that warehouse, go two blocks then take another left. The diner's lot will be on the right."

Quinn's hunger had fled. What if he discovered the

truth? Would his admiration shrivel when he discovered her stupidity? What if he rejected her, or worse, Reina? The idea of Tiago despising her added force to her already roiling stomach. She gulped what seemed to be her hundredth deep breath since getting in the truck with him. Maybe the happily-ever-after she'd indulged for the past two years was no more than another impossible dream.

Tiago remained silent, his expression a bit grim as he held her door and escorted her into the diner. She'd snatched the envelope before exiting the cab. He'd noticed but said nothing.

Once they were seated in a blue-and-white checked, retro vinyl booth menus in hand, Tiago sought her gaze with a familiar intensity in the set of his jaw and tight lips. His competition face.

"Quinn, I'm sorry if I've overstepped. I never meant to invade your privacy, only to find you so I could extend Coach's invitation."

She assessed him anew, noting the nervous tapping of his fingers, the tick of a muscle in his cheek, the brightness of his eyes, and the tiny curl above his ear that begged for her touch. Her anger evaporated. "Go on."

"This fall I'm beginning graduate work at MSU. I met with both rodeo coaches yesterday. They hired me as a graduate assistant. My second assignment is to recruit you back to the team for your senior year of eligibility."

Should she pump her fists or scream? Tension between her *Before* and *After* threatened to rip her apart. Choices like this drove her decision home, but she slammed the door on regret.

Her head shook of its own accord, her body taking over from her embattled brain. "I can't." Money drained from her account like sand through an hourglass. Her upcoming check would pay the rent, a few groceries. Little else. Despair scooted in next to her, elbowing her in the ribs.

"Wait." He raised his hand. "Hear me out. You'll receive a full scholarship––tuition, books, fees, board for both you and your horse. Everything's included. Coach says with you leading the team, Bobcat Rodeo would be set to win another national championship and those wins translate into donations for the program and the school."

Quinn's fingers tightened on the envelope. "But even if that were enough, it's one year. What about after that? I'd be right back where I am now. No job. No money to continue school." She closed her eyes and pressed her lips together. She hadn't meant to say so much. Letting Queen surface resurrected old habits.

The waitress arrived––gray peeking through her dark blonde curls––wearing an old-fashioned pocket apron over a blue-and-white checked uniform, pencil and pad in hand. Her cheerful manner broke the tension. "Lovely day, isn't it? I'm Karen. Can I start you off with a flavored soda?"

Tiago deferred to Quinn who ordered by rote. "One chocolate and one vanilla coke, please." It's what Cal always ordered at a similar diner in Shelby.

"Right away, sweetie. The bacon burger's on special today if you're interested." She moved away.

"I don't have a horse." Quinn sent the declaration across the space between them like the first volley in a gunfight.

Tiago shifted to rest his forearms on the tabletop, but other than the thoughtful crease that appeared between his brows, he didn't return fire.

Quinn's eyes narrowed. Few resisted her challenges. Maybe if she made enough demands, he'd back off. "I need to live off-campus. Will the university pay my rent?"

At that, he pursed his lips. "I'll have to check, but I'm sure there's a solution."

"Here you go." The waitress swept in with two chilled glasses and straws. "What else can I get you?"

Tiago glanced at his menu. "Quinn recommends the patty melts, so I'll try the cheddar on sourdough, deluxe."

"Fries with that?"

He glanced at Quinn who nodded. "The lady says yes."

Karen winked. "And the lady's always right." She aimed her pencil at Quinn. "For you?"

"The pepperjack melt with jalapeños, grilled onions, and that spicy sauce from the Cajun burgers."

"You got it. Fries?"

"Of course." Quinn's smile broke loose some of the gloom that had gripped her earlier, allowing her a full calming breath. "Thank you, Karen."

"My pleasure, sweetie."

"Wait, Karen, I heard you have milkshakes?" Tiago shot Quinn a grin.

The waitress's face brightened. "We do. And malts. Would you like one?"

"Get my friend a hot fudge malt."

Karen flicked her expressive penciled brows at Quinn. "Sounds like a winner. Just one?" She returned her attention to Tiago.

"I'll try a chocolate strawberry shake, please."

"My, you folks are adventurous. I'll have them right out." Her pen slipped behind her ear before she glided away.

Despite everything, a thrill wriggled in Quinn's stomach. "You remembered my flavor."

"I did. Is it worth anything?" The gold ring around his irises flashed.

He was teasing her. And she liked it. But banter was more dangerous than a battle of wits. Best she threw her guard up and pray it held. "Perhaps. If you'll tell me why I only rated second."

Tiago's forehead creased.

"You said I was Coach's second assignment. What was the first?"

"Ah." He grabbed a straw and tore off the paper, lowering it into tinkling ice. "Do you mind? I've never had a chocolate coke."

"Either is fine for me."

He smiled his thanks, then sipped. Nodded. "That's good. Wow. Who knew?" He took another long swallow, then licked his lips. "Have you ever tasted authentic Argentinean beef?"

"Not that I know of. Why?"

"Back in Nashville, where I'm from, my family operates an Argentinean restaurant with imported beef. If you like, I'll take you there, and you can sample some for yourself." Tiago leaned against the high back of the booth and crossed his arms over his chest.

His action drew Quinn forward, as if she couldn't allow more space between them. She shook her head. "Why would you do that? It's days away."

Tiago pursed his lips. "What if--"

"One shake and one malt. Your food'll be up in a jiffy. Enjoy." Karen placed glasses brimming with whipped cream and bright red cherries, then swept away before they could even thank her.

Quinn grabbed her spoon and brandished it at Tiago. "Continue."

He smiled. "What if assignment number one required me to return to Nashville, and I asked you to come along?"

"You lost me."

He sighed. "I'm supposed to scope out a set of twins for the rodeo program. Coach wants me to decide if they'll fit in here. Whether they're strong enough academically, mentally, attitudes, that kind of thing. You know more about MSU's rodeo culture, so I got permission to take you with me. While we're there, you can try out my horse."

"Try out your horse?"

"You'll need a horse. You could partner with Quilombo if he works for you. I used him mostly as a header, but I'm sure he'd be great on either end of the calf. He's trained for break-away roping, too."

Quinn's chest tightened. Could she trust her ears? Sharing a horse was like adopting someone into your family--not something done lightly on a whim. She stretched a hand toward him across the table. "You'd consider loaning me your horse?"

He met her, leaning forward and lacing his fingers with hers. "It would be an honor."

She blinked to keep the sting from forming into tears and swallowed. "But you don't know me."

His fingers tightened against hers. "I know you're one of the strongest people I've ever met--next to my own parents. I know you're also one of the most talented heelers I've had the pleasure of watching, and you're an excellent horse-woman. Anything else I need to know I can find out as we work together. If you agree, that is."

Quinn ran her teeth over her top lip. Was she seriously considering his offer? Oh, she wanted to, but she had respon-sibilities--a child and a mother who depended on her income. Pulling her hand from his, she retreated to her side of the table. A flash of something resembling hurt or maybe disappointment creased his face, but it was gone before she could acknowledge it.

He leaned closer and lowered his voice. "Tell me what you need to agree to a road trip."

She nearly spilled everything; his tone invited such confi-dence. She wanted to trust him. But she didn't dare take the

Queen-sized risk. So, she backed off. Put on her aloof face and her bland smile. "Nothing will make me agree to that."

She pulled out Mr. Dunn's envelope. "Time to see what's in here."

Tiago leaned away from the table, disappointment clearly etched his forehead and mouth. Even his eyes had dulled, the golden ring swallowed by shadow. While she slid her thumb beneath the seal on Dunn's offer, Tiago extracted a similar, slightly crumpled, envelope from his back pocket.

She tried unsuccessfully to keep her focus trained on her task, but the MSU seal flashed as Tiago tossed it in the center of the table. She eyed it, hesitating, her heart echoing her desire to disappear. Seconds passed. Then, in a casual movement, Tiago placed his thumb and forefinger around her envelope and waited, peering at her in a silent bid for permission.

Her will to fight gone, she dropped her hands. Tiago laid her envelope atop his, evened their edges, then slid them toward her. She tracked their progress across the table.

"Do you have someone who'll help you compare each offer? Debate the pros and cons?"

His voice was gentle, kind--kinder than she deserved after her little tantrum.

She wet her lips. "Missy will help me." It seemed a monumental admission until she realized he wouldn't know Missy was her mother.

"You trust her?"

Quinn considered this, wanting to take offense, but for the tiny niggle in her memories of the tearful aftermath on the day Bobby Brack said Cal wasn't her real dad. Missy's reaction had been odd, at first. Only later had she vehemently denied Bobby's charges and defended Cal. Those moments of hesitation reminded Quinn Missy hadn't told the whole truth until after Cal died. Too late because Cal had explained that same night after Missy stormed out.

"Are you unsure?"

Quinn started. Swallowed. "I trust her. She'll be fair."

Tiago nodded. "Let's table this discussion and enjoy what's left of this lunch. I think Karen's bringing our food. Good thing, because I'm starving." He patted his flat stomach and grinned.

And just like that, Quinn's nerves relaxed though her senses tingled. How did he know the right things to say to focus her attention on their undeniable chemistry and distract her so thoroughly? Whatever was between them threatened her very identity.

She should run and never look back.

CHAPTER 6

Tiago dropped Quinn off at Two Sisters around two with a promise they'd meet again on Monday. Four days without seeing her stretched impossibly before him.

He returned to the Fieldhouse, hoping to catch Coach McCloud and debrief.

"Come in. Have some coffee." Coach pushed away from his desk and stretched. "Time I took a break."

After Tiago recounted Quinn's cool reception, Coach laughed. "She wouldn't even take my calls, so I'd say you're making good progress."

"If she agrees to Tennessee, I'll feel better." Tiago set down his cup.

Coach nodded. "True. If you can get her to ride again, she'll remember how much she needs to be in the saddle. She had an amazing connection with her animals. Don't get me wrong, all our athletes are horse people and strong riders. But Quinn had that extra level of communication only a few reach. Dori has that special something. So does Rhiann James, our newest national champion. But none as strong as Quinn."

Tiago noted the pride with which Coach spoke about his athletes. "It's like you see them as more than competitors. The team members, I mean."

Coach wrapped both hands around his mug and surveyed the team photos adorning the office walls. "They're family. Sometimes they make me so mad, I want to shake them. Other times, my chest nearly bursts with pride at their accomplishments whether in the arena, the classroom, or life. But I get most emotional when they show kindness to one another, or when they reach out to someone outside our group with compassion or care."

He connected his gaze with Tiago's. "Rodeo can become all-encompassing. With so much focus on performance and improvement and competition, sometimes we forget what's really important. That life is more than rodeo. When my athletes do or say something that proves they've realized this and act upon it, my heart is lifted."

"Huh."

Coach's mouth twisted. "Huh? I give you my philosophy of life and all you have to say is, huh?"

Some combination of laugh and snort burst from Tiago. "Sorry, Coach. You made me consider my own priorities, and I realize I don't know what I stand for. I've tried to please my parents for as long as I can remember. I got into rodeo because my dad was a bronc rider and a roper. I majored in business so I could take over the restaurant one day. I came here because . . ."

"Because?"

Tiago shifted. The chair squeaked. The room's temperature shot up. His palms slicked. After several uncomfortable minutes, he found Coach watching him and swallowed. "I came to find Quinn."

Coach smoothed his moustache. "You found her. How does that affect your future?"

Tiago tapped the creases in his jeans. "I don't know. But having this job means my staying isn't dependent wholly on her anymore."

"Agreed. But what if she rejects you? Would you stay then? And what do you hope to gain besides Quinn? What fires your blood?"

"I guess that's what I'm here to find out." Tiago met Coach's gaze, a twinge of excitement working through his tension.

With a tooth-exposing smile, Coach stood. "Let's get to it, then. We've got less than a week to get you up to speed on all things Bobcat Rodeo. I want you to know exactly what we're looking for by the time you head to Tennessee on your little surveillance mission."

"You make it sound all spy-thriller instead of business interview."

Coach clapped a hand on his back. "Gotta keep the blood pumping one way or the other."

Tiago shook his head. "I guess."

"Ah, you'll loosen up if you hang out here very long. I've learned not to take myself too seriously. It always spells disaster. Come on, I'll show you what a normal practice day would look like and try to explain the kind of attitude and work ethic we're wanting to attract to MSU athletics."

Dori walked through the door, grinning. "Prepare to be tired, dirty, and a little sore tomorrow. Chet can't resist putting newbies through their paces. Even if you're a veteran, he's not above testing you. I'm giving you fair warning."

Before Tiago could come up with a witty retort, Coach nodded. "She's not wrong. Still want to come?"

The competitor he'd fostered in his college days rose up inside Tiago. He'd never shied away from hard, even when the results weren't what he'd wanted them to be.

He tugged his ballcap tighter on his head. "You bet."

Coach laughed with more intensity than Tiago thought warranted.

Later, when he returned to his motel, Tiago wasn't laughing. He was wishing he'd done more workouts in the year since graduation. Tomorrow would be worse, if Coach held to his word and took Tiago to the rough stock pens for what he called "a bit of a try out."

Chinese takeout in hand, he plopped onto the balcony chair. A warm breeze ruffled his still damp hair as shadows slid over the valley. Was Quinn at home? Would she have opened the envelopes yet? Did the Missy she mentioned have the ability to show Quinn the scholarship was the best choice? That he was the best choice?

But was he?

"What do you hope to gain besides Quinn? What fires your blood?"

Coach's words circulated with each pump of his heart. His father had sent him off with the same basic instruction: *"find your passion."* Only, with the Spanish pronunciation the idea seemed so much loftier. Pah-see-OWN! And still, the only pasión he'd discovered was what he felt around Quinn. Maybe God was punishing him for destroying his parents' dreams.

He extracted his container of Kung Pao chicken and the plastic fork from the paper bag. Too bad he couldn't reach into himself and pull out things he cared strongly about—the passion his father insisted he find. Had he ended his parents' passion by rendering his mother incapable of having more children? Images of his crying mother wrapped tight in his father's embrace filled his mind as the spicy scent kindled his taste buds. Not like Argentinean spice, but enough to blame for his watery eyes.

The distraction effectively turned his thoughts to the meal he'd shared with Quinn.

He forked a bite and chewed. Disappointing, compared to the patty melt.

It had burst with flavor, the diner cooks getting everything right. They could have used more waitstaff, though. Or maybe a hostess to pick up a few duties when the place was crowded. Their poor waitress had run her legs off to keep up, though neither her smile or peppy attitude had faltered.

If it had been his restaurant, he'd move the drink station nearer the guest tables to ease the waitstaff's workload like he'd recommended for Casa Vargas. Changes his father refused to adopt even after Tiago demonstrated their efficacy.

"Too frivolous," his father had said. *"We pay the staff well to work."*

Tiago swallowed. He'd never managed a restaurant, and he'd never get the chance to try if he didn't discover something that "fired his blood" as Coach put it. His father had made that quite clear the morning Tiago left for Montana.

He could almost see Tío Vasili's stern countenance reworking the paperwork for Casa Vargas, cutting Tiago out. Uncle Bertram salivating over the prime real estate should it pass to Tiago's mother's side of the family. Wasn't his cousin in culinary school somewhere? The cousin he'd punched for making lewd remarks about Quinn. How had Coach discovered that tidbit anyway?

He deposited the half-eaten meal on the small table and slumped in his seat. Honestly, he didn't know how his mother had turned out to be the generous, honest woman she was coming from a family as slippery and unscrupulous as hers.

His cell vibrated in his pocket, and he fished it out. Frowned. After thumbing the button to answer, he hit speaker and his mother's voice filled the air. His stomach lurched. Even at twenty-four, homesickness was real. He missed his family.

"I'm glad you called, Mom. I was just thinking about you and Dad."

"You're never far from my thoughts or prayers, Ti. Tell me all about Montana."

They chatted about mountains and sunrises for several minutes before Tiago mentioned the university.

Mom's pitch rose to an excited fervor. "Did you apply? Were you accepted? What will you study? Tell me everything."

Tiago laughed and complied. Thirty minutes later, he broached the subject he'd been dreading ever since answering his mother's call. "Mom, I'm coming home next week to pack my things, pick up Quilombo, and move to Bozeman."

A squeal reverberated in his eardrum. Good thing he'd put her on speaker.

In the background, his father spoke. "Laura, why do you carry on so?"

"Tiago's coming home, Joaquín."

"So soon?" Doubt darkened his father's voice. "Has he discovered his passion?"

"Not to stay, *esposo*. To gather his things and--"

To Tiago's utter dismay, his mother began to cry. He had the power to hurt her even thousands of miles away. His father spoke with the gentleness usually reserved for his wife. "Santiago, what's going on?"

Tiago stifled a sigh and stood, trying for a professional tone. "I've been hired by Montana State University as a graduate assistant to Coaches McCloud and Walstra of the rodeo team. They want me to combine a trip home to collect my things with some recruiting."

"I see. Chet McCloud's father comes to Casa Vargas

whenever he passes through the city. Upstanding man. I've met his son as well. Forthright and honorable. It seems congratulations are in order, *hijo*."

"I wouldn't slaughter the fatted calf just yet, Dad. Let's see how this plays out first. I might not be a good fit for the job. It's basically a trial run." Coach McCloud hadn't indicated anything of the sort, but Tiago's doubts crowded out any hope he might have embraced.

"Regardless, your mother and I will welcome you home for as long as you can stay."

"I appreciate that." Tiago wet his lips. "Do we have room for a visitor? I might be bringing someone with me."

"Of course we have room. Any of your friends are welcome here. You know that." His mother had recovered it seemed. "Do we know this person?"

"Unlikely, Mom. She's from Montana."

"She?"

"We're just friends, so don't get any ideas." Tiago paced the two steps from one end of his balcony to the other. "I'm not even sure she's coming, but I wanted you to be prepared in case."

"She can sleep upstairs in the Blue Room. I'll air it out. No one's stayed there in some time. I'll have to be sure we're stocked up." Her words faded.

His father laughed in that low, sultry, purely Argentinean way that made his mom act all lovey-dovey every time he did it. She called it his *machismo cariño* and claimed it was irresistible to American women. Tiago had always believed it was what made his mother fall for his father when they'd met in Tío Vasili's law office when she was but a university intern and his father a recent immigrant.

He tuned back into his father's voice.

"––mother's making lists. You'd better hope that woman comes with you, or we'll be buried in food and flowers."

Oh, he hoped. He hoped a lot.

U

"So? What do you think?" Quinn sank into one end of the brown-and-orange striped sofa Missy had rescued from the eighties. Missy perched on the other end, avoiding the pokey spring, offers in hand. Reina sprawled between them scribbling on a large sketch pad with a purple crayon, her above-average development evident. Quinn smoothed a dark curl and was rewarded with a bright, toothy smile.

Missy rustled the papers, comparing them. She squinted, then closed one eye. "I'm gonna have to get those readers at Walmart next time we go shopping."

"Or maybe you should keep one of the eye appointments I've made for you." She gave her mother a raised brow look.

Missy rolled her eyes. "Whatever."

How was it her mom sounded younger than she did? "The offers," Quinn prompted.

"They're thought-provoking, to say the least." She skimmed her teeth over her lip.

Quinn hid a smile. She came by the habit honestly. "And?"

Missy huffed, causing Reina to drop her crayon and pull at Missy's neon-painted toes. With ease, she gathered the child into her lap and held the pages out of reach of the toddler's grasping hands. "How much do you know about this Dunn fellow?"

Quinn shrugged a shoulder and tickled Reina's foot, eliciting a giggle. Love swelled in her belly. She clasped her hands around her knees and smiled wistfully at her daughter, deliberately squashing the feeling before it could explode her heart.

Reina pointed and cooed.

"Earth to Q." Missy flapped the pages to regain Quinn's attention.

She made a face. "Not much except his family founded Dunhorse Ranch and have run it successfully for several generations. I've met him several times when I rode out with Doc Liza or Doc Macie to check their mares or foals."

"How does he treat you?"

"Nice enough, I guess."

Missy screwed up one side of her mouth. "Nice is okay, but does he respect you?"

"I mean, he offered me a job? Doesn't that mean he respects me?"

"Not necessarily." A shadow crossed Missy's face, deepening the lines around her eyes and mouth. "Sometimes a job offer is a way to gain access to you. Did you feel comfortable with this guy?"

Quinn considered this, a cold creeping over her skin. The men from the stock pens flashed across her mind, followed by the sight of Tiago's face and the safety of his arms. She closed her eyes and pulled a long breath in through her nose. "I don't know. I think so."

Missy grunted and raised one page as if weighing it. "The rodeo scholarship pays for nearly everything a typical college rodeo student would need. Of course, you're not typical." She winked at Quinn. "Never were."

Quinn didn't know how to handle this affectionate, teasing side of Missy. She'd grown up with an aloof, serious version of her mother. Cal had been the one to hug and tickle or offer comfort. Had she been so flawed Missy couldn't love her? Was it pity that made her step up now? Both thoughts left Quinn empty and confused. Some of the distance between her and Reina was due to the worry Missy would withdraw if Quinn showed too much love, though at times it roiled like a tempest within her.

"What about a horse? How would you find one we could afford?"

Tiago's offer teetered on the tip of her tongue, but she swallowed it. Too soon to mention that. "I don't know. That's a con for sure on the scholarship."

Missy nodded as if keeping a mental tally. "The hours are a con for the foaling manager job. You'd be on call and expected to practically live at the ranch during foaling season. That would limit your time with Reina."

She hadn't thought of that.

"You couldn't take more than a class or two at a time, either. Likely online due to the time constraints. It could delay your entrance to vet school by years."

Quinn ignored the unlikelihood of ever becoming a vet for Missy's sake. "If I accepted the scholarship, I could be done with my undergrad in one, but during rodeo seasons I'd be gone quite a bit, sometimes for multiple days."

"Reina and I could come with you."

Great. Her reckless stupidity laid bare for the world to see, and exposing her daughter to ridicule wasn't an option. "Maybe we can pretend she's yours." But even as she made the suggestion, she dismissed the lie. *Forgive me, Lord.*

"That's not what you want."

Quinn shook her head. "You're right. It isn't. I feel so vulnerable where she's concerned."

Missy passed the pages to Quinn, then settled the baby against her shoulder. She pressed a kiss to the halo of curls, cradling her tight. Reina's eyelids fluttered like butterfly wings and settled dark lashes against sun-toned cheeks.

Something uncurled inside Quinn, satisfying as a good stretch after a nap. The sense of God's Spirit washed over her in strength and peace.

Missy's mouth curved into a smile at Quinn's long sigh, but her eyebrow quirked in question.

"I'm content. Right here and right now. With you and Reina. With this small house in this decent neighborhood. I don't want things to change." She settled into the couch's embrace, into her faith, as if she'd stay forever.

Missy's smile became a sad caricature. Her eyes misted over as if she were sifting through memories, their color lightening to almond. "I've always admired your choices, Quinn. You possess a strength I wish I'd had. My weakness became a thorn that pricked my conscious daily, but I cling to hope through you and this little one you chose to bring into the world despite everything." Her words choked off.

What Quinn's younger self wouldn't have given to hear those sentiments, but right now with the pressure of the choices ahead of her, she couldn't afford to succumb to emotion.

Quinn jumped from the couch, cheeks hot, and rushed to the kitchen for water. All comfort had vanished. She was proud of her mother. Admired her even. But why had Missy waited so long to love her?

She filled two glasses and returned to the living room, setting one to her lips so she wouldn't have to meet Missy's gaze, the other on the flea market coffee table. Quinn wasn't brave, she was a coward. She perched on the edge of the couch; afraid it would burn her again if she let it hold her.

Wasn't that how it always worked? The minute she grew comfortable, the world yanked the saddle from beneath her and sent her spinning like a cowboy ejected from a bronc. Soon, she'd hit the dirt and end up bruised or broken.

Missy leaned forward, quite a feat with Reina asleep on her chest, and touched a warm hand to Quinn's goose pimpled arm. "I wish I'd shown you more affection when you were little, but I let Cal take that role. Guilt held me back. I feared you'd sense my betrayal if I held you too close or too long."

Quinn set the glass on her knee. Her stomach pinched, a knot forming. What loop would this conversation send her on? She almost walked away, but an invisible force encouraged her to remain—to hear her mother's confession. A sense of compassion rose and she let it soften her expression, then met Missy's gaze.

Her mother's shoulders relaxed a fraction. Her chin quivered. "I nearly lost you. Before you were born. Before I knew I wanted you." She hesitated. Looked down to where her fingers splayed pale on Quinn's dusky skin. "You never met your grandparents because they were addicts and alcoholics. Dad walked out when I was five. Mom blamed me. I was an accident—never wanted. Always a nuisance. As soon as I could, I sought solace elsewhere. Not in substances, but in people. Men. Boys, really. None of us old enough to handle emotionally what our bodies said we could handle physically."

"You already told me all this—after Cal's funeral." Quinn covered her mother's hand with her own, the compassion turning to empathy. "You said Cal changed everything for you." *Please let that remain true.* A giant wave of fear hovered just at the edge of Quinn's thoughts, her faith in a good God and her hope the only things holding it at bay.

Reina wiggled and Missy pulled her hand free to rub the toddler's back, making shushing sounds and rocking slightly.

An arrow of jealousy hit Quinn. Why couldn't she be the mother to her own child? Was Missy's past doomed to be repeated? Quinn didn't want that, but couldn't bring herself to reach out for her daughter. Instead, she looked on while another gash opened in her heart.

Reina turned, her lips making little sucking motions in her sleep. Missy caught Quinn's gaze, then looked away. "There's more."

The knot grew in Quinn's stomach. She sucked in a shaky breath and waited.

Missy leaned back, putting distance between her and Quinn, gently rubbing the baby's back. She seemed young, vulnerable.

When Quinn could stand the tension no longer, she made to rise. "If you're not––"

"I tried to abort you, but the pill didn't work like it had before. Two months later, I bought a home pregnancy test and took the proof to your father. He threw me down his front steps, calling me names. I stumbled away––didn't really know where I was going––and collapsed on a bench outside the drug store. I considered harming myself. It wasn't my best moment." Missy sniffed and wiped her eyes with her oversized t-shirt.

Quinn wanted both to throw her arms around her mother and sob and to run away with her hands over her ears. *Give me strength, so I can be strong for her.*

Missy pulled herself together and found Quinn's eyes. "Lucille says I walked through the valley in Psalm twenty-three that day. And God sent her to walk with me."

"Lucille is the woman who introduced you to Cal."

"First, she introduced me to the Lord. I met Cal at church nearly two months later." Missy paused, shifting beneath the baby's weight.

"Why didn't you tell me this when everyone insisted I should abort Reina?" Quinn forced her hands to unclench.

"It had to be your choice. Raising a child is hard––harder without a helper. I had Cal. You had so many successes. Dreams. Maybe . . . maybe, I wasn't sure I wanted you to keep the baby."

Quinn rocked back as though she'd been struck.

Missy hurried to bridge the chasm between them. "I was afraid. I've always been afraid, but you were so brave––so sure--since you were little. You were Cal's Queen. Bold. Fearless. You gave me the courage to overcome my guilt and take a chance on love. With Cal first, and again with Reina. With you, now, too."

"I'm not that person anymore." Quinn managed a hoarse whisper.

After a long moment, Missy nodded at the offers lying abandoned on the couch cushion. "What will you choose?"

Rising, Quinn took another drink and wandered to peer out the window onto the quiet street. Her gut roiled, the knot extending to her limbs. Her own mother hadn't wanted her. *Help me, Lord. I don't want to cause pain. Help me let it go.*

But even as she prayed, her mind demanded more. She hated lies. Hated the problems they caused. Even the shroud she'd drawn around the events surrounding her child's birth was coming back to haunt her now. Everything needed to come into the light, but Quinn didn't know how to open up. To expose them to the darkness of that moment. It seemed a cruel thing to do to one so innocent. Easier to let Reina believe her mother had never lost control or been rendered vulnerable and helpless. That she hadn't been conceived in violence and fear.

The springs creaked as Missy rose and padded away, presumably to settle Reina in her crib. Quinn was still at the window when her mother returned, flipping on a dim lamp and coming to stand beside her. Their reflection revealed the foot or so of height differential as well as Quinn's willowy slenderness compared to Missy's rounded curves. Straight ebony hair trailed over Quinn's shoulders to the center of her back. Missy's strawberry waves ended at her chin.

The high cheekbones, strong jaw, and almost hollowed cheeks in Quinn's facial structure hadn't come from Missy. "Was I hard to love because I look so much like my father?"

The question rushed from Quinn's mouth before she could stop it.

The jaw dropped in her mother's reflection, then clamped shut. Quinn knew that look of stubborn determination. She'd seen it the night after Bobby's schoolyard taunts. She wouldn't be getting an answer today, either.

Missy's mouth flattened. "Since becoming a Christian I learned I've always had value because I am made in God's image. The man who sired you treated everyone like he determined their worth. He was wrong. I was bought for a price. Jesus died for me and saved me from my sins. All of them. I wasn't created to be insignificant and neither were you. Change comes whether you let it happen or help shape it. Please stop hiding in the shadows, believing it'll keep you safe. Let me be your helper, so you can become who you were created to be."

Quinn had no words. She spun, aiming for the hall that led to the single bathroom and her tiny bedroom. Steadying herself with a hand on the far wall, she half turned. "Tiago asked me on a recruiting trip to Nashville. If I go, I'm taking Reina with me." She tapped her palm on the faded border, then let the shadows of the hall swallow her.

Missy's voice chased her like a hunting hound. "He's seen Reina. The day he stopped here looking for you. I let him think she's your sister."

Undressing seemed to unleash a cacophony of thoughts to jab at her mind. Flashes of faces and feelings fought themselves for dominance. Anger. Frustration. Guilt.

She stared at herself in the bathroom mirror as she brushed her teeth. Who was she? Uncertainty deepened the shadows beneath her eyes and further hollowed her already-thin cheeks making her look like a specter. The odd green-gray of her eyes added to the haunted quality.

If her father was evil, did the tendency toward evil run in her genes?

She'd never considered herself beautiful. Interesting or unusual, perhaps. So why would a handsome cowboy from a successful family travel nearly two thousand miles to find her? Did he have an ulterior motive?

She rinsed her mouth, expelling the suspicious thought with the rest of her toothpaste. She grabbed a floral-printed hand towel and dried her face. The towel was a remnant of growing up in Shelby when Cal, Missy, and horses were her life. She gave herself a moment to grieve for those times, then heaved a breath.

Go.

The whisper entered her heart, furrowing her brows. She switched off the light and navigated the three steps to her room from memory. Closing her door, she clicked on the bedside lamp and pulled back the covers.

Could she even consider Tiago's offer? Liza would be back on Monday. Macie next Wednesday. She was caught up on her classwork and could let the professor know she'd be gone for a bit with no problem. Could she really take Reina? What would Tiago say? Would he reject them like her father had? Think less of her?

It would be a good test. A growing freedom expanded her chest. After spending time with Tiago, she'd know whether he was genuine or a fraud. And he didn't present a physical danger, only an emotional one.

Hope overflowed into excitement that turned her cold. She slid between the sheets, a prayer on her tongue. *Protect me from myself, Lord. Guide me through my tendency to be bold and brash––to plow unthinking into unknown territory that leaves me broken and wounded. Most of all, protect my daughter from my rashness. She is a most precious gift.*

She'd prayed this prayer daily following her discovery

that she carried a rapist's child. Lately, it had come less frequently, but tonight, the fervor returned. She stood at the bottom of a mountain and both roads led upward into shadows. Which should she choose?

U

Quinn jerked upright, covers wound around her body, with the feeling she'd barely slept. Dingy light edged the curtains of her single window. She fumbled on the nightstand for her phone, eyes squeezed shut, then realized she'd left it in her tangle of jeans on the floor. Forcing her eyes open against the red glare of her old-fashioned bedside alarm, she groaned. After six already?

Monday. Lunch with Tiago. Today!

Her feet met the floor with less than an hour to get to work. She rescued her phone and plugged it in to charge while she gathered clean jeans and her last clean scrub top. Ugh. Laundry tonight--her least favorite chore.

She tiptoed to the bathroom, dressed, and grabbed Missy's pre-made peanut butter and jelly sandwich on her way out the door. Reina's soft cries hit just as the door closed, tugging at her middle. Missy would handle it. She steeled herself and walked to her truck, unlocked the door, and climbed in, tossing her bag in the passenger seat.

If she took Reina to Tennessee, there'd be no one to help. She'd be on her own. Missy's words taunted her. *"I let him believe she's your sister."*

Quinn sat still, arms folded on the steering wheel. An edge of gold highlighted the tops of the mountains in her rearview mirror, reminding her of God's faithfulness. He would never abandon her, and His truth was unassailable. He would see her through. Calm descended and she inserted the key into the ignition and turned. The engine coughed and chugged, then died.

She tried again. Nothing.

Panic flirted with her calm. She pushed it down. Closing her eyes, she uttered a silent prayer. Turned the key.

Just a weak sputter before the engine caught, but the uneven rumble allowed Quinn to sag back in her seat with gratitude on her lips.

She'd have to find a mechanic or another vehicle. Either would cost money she didn't have. She shifted into drive and worried her lip as she headed the truck to the intersection. Doubt and indecision clouded her thoughts. Regardless, she had to choose her path today. Tiago would expect an answer, and she had no idea what she would say.

"It was no problem. Think nothing of it." Tiago placed a napkin in his lap, fascinated by the pink creeping up Quinn's cheeks but trying not to add to her sense of vulnerability. When she'd called to say she was stranded at work with a nonresponsive truck, he'd volunteered to pick her up and arrange for mechanical service.

She'd accepted the ride but said Polly had already called a mechanic friend who was supposed to look at it sometime that afternoon. The worry in her voice had overshadowed the confidence he remembered from her rodeo days. Seated across the small table in an outdoor bistro, she seemed diminished from the last time they'd met at the diner. Compared to the brash, over-the-top "Arena Queen" ego the press had assigned her, she was a shrunken shell of her former self.

Not that Tiago had bought into her public persona. He'd recognized the softness in her eyes when they'd connected after her rides, the warmth in her smile. The passion the press took for arrogance, he saw as love for the sport and a determination to perform well.

He'd seen the same drive and determination in his father as he strove to expand and improve his customers' Argentinean experience at Casa Vargas. He'd seen it in the tenderness and absolute devotion his parents shared with each other. He strove to ignite such a quality in himself.

"Have you been here before?" The tentative way she asked emphasized the fragility of her emotions.

Tiago wished he knew what was at the heart of these changes. Somehow, he was certain the truck was only the final weight that tipped the scales. After the way she'd shut him down at the diner, he shied away from the delicate topic foremost on his mind.

"Dori recommended it." He panned the patio lined with smooth pavers and a dozen round, umbrellaed tables, most occupied. The area contained several other upscale eateries and shops. Patrons strolled in small groups carrying reusable shopping bags.

"Dori's great. She helped me learn the goat-tying event. I'm glad she decided to take up coaching. She'll be fantastic." Quinn unwrapped the silverware and smoothed her cloth napkin, then glanced up. "You'll be good, too. You stayed so calm in the ring. Each movement controlled, precise. The perfect header. Too bad your heeler's timing wasn't better."

Tiago's brows furrowed. "My heeler won gold our senior year. He was one of the best ropers on the team."

Quinn nodded. "True, but he missed too many catches as a heeler. Timing issues."

"Huh. I always thought I was the slow one."

She huffed. "If I'd had a header as consistent as you, my job would have been simpler. Not that my headers were bad, but we incurred too many penalties and missed catches. Made for more pressure on each run."

"Like the short-go your freshman year at the CNFR."

Her eyes rounded. "You remember that? From four years ago?"

"Of course. You only had two clean runs yet lost by less than a second."

She laughed. "Fastest two runs ever."

The tension had left her face and shoulders, and she'd stopped fidgeting with the utensils. In fact, her gray eyes radiated the joy he'd loved most about watching her perform.

Their order arrived, and she attacked her mesquite-roasted chicken sandwich with gusto. His pulled pork exuded a satisfying hickory-smoked scent. He wiped sauce from his lips. "This is good. How's yours?"

She shielded her mouth with a hand and nodded. "They got the spice just right."

"Are you a fan of heat?"

"Yes, but I like to taste the other flavors, not have my mouth lit on fire."

"Understandable. My dad's been working on a sauce for brisket that approximates these flavors. Something a little smoky but with an uncommon kick that isn't mesquite or jalapeño."

Interest sparked on her face. "Do you collaborate with your dad on recipes and restaurant things?"

"Some," he hedged. "What about you? Were you and your dad close?"

A shadow crossed her expression, then vanished, and Tiago wanted to kick himself. Her dad had passed away not long after she'd dropped out of sight. He'd managed to smother their conversation. Again.

She surprised him by flashing a smile. "My dad taught me everything he knew about horses, riding, and rodeo. And when he reached his limits, he found others who could add to my skills. He had an incredible heart. So full of compassion, it broke in two and killed him." Her throat convulsed, and her eyes glinted with unshed tears.

"I'll bet he was proud of you and your accomplishments."

"Mostly. He didn't like my image--said pride is the most difficult stumbling block to overcome. That we should humble ourselves before the Lord and before our fellow man." The pink crept into her cheeks again as she bowed her head.

"My mom's always quoting scriptures. She's even got my father doing it from time-to-time. Her faith is an inspiration. I'm afraid mine's a bit lacking."

Quinn's head cocked in an adorable way, dislodging a strand of ebony hair across one cheek. Tiago slid his hand beneath his thigh to keep from tucking it behind her ear, fearing she'd bolt if he succumbed to temptation.

"How's everything here?" The waiter alternated his raised brow between them.

"We're fine for now. Thank you."

The man nodded and moved to clear the next table.

"What do you mean? Do you not believe in God?" Quinn's features scrunched together.

"I believe in Him. It's . . . I'm not sure He's listening." He paused, trying to find the words to express the condition of his soul.

She held up a hand. "You don't have to explain. I'm told I ask uncomfortable questions." She polished off her sandwich.

"I'm sure God hears me, sees me, knows my thoughts, but I don't deserve His attention." Why had he admitted that? It was too intimate. Too much.

"No one deserves His attention."

Not what he thought she'd say.

She pushed her empty plate aside. "None of us is good enough to warrant the Creator's attention, let alone the notice of the One who defeated death in our place. But He invites us into an intimate relationship, so we can have access to all the blessings He longs to provide. I was recently reminded we are His beloved children, bought for a tremendous price, so we can abide in Him. Of course He sees us. And He hears us. But He doesn't always indulge us and, like wayward children, we often must learn lessons before we can handle His best blessings."

Tiago blinked. The truth smacked him in the face. Had he been asking for the wrong things? Was it too much to ask to know the purpose for which he'd been created? He didn't think so. Regardless, he'd need time to ponder Quinn's words. Her conviction had been transparent. She believed in Jesus as her Lord and Savior as strongly as his mother. They were well-suited.

"Have you considered road tripping to Tennessee with me?" He had to change topics before he said something that turned her away, though this might do the trick as well as religion.

She stirred her strawberry lemonade, the swirling bits of fruit drawing her avid attention.

Her avoidance stole his breath. He gripped the edge of the chair to keep himself upright, while his heart tattooed her extended silence onto his ribcage.

At last, she looked up. Gray irises locked onto him, drawing him into their intense gaze.

"I have."

He leaned forward, stomach knotting at the shadow lurking in her expression. "And?" Her blink released him, and he drew air. Her scent, sweet and tart like ripe apples, reached him, intoxicated him. Made him want more. *Please,* he begged silently. *Give me this one thing. Even though I don't deserve it.*

"When do we leave?"

Iron bands seemed to wrap around his chest. Did that

mean she'd go, or was she merely asking for information? "Wednesday at seven," he choked out. Swallowed. "If you can be ready that soon."

She clenched her jaw and fiddled with her napkin, creasing then smoothing it. The wait nearly drove him mad. Her jaw clenched a final time, then relaxed as if she'd made some sort of decision.

"I think so."

Relief swept through him, releasing the crushing tension. Thank God. *Thank You, God,* he amended.

Her throat convulsed. "Could I . . ."

"Could you what?" An edge of anticipation rattled his raw nerves.

She shook her head. "I've a few loose ends to tie up. Will I need anything special?" Her expression revealed nothing.

Was she concerned because of his family? "I doubt anything requiring fancy dress will come up, and if it does, we'll be in Nashville. Shopping is plentiful."

He sent her a reassuring smile. Her return attempt didn't quite reach her eyes. He almost smacked his forehead when it occurred to him she might be the only support for her mother and little sister after her father's death. Was lack of funds what prevented her return to MSU for her senior year? Something didn't add up, but he'd worry about it later.

Seeking to reassure her, he added, "Remember, this is a paid vacation of sorts. You're working for Bobcat Rodeo as we interview prospective athletes. You'll have a small budget for expenses and receive a stipend for your services when we return."

"It's very generous."

"Not at all." He shook his head, then smiled at the waiter and pointed to his partially-eaten sandwich. "You have knowledge I don't. I need your perspective on whether these twins will fit into the program. Plus, we need to see how you get along with Quilombo." He winked, and her laugh evaporated the weight he'd not realized lay across his shoulders.

The waiter returned with a box and the check.

Tiago slid a card from his wallet and handed it to the waiter.

"Okay. You've convinced me." She slurped up the rest of her lemonade, fishing out a large strawberry. "You're sweet." She popped it into her mouth and bit down.

At the return of his card, he signed, then stood, pushing in his chair and picking up the box. "Do you prefer strawberry ice cream as well?"

She made a face and matched his movements. They maneuvered through the maze of tables toward the street and his parked truck. "No way. Vanilla with hot fudge, remember?"

He chuckled. "I forgot. And malt, yes?"

Her eyes widened with exaggerated emphasis. "Lots of malt."

He was going to enjoy getting to know her the next two weeks. But what would happen once they returned to Montana, and he had to decide on a discipline to study. She had clear career goals. Would his lack of direction send her running?

Perhaps, he could try trusting God that this time, things would end up in his favor. If they didn't, he could always pivot and come up with another plan.

He took in Quinn's smile and enticing gray-green eyes. His fingers itched to comb the length of her sleek ebony hair. Oh, Lord. He was already a goner. No room for screw-ups. He had to find a way to win Quinn's heart or his might never recover.

CHAPTER 8

Quinn circled the living room with a bouncing step, patting Reina's back. Nothing seemed to quiet the tiny whimpers issuing from her daughter's throat. Quinn understood how the toddler felt. Her own stomach was knotted tight. She'd twisted the bedcovers into pretzels before rising at four and brewing herself some tea.

An hour or so later, she'd stood before the living room window staring into the streetlight when Reina's fussing began. Hoping to keep from waking Missy, Quinn put down her cup and rushed into her daughter's room, shushing and cooing. Reina had reached for her, chubby arms extended and a bit warmer than they should have been when Quinn boosted the girl onto her hip.

Hopefully it was another bout of teething and not a virus.

"Jesus loves you, this I know," Quinn intoned, reaching for the damp washcloth on the back of Reina's neck. No longer cool, Quinn entered the kitchen and rewet the cloth with cold water. She wrung it out as best she could one-handed, then reapplied it. The baby didn't feel as warm and seemed drowsier. Maybe the dose of fever reducer was working.

Crossing back into the living room, she stepped on the squeaky floorboard and froze. She'd been doing so well staying quiet.

Missy appeared in the doorway, hair disheveled and pajama top askew. She squinted at the mostly-dark window, then at the spray of light seeping in from the kitchen's over-the-sink fixture. "What time is it?" Her jaw gaped in a yawn.

"Nearly six. Reina was fussing, but I was already up." Quinn smoothed the springy curls on her now-sleeping daughter and resumed her circuit.

"You should have woke me." Missy ran a hand over her face. "But if you're good, I'll get the coffee going."

"We're fine." Quinn whispered the words. They were meant for Missy, but somehow seemed to sink into her own soul. Love swelled in her breast, but as always, she tamped it down before it overwhelmed her. A surge of love had killed her father. Either that or his vast disappointment in her. Either way, she couldn't lose herself in anything so dangerous. She cared. That had to be enough.

She forced her steps into the combination nursery and Missy's room, stopping at the crib. For several long moments, she rocked Reina, relishing the weight of her daughter in her arms, before transferring her to the mattress. Quinn removed the washcloth and let her fingers linger on the soft skin of her child's cheek. Her child. Not Missy's. Quickly, she covered Reina with a light blanket and stepped back.

Missy needed Reina more than Quinn. Since Cal's burial, she'd poured all her focus into caring for Quinn's daughter, and lately, Quinn herself. Missy was happier now than ever, even when she and Cal had learned to lean on each other after the rough years that were part of Quinn's earliest memories. Cal had confided in her that once they'd learned to trust each other everything else had fallen into place.

As an adult, Quinn believed it had a lot to do with Missy's growing relationship with Jesus, too. Maybe Cal's growth in that area was just as significant.

A shadow blotted out the dim light flowing into the room. Quinn pressed her fingers to her lips, then transferred the kiss to Reina's temple. "Be well." *She's in Your hands, Lord. I trust You with her life.*

Quinn retired to the kitchen while Missy fussed over the sleeping toddler.

When Missy joined Quinn, she filled her mug with coffee and added cream. "Her skin feels normal, and she's peaceful."

"That's a relief." Quinn had already poured and doctored her brew with sugar. She indicated the truck keys dangling from a hook inside the door. "The truck runs surprisingly well since Polly's friend worked on it. Almost as good as new."

"He didn't charge much, either." Missy sipped her coffee.

Quinn said nothing, thinking of the two-hundred-dollar dent in her daughter's inheritance. She'd promised not to dip into that money unless she absolutely had to, and this had been necessary since her check from Two Sisters barely covered rent and living expenses. No way could it have withstood the repair bill, however reasonable.

Thankfully, next week's check would have the extra hours and bonus pay Doc Liza had promised for Quinn's extra duties. That, together with the substantial sum from MSU, would tide them over until the next rent payment. Quinn squeezed the coffee mug to release the building frustration.

Missy grimaced. "What did that cup do to you?" She tugged it free and threaded her fingers through Quinn's. "God will provide. Trust Him."

"I'm trying. Really, I am."

"I know, Queen. We must persevere, even when it's hard."

Quinn stiffened at Missy's use of Cal's nickname—the one the press had latched onto and turned into an insult. She swallowed to loosen her throat. "Please, I never want to hear that name again.

With a squeeze, Missy released Quinn. "I'm sorry. I didn't think." A beat, then, "Are you still planning to take Reina?"

Quinn shook her head, not missing the quaver in Missy's voice. "Not when she's sick or teething. She's better off here." A guilty sting followed the relief the decision brought. She stuffed it down like she banished all her unwanted emotions. Besides, she'd chickened out and hadn't asked.

Missy nodded, finger tracing the pattern on her cup. "Children complicate things. Some men can't handle it."

Was Missy thinking of Quinn's biological father?

Her mother's gaze strayed to the microwave clock. "What time is that handsome cowboy picking you up?"

Quinn jerked straight, eyes on the glowing numbers. "Shoot. I only have thirty minutes."

Missy's laugh felt forced. "Good thing you're not one of those fru-fru girls. Better get moving. I'll make you an egg sandwich to go."

Quinn rushed from the room, then ducked her head back in. "Thank you. For everything."

"That's what moms are for. Now shoo. When you keep a good man waiting, you risk having another woman snatch him from your hand. An old wives' proverb."

"Where do you get this stuff?" Quinn shook her head all the way to the shower, realizing with a pang how much she would miss her mom's presence.

Quinn skipped down the stairs from the kitchen door, small suitcase in one hand, egg sandwich in the other at one minute after seven. The sight of Tiago casually leaning against his truck door, one jean-clad leg propped over the other, crossed arms straining the fabric of his black t-shirt, nearly tripped her. The Bobcat ball cap perched askew on his head added a jauntiness to his personality she'd not experienced in their previous meetings.

His gaze tracked her movements until she stopped in front of him. Then they locked onto her face, and the intensity she'd sensed beneath the surface bore into her. Without breaking eye contact, he unfolded his body and relieved her of her suitcase. His hand rested lightly on her shoulders as he guided her to the passenger door, opened it, and helped her inside.

The closed door broke his hypnotic gaze, leaving Quinn feeling bereft. The places he'd touched tingled from the contact, and her stomach was as quivery as a rodeo queen contestant before the final announcement. If she kept this up, she'd crash from adrenaline overload and be snoring before they left Montana. What a good impression that would make.

When Tiago opened the rear door to stow her suitcase, the breeze wafted his clean scent around the cab. She resisted pulling an extra-long breath by glancing about. Everything sparkled as if he'd spiffed it up just for her. Likely not the case, but it felt good to dream.

The smile he sent her through the windshield as he crossed to his own door nearly melted her heart, but she'd had lots of practice quelling such feelings and set about stuffing them down. She'd barely succeeded when his scent hit her full force and her emotions tumbled free once more. This trip might be more of a challenge than she'd thought. She gripped the armrest to anchor herself, then allowed her gaze to stray his way.

He fixed his dark eyes on her. "Ready for the journey?"

Why did those words feel prophetic? Quinn focused on the street ahead. "Let's go."

Her voice carried an eagerness the rest of her didn't feel. In fact, she nearly flung open the door and fled to the safety of her familiar life. How was she to hide when he seemed able to peer into her soul?

The truck roared to life, and the world inched into motion. Quinn expelled a breath and tried to relax. *"Enjoy,"* her mother had said. But danger lurked within the bounds of enjoyment, and she wasn't sure she could keep from reverting into Queen—her bold, brash self. Queen—who chose dangerous paths. Sought them, even. Reveled in the thrill.

She couldn't afford to be that person any more. Others depended on her, and she owed it to Cal. But perhaps she could have a friend. A friend would be a welcome change.

"You're awfully quiet over there." Tiago glanced at her, then returned his focus to the road. They'd left her small neighborhood behind headed to I-90, the interstate they'd follow east to Sioux Falls, South Dakota, then south, and east again at Kansas City, Missouri.

She'd studied the map in detail the night before, eager to see what territory she'd be traveling through. Her never-quite-conquered sense of adventure had skipped circles around her recently-cultivated sensible, responsible nature. But she'd squashed it. After all, the trip was for business, not pleasure. Still—"I'm thinking about the new landscapes I'll get to see since I've never been farther than Wyoming." Would he think less of her for her lack of experiences?

A smile spread across his face. "Then it will be my honor to introduce you to some of America's more prominent sights as we go."

Some of her excitement bubbled up, lapping at her empty

places. "Don't we have a schedule to keep?" Her enthusiasm teetered on the precipice awaiting Tiago's words.

"Not that I'm aware of. Will your mom and sister be okay without you? Is there something else pulling you back?" He cocked an eyebrow.

She swallowed but avoided his gaze. "I've got time off work, and I'm ahead in class." She'd spent the last two nights completing two weeks' worth of assignments, just in case. Her palms grew sweaty from the effort to sound casual. She wasn't lying, but no matter how much she justified withholding her daughter's existence, she couldn't escape the feeling God was saddened by her lack of trust.

I'll tell him, Lord, just not yet. She sent the thought skyward with a plea for grace on this sticking point. *A little longer. Please.*

Tiago merged onto the interstate and concrete hummed beneath the tires. They approached the mountains ringing the Gallatin Valley. Sun in their eyes, they both reached for the visor at the same time and an awkward laugh escaped.

Quinn scooched up in her seat to take advantage of the shade. It couldn't hurt to relax and enjoy the experience, could it? She sent Tiago a shy smile and caught him studying her. A thrill zinged through her chest. She wanted everything to work out. If only she knew how to make that happen.

Trust in Me. The verses she'd read last night floated above her raging emotions, and a warmth flowed through her, quieting her spirit.

I do, Jesus. I trust You.

The one she didn't trust was herself.

CHAPTER 9

Tiago had a hard time keeping his eyes trained on the road. When Quinn bounded from her house in jeans and a greenish-gray top that mimicked her eye color to perfection, he'd exercised all his will not to rush forward and sweep her into his arms. After a quiet beginning, her comments on the scenery interspersed with adorable, shy smiles had maxed his awareness meter. When she removed her sandals and rested green-painted toes on his dashboard, he over-heated.

A sign caught his attention. "What say we stop in Billings for a short break?" He grinned. "Some of us didn't have a sandwich to start the day."

Quinn chuckled. "Some of us don't have a live-in mother who insists her daughter eats."

"Even when I was young, my mother rarely cooked. That's dad's job, and he takes it very seriously. Beware if you enter the domain of Joaquín Vargas."

She sent him a mock salute. "Thanks for the warning."

Tiago took the exit and stopped at the first truck stop he

found. He topped off the tank, then pulled into a spot for the convenience store and some sort of off-brand establishment whose sign promised steaming coffee, omelets, and biscuits and gravy.

When he slid into the booth across from Quinn, his stomach growled. The only visible waitress brought coffee in plain white mugs, then left them to peruse their menus. "Anything strike your fancy?"

Quinn peeked around the edge of the laminated sheet. "Not yet. But I'm not the one with the grumbly tummy." She flashed a smile, then retreated, using the menu as cover.

By the time the harried waitress returned, they had drunk most of their coffee and chatted about how they would improve each of the exactly twelve offerings. Quinn had good instincts concerning food, adding to the list of things Tiago admired about her.

Rather than speak, the woman held up her ordering pad and waited, mouth pinched and forehead wrinkled.

Tiago's father wouldn't tolerate such insolent guest treatment from Casa Vargas' staff. They'd get one chance to toe the line or be let go.

"Good morning, Terri." Quinn's upbeat tone sounded genuine.

How could she welcome someone who'd basically snubbed her? Tiago checked the nametag. Sure enough. "Terri L." was emblazoned on the plastic oval. He peered closer. Was the 'I' dotted with ketchup? Hot sauce? Meanwhile, Quinn carried on, even though the woman grunted her answer.

"You seem upset, Terri, or maybe it's nearing the end of your shift?" Quinn's smile grew. "I'm Quinn. It's nice to meet you."

Terri's expression quivered, then slowly shifted. Her eyes

narrowed. Then her entire body curved away as if Quinn might be about to slap her. Or kidnap her.

"Congratulations on the championship. What position does your son play?"

The woman's eyes widened, jaw going slack. "M-my youngest is the new quarterback. His brother graduated last year with a scholarship. Good thing 'cause this dump don't pay enough for him to go." She harumphed. "What can I get ya?" She leaned in. "Stay away from the omelets. Cook's bad at cracking eggs."

"May I have the hashbrowns with sausage patties, please? No eggs or toast. And a small orange juice, if it's not too much trouble." Quinn beamed a smile. "I hope your son has a stellar season this fall."

Tiago worried Terri's make-up might crack she smiled so big. When she turned her pencil and pad on him, laugh lines creased the outer edges of her eyes, replacing the signs of over-work that had lingered there before.

Why not try Quinn's approach? "Hello, Terri. Two eggs over-easy, bacon, and wheat toast, please."

"Comin' right up."

Was he imagining it, or was Terri's step lighter as she carried their order to the kitchen? He stared at Quinn, who was fiddling with her napkin.

She started and pulled her hands from the table. "What?"

"How could you know her sons played football?"

"Oh, that. She's wearing a football championship t-shirt with the name 'Long' printed on the back. It wasn't hard to assume it belonged to a son. I took a chance and guessed right."

"Why engage her like that? I wouldn't have."

Quinn shrugged. "I heard her arguing when we walked in. She seemed so mad; my goal was to distract her. Maybe make her feel seen. Help her recall the good things in her life. It could have backfired if I'd been wrong."

"I only thought to dismiss her without looking for reasons for her surly attitude. I notice workflow and efficiency. Not the stress level of employees."

"I never used to notice others until--" She swallowed hard and jerked her eyes away. Her fingers returned to the napkin.

Tiago placed his hand over hers, stilling them. "I'm sorry about your father. I know losing him had a huge impact on your life. I wish I could take away the sting."

Her gaze flicked to his then darted away again, like a hummingbird. Fluttering her wings. Seeking the nectar that would sustain her. Or maybe she'd found it. Maybe it was him who needed sustenance. "I wish I had your faith."

Quinn narrowed her eyes, as if expecting a taunt. Her guard lowered as she took in his serious expression. She ran her teeth over her lip, a nervous tell.

He squeezed her hand for encouragement--and to feel the silk of her skin beneath his fingers. Even that small contact lit a spark in his belly. He tried to refocus, but her lips distracted him, full and oh, so, kissable.

Her hands slipped from beneath his, and she swatted his forearm. "Stop looking as if you want to eat me. We're speaking of holy things."

Tiago straightened, abashed. "You're very distracting."

She frowned at that, but let it go. "My faith comes from Cal and my mom, Missy."

So Missy was the woman he'd met with the adorable little girl, and the one Quinn depended on for advice.

"Something else you need to understand. I've always called my parents by their first names." She shrugged. "Anyway, shortly after Missy discovered she was pregnant, she met an older woman named Lucille."

"Was this in Shelby?"

"In Eureka. Way up near the Canadian border, north of Kalispell and west of Glacier. Cal is from around there too."

"Glacier? You mean the national park?"

"I forget you're not a Montana native. Yes. Incredible hiking and camping."

Tiago folded his arms on the table and leaned forward, eager to learn more.

She wrinkled her nose. "I always got the feeling they went through some really tough times. Missy's told me a few ugly childhood memories. She was left to fend for herself a lot." Quinn's eyes glazed over. "I don't want that life for--"

Terri arrived with their food, startling Quinn. "Here you are. Enjoy." With rounded shoulders, she set the plates before them and offered a tired smile. "I'll be back with coffee."

An odd look crossed Quinn's face before she straightened, eyes bright. "Thank you, Terri."

"Yes, thank you," Tiago jumped in. The woman was obviously exhausted, but her attitude switch amazed him. All because someone had gone out of her way to connect. Seeds of ideas began to germinate in his brain. He'd need time to nurture them, but they stirred an entirely different type of excitement in him from that generated by Quinn's presence and new openness.

U

Contentment cradled Quinn in leather as rolling green land sped past her window. They'd left Billings behind along with a generous tip and wave just over a quarter hour ago. She understood how a beloved horse must feel after a meal and a grooming. Her and Tiago's conversation hadn't been as intimate, yet his eager attention had drawn out her words.

Normally, she refused to speak of her beginnings.

Reporters had plied her with questions she never answered. She was thankful the arrival of their food had stopped her from revealing Reina's existence.

He hadn't reopened the subject––another surprise––but one which completely disarmed her. Had he forgotten, or was he respecting her privacy? Or had he already guessed? The last thought curdled the food digesting in her stomach.

"Have you ever been to the Little Big Horn Memorial?" Tiago glanced at her for a moment and tipped his chin toward a large sign in the distance.

She followed his gaze to the advertisement, swallowing the rising bile. Shook her head.

"Do you like history?"

He couldn't know about her else he'd press for details. She released her worries in a long exhale. "When it's told like a story. Not like school." She wrinkled her nose with the memory of Monotone Morris, her high school social studies teacher. "I could do without memorizing a bunch of names and dates only to forget them all after the test."

Tiago laughed. "History was like that for me until my junior year when we got a new teacher, Miss Sanderson. Man, could she tell a story. Had us all eating out of her hand. Sometimes we were so mesmerized we missed the bell signaling the end of the period."

"I envy you. I couldn't recite any of the information we supposedly 'learned' in Morris's class. Multiple choice questions and the ability to embellish saved my grade."

Quinn curled her left leg onto the seat and leaned against the door for a better view of Tiago's face. More forgiving than the landscape of rocky undulating hills––a blend of strength and kindness she'd seen in Cal, but rarely anywhere else. Maybe Coach McCloud, too, but he wasn't as in tune with her. Not that he should be. He had an entire team to worry about. Somehow Tiago's face had always been the one she sought for approval and comfort. Even if it had been across an arena.

"You got awfully quiet."

"Sorry. Thinking."

"About what?" Tiago's tone was low but sincere. Was he really interested?

"Missy told me once Lucille saved her life."

He flashed the grin and nod he'd always sent her way when they connected after one of her events. "How so?"

She pulled her other leg into the seat, turning her knees into a sort of mountain between them. While part of her longed to share her childhood, another part needed to hide from her past. And maybe her present as well.

"She never elaborated, but I believe it's because Lucille knew Jesus." Quinn laughed. "More than knew Him, she lived Him and shared Him. Years later, when I was thirteen, I met this incredible woman named Ellee who said Lucille and Lucille's husband mentored her through a really dark time in her life. I think that's my mother's story too."

Tiago gave her knee a quick squeeze, then returned his hand to the wheel. "I'm glad they each had someone to help them."

"Me too."

"How did you meet Ellee?"

Warmth toward the woman who'd befriended her when she'd most needed someone expanded Quinn's chest. "Cal called Ellee to get me back on my horse."

"Get back on?" Tiago shook his head.

"Seems crazy, doesn't it? We couldn't afford a broke horse, so Cal bought me a rather wild and somewhat crazy two-year-old filly no one had been able to tame, let alone break."

Tiago gave a slow nod. "Let me guess, Delilah?"

"Exactly. As difficult as she was to handle during rodeos,

she was ten times worse at two. Every time I thought I'd won her over, she'd back off again, getting all skittish and jittery. We finally got her used to the saddle, and I thought she'd let me ride." Quinn huffed. "Boy, was I wrong. She bucked me off in record time, and I was done. I told Cal I'd never sit on that black devil's back again. Not that I could move for the next three days anyway."

They shared a chuckle, before Quinn's mouth pulled taut. "About this time, my school-days nemesis started up his old taunts, saying I had no real dad." Quinn couldn't contain her grimace.

"What happened?" His hand returned to her knee, courage seeping through their connection.

"It was too much being the week after my ignominious dismount––my failure. I fell into what can best be described as an angry depression."

"Is the guy still around?" Tiago's grip tightened.

"Easy, Tiger. I took care of him long ago, and he's beneath your consideration."

The frown said he wasn't satisfied. "So you refused to ride?"

"Yep. All the rejection spiraled me into darker and darker places. That's when Ellee stepped in. She convinced me to go to the barn. Not to ride, just see how Delilah was. Ellee could be persuasive. Her confidence level was a bit overwhelming at times but inspiring, too."

"Sounds like an amazing woman."

"She is. I credit her with my ability to read horses. To consider their desires and work with those to persuade the animal to cooperate."

"How did she learn?"

"She was a jockey before most of the Montana tracks closed. Said she couldn't gallop one of Lucille's horses without him running off until she learned to draw her strength from God. They ended up winning some important races, but not without several really big setbacks."

"So your incredible resiliency comes from her?"

He thought her resilient?

Tell him.

Quinn recoiled, planting her bare feet on the floor. His hand returned to the wheel, and she regretted her instinctive reaction.

A sign appeared ahead. Little Big Horn Memorial 5 miles.

"Can we stop?"

"If you like."

She felt his gaze and nodded. She'd often been asked if she were Blackfeet or Absarokee--commonly called Crow--because of her facial structure and skin tone. Her stomach twisted. Her father could have been either given Eureka's proximity to tribal lands.

"Do you have native ancestors?"

Tiago's gentle question sparked Quinn's anger at being denied information for so many years. She twisted a lock of hair around her finger while shoving the overboiling feelings down. If only she were brave. "Cal was my dad. He raised and cared for me my whole life, but neither he nor Missy spoke about my heritage."

The prick of tears stung her eyes. Then the feel of Cal, cradling her, explaining how he took Missy in, his joy when the adoption went through. How he loved their family--loved her. And yet, Quinn was the result of a failed abortion. Her own mother had tried to eliminate her. Granted, Missy hadn't thought her a person, but even so, the knowledge was hard to accept.

Warm pressure gripped her arm. She bit her lip and glanced through a curtain of hair. Concern darkened Tiago's already brooding gaze, prompting her attempt at a reassuring smile. It fell flat. She squeezed her eyes against the growing moisture.

His hand left her arm, and she huddled against the door. Would he abandon her in her moment of weakness?

Like Cal?

The thought hit her from nowhere with the force of a raging bull. Everyone in her life had abandoned her. Or tried to.

The truck slowed and she swayed as it changed trajectory but didn't open her eyes, too devastated to care where they went. The pavement shifted beneath the tires, crunching as if on gravel, then increased speed.

"Quinn, talk to me." Warmth radiated from where his hand touched her hunched back. "Despite your belief in my superhuman abilities, I can't read your mind."

The quiet earnestness of his voice, his touch, and the attempt to distract her, broke the tenuous hold she had on her fears. They slammed through the cracked dam, thunderous in their rush to fill her––to exist in the open where she'd denied them for so long. Quinn buried her face and sobbed as Tiago's fingers drew circles between her shoulder blades.

The truck slowed. His hand disappeared, and the window lowered. A gruff voice spoke. Clothing rustled. The window whirred, and the truck moved forward. Her sobs slowed to hiccups, tears to a trickle. She sniffed.

Something touched her palm. She wiped her face with the scratchy napkin, then pushed upright, a hand on the dash. A tableau of rolling hills spread before her. An old building crouched on her right, and signage indicated trails and markers denoting various battles.

Tiago pulled into a space and shut off the engine. He appraised her.

"That bad, huh?" She blew her nose and gave a final sniff. "Could we find a restroom first?"

His smile and nod reflected a heroic nature that tugged at her guilt. He deserved someone brave. Someone more like him.

She stepped out to overcast skies. A stiff breeze gusted up the valleys and onto the hilltops, fussing with her hair. She shivered, though the temperature hovered around eighty. Tiago took her elbow and steered her toward a small building bearing a restroom sign.

Rows of white grave markers stood in stark contrast to the emerald prairie grasses surrounding them. The etched names shadowed by collected dirt and moss made Quinn shiver once more. Tiago tightened his hold.

The cool water revived Quinn, and she determined to soak in the atmosphere of this place. Use it to connect with the Almighty and ask for strength and wisdom. She needed both in spades because relying on Tiago had to cease. He wouldn't stay with her after she destroyed his idealistic view of Queen—of her.

She drew in a slow breath, fortifying her defenses, though nothing could repair the damage done to her walls. She feared returning to the emotion-driven woman she'd been before those men brutally attacked her. Missy was right. Much as it seemed like that girl had it all together, she'd been scared, only hiding in plain sight. The over-the-top persona of being daring and brave had been just that—a persona. A place to hide the truth that she was still the terrified little girl running from Bully Bobby's taunts because she feared they were true. Silencing him with violence, so she could remain in denial.

When she emerged from the building, Tiago's penetrating gaze swept over her. Would he see through her?

He hurried the few steps to join her holding a folded map.

"It appears we can begin here, walking among the markers, or take a path to visit several of the battlefields and the Native American Monument."

Quinn peered around. Couples strolled along the rows, pausing now and then for a picture. Beyond the museum rose the path promising an overview of the battlefields, no people in sight. Solitude and open spaces beckoned. "Let's start there."

His irises flashed gold. He made a show of proffering his arm as if they were in Victorian England, not the wild Montana countryside.

Tiago swept his cap from his head and gave a little bow.

She suppressed a giggle––her emotions careening all over. Her next giggle bubbled free as she slid her hand into the crook of his elbow.

He really was her hero.

The wind rushing through waist-high grass, the birds, and the connection with this intriguing man relaxed her spirit. As Tiago guided her along the path, they stopped to read the story that had unfolded on the ground dropping away before them. A tragic number of lives had been lost, bringing a silent prayer to her lips.

They continued climbing, stopping several more times to read and ponder the senselessness of it all, the lack of respect for another's way of life. At the top of the hill, they reached an interesting circular structure whose sign read, "Indian Memorial."

An inward tug separated her from Tiago and drew her forward through a narrow gap in the walls. She peered at and then through the exquisite metalwork outlining three warriors riding to battle, to the tall grasses beyond and on to the horizon where gathered clouds met earth. The memorial's theme, "Peace through Unity," resonated with her. That sense of destiny as much as the touch of Tiago's fingers on hers, sent a shudder up her spine.

She grasped his hand, interlocking their fingers. Peace through unity. Was this God's way of telling her to stop isolating herself? To stop hiding? Together they moved around the inside of the structure reading the weighty words.

Neither spoke, but their grip tightened. When she read the etched plaques set in the wall, she faced the bronze sculpture, this time noticing the woman handing her warrior a shield. "What heartbreak the women bore as they scoured the battlefields for their dead and dying husbands, brothers, and sons."

Tiago pulled her close and she tucked her head into his shoulder. He hesitated, then wrapped his arm around her, anchoring her in place. "One thing I love about you is your ability to see to the heart of a person. Like with the waitress earlier."

"I've had to learn the truth isn't always what is visible, beginning with myself." She expected fear to chase her boldness, but instead, freedom buoyed her spirit.

Tiago guided her through the Spirit Gate, one of four entrances at each cardinal direction into the memorial allowing for free movement of the spirits of the dead.

Quinn knew nothing about spirit movement, though she believed in a spiritual realm and spiritual battles. Evil had fueled her own attack.

"I don't recall a time where you treated anyone harshly."

Her brows crashed together. "But we never met."

His lips softened into a knowing smile. "We met every time you found my face after tying a calf or roping a steer. You saw me when no one else did. More than that, you made me feel important, and it changed the way I looked at myself.

Exactly the way it affected Terri this morning. You have a gift, but I'm afraid you're locking it away."

Wow. He'd pegged her. "I think you're the one with the gift. And I think you lied about the mind-reading gig." She slanted him a glance, lips quirked.

"Pure coincidence." They moved down the paved path toward the cemetery.

"I don't believe in coincidence. Or luck."

"You and my mother will get along splendidly. She's constantly preaching those same words."

He grinned so Quinn knew he was teasing, at least in part. But the words sobered her, set her mind spinning off in directions she hadn't allowed in years. She cocked her head. "My mother didn't lie as much as suppress the truth about my beginnings. I believe Ellee knew more than she let on, too. Once she spoke of my grandmother as if acquainted with her, but I was young and insecure, so I never pressed.

"Maybe they had good reasons not to tell you." Tiago's even tone––his ability to stay calm in every situation––was one of her favorite things about him. She'd drawn encouragement from his steadiness in her rodeo days, and it bolstered her now.

"You think Missy emphasized Cal was my 'real' father so she didn't have to lie? He *was* in all ways but blood. But why not tell the truth sooner?" Her stomach pinched. She was guilty of the same subterfuge.

"Maybe she didn't know how." Tiago's words hit home.

Quinn squirmed. In one sentence, he'd laid bare the very problem she wrestled with. She couldn't go there.

"I saw you break up a fight between two cowboys once. One was popular, high-ranking, the other a no name. The gathered crowd obviously favored the popular guy, but you showed no bias toward either of them. I've never forgotten."

Tiago turned wide eyes on her. "You remember that?"

"It was the first time I saw you unfiltered by dust." She waited, but when the muscle flexed in his jaw, she nudged him with her elbow. "Care to tell me the story?"

He drew a loud breath, eyes remaining on the view. "My freshman year I didn't qualify for the CNFR, but I attended to support the others. When I heard shouting, I crowded around with everyone else."

"But you didn't gawk or egg them on."

He huffed in self-deprecation. A habit he employed with frequency. "No, I waded into the middle of the mess and nearly got my butt kicked. But at least that time I didn't punch anyone."

"You broke them up. Sent them packing in different directions. It was magnificent."

Tiago faced her. "That's what you saw?"

She frowned. "Isn't that what happened?"

"I recognized my cousin and convinced him to back down by threatening to tell his father he'd been brawling in public. My uncle's a jerk, but he hates open displays. He'd take somebody down in a dark alley but shake hands with them in a crowd. He's that kind of lowlife."

They moved to the side of the path for an oncoming family. Each young parent held the hand of a child and smiled warm greetings as they passed. The eldest youngster——a little girl with dark pigtails——turned back. "Hi." Her high, sweet voice brought the separation from Reina bearing down on Quinn's chest. She tried to smile but feared it came across more like a grimace.

Tiago grasped her shoulders. "Quinn, what's wrong?" His soul-touching eyes threatened to swallow her in their depths, daring her to trust him. So much warmth, she nearly broke.

"Children complicate things. Some men can't handle it." Missy's words. Would the truth drive him away? Or maybe it would be her lack of trust? Regardless, this instance revealed how

much she needed to put distance between them. She'd relaxed too much. Shared too much––and yet, not enough. Her heart was becoming too engaged––too entangled. How would she recover if another person she cared for abandoned her?

Her shoulders shook, not hard, but enough to focus her attention on the one place she didn't dare allow them to linger––Tiago's gaze. Creases across his strong forehead and around his eyes and mouth made her feel cared for, but she couldn't keep him in agony––had to say something.

"It's . . . I was reminded how my biological father didn't want me." Missy hadn't wanted her either. Thinking of Missy's confession brought so much pain Quinn had to move on or get sucked into a maelstrom she didn't know if she'd have the strength to escape.

She clasped Tiago's hand and pasted on a smile. "Let's walk through some of the headstones before we leave." She tugged him along the path, stepping from it onto the first bright grassy strip. Flanked by the long rows of stones, each with a name and date, new emotions clogged Quinn's throat.

Tiago walked silently beside her wearing a pensive look, mouth askew and eyes unfocused. They reached the end of the row and rounded into another.

She steered him around the few broken branches and gopher hole hazards they encountered, unwilling to break the solemnity of the setting. Eventually, she pointed them toward his truck.

He grasped both her hands and tugged her close, then turned her to face him, their eyes almost level. She gasped, staring into the hope that sparkled the gold ringing his irises.

When he spoke, his voice resonated in the pit of her stomach. "My relationship with God has been a bit one-sided––at least lately. But my mother's favorite saying won't leave my head. You need to know that no matter how many people fail you, Jesus never will." He exhaled slowly, tucking her hands against his chest.

The rhythmic rise and fall and the rapid beating of Tiago's heart fascinated Quinn. She barely breathed herself, unwilling to ruin this moment with a sudden brash move.

"I tried to ignore the nudge the whole time we walked." He freed one hand to encircle her waist. "He wouldn't let me off the hook."

His breath feathered across her face, smelling of the trail mix he'd brought for their journey. Sweet and salty. Unconsciously, she leaned in and rose onto her toes. By the time she realized her brazenness, he'd tightened his hold.

A moment of panic, then realization she was safe. Heat coursed through her––foreign, but welcome and slightly intoxicating. Maybe protected but not safe. Not when she wished he'd kiss her lying lips so thoroughly she'd forget the confession that had cracked the bedrock of her life.

"Queen." His gaze roved her face, settling on her lips.

She stiffened at the nickname. Then the screech of air brakes startled them both, followed by the cessation of a diesel engine Quinn hadn't noticed before. Mingled voices carried down the hill.

With excruciating gentleness, Tiago's fingers traced the curve of her cheek. "I'll not have our first kiss be in public."

He released her and she nearly stumbled without his support. His hand snagged hers, steadied her, then let go. "You okay?"

Quinn recoiled, terrified by the intensity of her feelings and the odd sense of loss without his touch. Like she felt without Reina but different. Distance. She needed distance. "I'm fine." Another lie. She strode toward the truck, new heat searing her insides.

Maybe cultivating her cautious side was a mistake. A little

courage might be useful about now. And she knew Jesus wouldn't fail her, didn't she?

But if she truly trusted her Savior, wouldn't she do what he asked? She'd taken up lies as her shield instead of faith. She swallowed, recognizing the battle Tiago had fought to bring her those words. She'd thought she was the only one, but maybe he struggled too.

"Our first kiss."

They hadn't even made it out of Montana, and she was sinking under Tiago's spell. But she was a liar. He'd called her Queen. He thought he knew her. What would happen when he found out she wasn't who he believed her to be?

The truck ate the miles as day faded to twilight. Conversation had focused on mundane topics, and Tiago could admit he was relieved. He wasn't the only one drained by the day, if a sleeping Quinn curled into a kitten-like ball meant anything. Her withdrawal had hiked his compassion and his concern. He wished she would share whatever was bothering her, but at the same time, he didn't know how to put his own feelings into words, so couldn't blame her for skirting worries and fears.

He doubted Quinn realized her allure. She spent so much time reading and responding to others' needs, she likely didn't notice the reactions she invoked, especially in men. When she relaxed and let herself be herself instead of forcing the press's Arena Queen to the foreground, her vibrancy and presence made her the most compelling woman Tiago had ever met.

If only she'd stop pushing him away.

Near Sioux Falls, he pulled into a truck stop to refuel. The lights and changes in motion must have awakened Quinn, because she stretched, much like the kitten he'd been comparing her to, and yawned.

"Are we there yet?" Her voice held that just-awakened muffle and made her attempt at humor even more adorable.

He wished he could gather her into his arms and kiss her fully awake, but other than her connection with him, he'd never known her to encourage men's affection--even friendship--and he doubted she'd welcome such a move. At Little Big Horn, she'd seemed to be opening up, until he'd almost kissed her and her body went rigid. No, definitely not a good idea. At least, not yet. "Have a good nap?" he asked instead.

"Where are we?" She sat up and combed fingers through her long hair. The ebony strands caught the light, shining like black diamond.

Tiago's throat tightened at her beauty. He focused on the gas pump and cleared it. "South Dakota. Are you hungry? There's a food court of sorts here." The hunger he felt had nothing to do with food, but he was proud of how even his voice had sounded. The passenger door opened, then closed. He refused to look at her. Didn't want to feed the growing heat in his belly.

"I'm going in to find the little girl's room."

"I'll finish fueling, then park and find you."

"I'll try to decide what I want in the meantime."

She spoke with such confidence, the problem that had chased him out of Nashville resurrected. *Find your passion.* The only answer he had to his father's quest was Quinn, and Tiago didn't think Joaquín Vargas would find it sufficient. But for Tiago Vargas, Quinn was enough. If only she returned his affection.

The pump clicked off. Tiago topped off the tank, then replaced the nozzle. After he'd pulled forward to a parking space, he ventured inside to look for Quinn. As soon as he entered, the space felt wrong, his sense of equilibrium thrown off by the layout and flow. Muted conversation, presumably from the occupants of the vehicles lining the half-full parking area, flowed around a block wall packed with touristy items. Postcards, keychains, shot glasses, stickers and the like forced him to choose left or right.

The architects should have left that area open with the array of businesses visible so anyone entering could see the choices. All he could figure was the building must be old. No modern design would have directed traffic in this pattern.

He randomly chose left, thinking about the traffic flow and layout section of his marketing design class. He'd dug in with enthusiasm, choosing to present a plan for a retail and restaurant space as his project. The professor's compliment on his ingenuity in meshing aesthetic appeal with practicality and accessibility had fueled him for weeks.

He rounded the wall and searched for Quinn against a backdrop of standard fast-food fare. That project had been the first time any interest sparked from his studies. While he'd performed well in all of his classes, rarely had he been intrigued by the material.

Tiago navigated past clumps of people. Families, couples, truckers, a few teens who could be locals, but no ebony hair shining in the neon signage. He stopped and turned in a slow circle, surveying each nook and cranny. There, leaning into an alcove near the restrooms with her phone to her ear, one foot propped on the wall, was Quinn. He released his breath and forced his fingers to unclench. Allowed his heartbeat to return to normal.

Rather than interrupt, Tiago took the moment to study her. Her bowed head brought a curtain of hair to shadow her face, but he could picture her thin straight nose, prominent cheekbones, strong chin, and mesmerizing gray eyes. He'd memorized her features after two years of long-distance connections at rodeos and a bit of social media stalking. Nothing creepy, but he kept track of her successes and failures.

Quinn slumped, and she grabbed the phone with both hands. Tiago took a hurried step forward and nearly plowed into an elderly woman carrying cherry-topped milkshakes in each hand.

His arm flew up as if to ward her off, foolishness heating his neck immediately afterward. "I'm sorry, ma'am. I wasn't watching where I was going."

She glanced at him, then moved away, muttering, "Young people. Always in a hurry."

He raised his brows, then continued forward, but when he looked up, Quinn was gone. He took two more steps, casting his gaze into every corner he could find. Still no Quinn. His pulse skyrocketed. A tap on his shoulder spun him around.

A smiling Quinn opened her mouth to speak, but he closed the distance between them and threw his arms about her, squeezing hard as a volatile cocktail of panic and relief circulated in his blood. Hands shoved hard on his chest, forcing him back. He dropped his arms, a different panic beating at his ribs.

Grabbing her hand, he led her toward the food court, his gaze searching. There. A white DQ on a red background. He stopped at the counter.

"Order when you're ready," a teen with a horrible case of acne told him from behind a mask of boredom.

Tiago peered at the name badge. "Brian, we'd like two large hot fudge malts, please." He glanced at Quinn for the first time since his spontaneous embrace. "Would you like something to eat?" *Please let this work.*

Her mouth opened, then closed, and she eyed him with a sideways glare before turning her attention to the menu.

A silent sigh released the tension in his shoulders. He'd been so afraid he'd frightened her with his brazen invasion of her personal space. She wasn't ready for his advances, though her curves had molded to him as though made for him, and his arms ached to hold her once more.

"I'll have the chicken strip basket, please." Quinn flashed her lovely smile and poor Brian's mask melted.

"Make that two." Tiago paid, and they carried their food to a vacant booth.

Quinn looked around and wrinkled her nose. "This place is so dark. How am I going to know if I drip gravy all over myself?"

Tiago chuckled, then considered the cramped common dining area. "If they took out that wall and opened this up, they'd be able to space the tables and booths farther apart and also allow for skylights and other low-cost lighting options."

Quinn considered him, chin and forehead puckered. Then she placed a chicken strip on her garlic bread, smothered it in gravy, and rolled it like a giant burrito. Holding her creation with both hands, she lifted it toward her mouth. Pausing, she speared him with a look that seemed to shoot lighting from her intense gray eyes. "You're good at that."

He nearly didn't have enough breath left to speak and only managed to croak out a single word. "What?"

She'd already taken a huge bite, gravy oozing out. He covered his eyes with a hand, then peeked at her between his fingers. She chewed and stifled a laugh, then wiped her chin with a napkin. When she'd swallowed, she flicked her eyebrows at him. "Don't knock it till you try it."

"Oh, yeah?"

She nodded, one hand holding the remaining garlic bread. She raised it to take another bite.

He was quicker. He grabbed her hand and leaned over,

teeth closing on the intact end. He expected to force the food down. But somehow, the buttery garlic mixed with the spices of the chicken strip and the peppery gravy to create an explosion of flavors, sweet and savory, smooth and sharp, that made his taste buds dance.

"Right?" She licked gravy from her fingers, shooting flames up Tiago's spine.

What had Tiago gotten himself into? *Mercy, Lord!*

Quinn curled up in the king bed––body exhausted, mind spinning. The hotel was nicer than she would have chosen, but Tiago had insisted. They'd driven to Kansas City, rejuvenated by their food and antics at the Omaha travel plaza. He'd tried to put her at ease using her favorite ice cream, and he'd taken her gravy-and-garlic-chicken wrap seriously.

The way his eyes had sparkled golden when he'd stolen that bite prickled the skin on her arms and sent a tingle through her body. So goofy. So handsome.

She was so not in a place to take on another relationship.

The conversation with Missy slapped her silly dreams back to their place––in fantasyland. Quinn had a daughter to provide for and a mother to worry about. Why had Missy been so cryptic on the phone? Was she keeping some other catastrophic piece of her past a secret? The night before Quinn left with Tiago, she'd seemed willing to spill details, but Quinn had been too caught off guard by Missy's bombshell to ask questions.

In the hours and distance since, especially after her emotional connection with the Indian Memorial at Little Big Horn Park, she wanted more.

"Perhaps it's best if you don't know any more. It's enough you

understand why I'm so desperate to be here for Reina after being so distant from you."

Missy's words made Quinn want to punch something, though she'd never been prone to violence even in her Queen days. How could she deny her mother a chance to make up for her mistakes? And yet, Reina was *Quinn's* daughter, one everyone––including Missy––had encouraged her to abort.

The daughter she couldn't seem to claim where Tiago was concerned, which made no sense because if he wouldn't accept Reina, he couldn't have her. A chill wiggled its way up her spine.

Quinn curled onto her side and scrunched one of many pillows beneath her head. *Please, Lord, share your wisdom. Help me make the best choices for all of us.*

The next morning, her phone alarm punched through the familiar dream. An exhausted Quinn woke tangled in sheets and covers, drenched in sweat, and clinging for all she was worth to the only pillow remaining on the bed. She stretched her arms wide, inviting Jesus into every part of her and spent time in prayer asking for strength and peace.

When the emotions painted by the vivid images of her darkest moment had been replaced by the love flowing from her relationship with Jesus and reminders of the exceptional good that had resulted, she rose and showered. Thirty minutes later she met Tiago at her door, bag packed and ready to roll.

"You wear lavender well." Tiago slanted her an appreciative look before slipping her bag from her hand and leading her down the stairs and out to his truck.

"You don't look bad yourself." The words slipped out before she could stop them. Her ears warmed. Good thing her hair covered them. She rarely blushed, but if she had much more of this view, she might. My, he fit those jeans. Quinn resisted fanning herself as she settled into her seat.

The sun was partially hidden when they pulled onto the interstate headed east to St. Louis. Quinn delighted in the palette of colors climbing above the cloud bank. Rose, saffron, lavender, and finally, a fiery orange that split the pastels with its vibrance and shooed away the twilight to usher in the day.

What was Reina doing at this hour? Was she sleeping peacefully, or had she noticed Quinn's absence and fussed? Frustration ate at her morning's peace. Wanting to distract herself from obsessing when she could do nothing about the situation, she searched her mind for something that might initiate conversation with a tight-lipped Tiago.

"Tell me about your family. What should I know before I meet them?"

Tiago shifted his hands on the wheel and sent her a glance. "Do you want the surface level stuff, or are you digging for all the sordid details?"

"The sordid details, of course." She flashed him a raised brow and wiggled her body into the comfortable leather.

He adopted her teasing tone. "I'm not sure you can handle that much insider knowledge."

"Try me."

His countenance grew serious. "Do you really want to know?"

Quinn studied him, an unsettled feeling growing in her gut. She scooted as close as her seatbelt would allow and touched his arm, keeping the contact light. "I would like to hear whatever you'd like to tell me. No more and no less. I'm here to listen and support you."

He covered her hand with his own, pressing her fingers into his bare skin. The dark hair was rough beneath her palm, and the contact conjured a storm in her middle. The pressure from his warm hand nearly sent her into a loop-de-loop.

"You've no idea how much I appreciate hearing those words, Quinn."

He held her hand a moment longer, then released it and focused his attention on the highway traffic. Semi-trucks, SUVs, and delivery vans clogged the road, a few cars and farm trucks interspersed between them.

Once the traffic settled, his shoulders loosened, and he drew a long breath. "I always get nervous when the road is that crowded, thinking some other driver will lose control and cause an accident I'll get swept up in." He grimaced. "I know. Morbid thinking, but I can't seem to help it."

"Would it be better if I asked specific questions? You could always skip the ones you'd prefer not to answer."

He gave a curt nod. "That should work." His sideways glance seemed to beg for mercy.

Oh, my. "How did your parents meet?"

"They met when my mother was interning at my father's uncle's law firm. The way she tells it, she saw him first and decided on the spot he was the man she'd marry. My father disagrees, saying he's the one who fell in love first. Either way, they married six months later despite my mother's family's disapproval."

"Why didn't they like your father?"

"Multiple reasons––many the same ones Mom lists as the ones that drew her to him."

"I'm intrigued."

He flashed one of his gorgeous smiles––the kind that made her insides quiver. "My father immigrated to Tennessee from Argentina on a rodeo scholarship to attend UT Martin." Tiago glanced at her, but when she didn't react, he continued. "He'd only been in the states for a few hours when he met Mom, but she says his English was easy to understand, and she loved his accent. Loved his machismo—— that Latin flair bordering on arrogance. Confident, gallant, polite, and charming is what she calls him even today after twenty-nine years of marriage."

Quinn's heart swelled as she listened to Tiago's parents' love story. Not only the beauty of it but that he could recount it so well. Her throat thickened over the shadows obscuring her past. She tried to swallow the surge of bitterness and envy, but it refused to go away. She was blind to the scene whizzing by the windows, every consideration turned inward.

"Are you okay?" Concern clouded Tiago's voice. "I didn't mean to upset you."

She gave a quick shake of her head and swiped at the stupid tear escaping down her cheek. "It's lovely." She shifted, risking a glance. "Do you have a big family? I've always wondered what it would be like."

Something dark crossed Tiago's face, but it vanished in an instant. "I'm an only child, but my father's uncle has six children, who all have children of their own. My grandparents, two uncles, and an aunt live in Argentina along with multiple cousins. We rarely get together in one place, but it's a large group."

"What about on your mom's side? You said they didn't agree to the marriage. Have they softened over the years?"

His lips twisted. "Softened? No. Resigned themselves?" He lifted his palm and shrugged. "Uncle Bertram, Mom's older brother and heir to the family real estate business, hasn't ever gotten over the fact that an immigrant bought the property Casa Vargas occupies out from under him. While he's learned to play nice on the surface, I'm certain underneath he's plotting a way to get it back."

Quinn's brows drew together. "That's horrible."

"And my father refuses to do anything about it. His sense

of honor requires he respect his wife's brother, regardless that he's a beady-eyed, self-serving lizard. No offense to lizards as a species."

A single beat of laughter blew out with her breath. "Holidays must be fun at your house."

Tiago's voice warmed and deepened as if recalling fond memories. "They are usually. We tend not to invite the Renault side very often."

They rode in companionable silence until Tiago pointed out her side window. "There's the arch."

The sun's orb fit beneath the top of the horseshoe-shaped silver structure, reflecting spun gold over the landscape and sky. A strip of river rippled beyond, spanned by a bridge.

"So different than in pictures." She shaded her eyes with her hand and took in the magnificence of the scene.

Tiago shifted lanes, taking the exit. "Let's go see it."

"But--"

He cut off her protest. "We won't stay long."

They spent the next forty-five minutes taking the first elevator of the morning to the top, gasping and laughing at the sights from the observation deck, then walking to the river where the paddle wheeler docked. They took the obligatory selfie with their heads framed by the arch and a few others with the city and park as backdrops, before strolling back to the parking garage with a late breakfast--slaw-topped barbeque sandwiches they'd charmed from the skeptical waiter at the Hyatt--in hand.

Minutes later, they crossed the bridge into Illinois on Interstate 64. Quinn couldn't process Tiago's seeming delight in presenting her with new experiences. As they chatted about rodeo days, food, and horses--while avoiding any mention of family--Tiago's habit of building others up while diminishing himself roused Quinn's protective streak. She longed to take down a peg whoever he'd compared himself to and come away lacking.

A bit of Queen's redemptive fire ignited. Around the rodeo she'd taken sweet revenge on many a bully on behalf of one victim or another. Through her wits and stealth, she anonymously orchestrated small, harmless stunts that satisfied her sense of justice and provided others a good laugh.

Remembering her attack doused the flame. After that night, she'd never again pull a prank on an unsuspecting victim, deserving or not.

"Ready to stretch your legs a bit?" Tiago pointed to a green sign. Paducah 2.

"Fresh air would be nice."

Tiago directed the truck along the exit ramp and followed the arrows left to a cluster of gas stations and fast-food restaurants. After refueling and using the facilities, they found their way downtown and ended up on Water Street where they paused for a view of the Ohio River.

"When I see huge amounts of water like this, I always wonder where it originated." Tiago stood so close to Quinn their shoulders touched.

His tension transferred to her, stirring her as much as his words had. She pressed into them. "The mountains make me shake sometimes with their ruggedness and utterly unapologetic, ruthless beauty. But water does something similar. Especially when it's moving with the force of the Mississippi or the Ohio. I've never seen the ocean, but I can imagine the weight and power it contains."

Tiago's fingers brushed hers. A tentative touch. When she didn't flinch, he wrapped her hand in his. Quinn's accelerating pulse beat options against her temple. Bolt or lean in?

She did neither, holding her body immobile, though her brain refused to be still. Warmth radiated from their connection, running up her arm and threatening to reach her heart.

Not the zinging sting of electricity but more a hearth fire meant for refuge and comfort.

Sustenance.

Quinn jerked her hand away but maintained contact through their shoulders. Prior experience taught that each time she began to rely on someone, something life-altering occurred. She couldn't handle another shift.

Tiago tensed. Did her withdrawal anger him? Confuse him? Hurt him?

Lord, help! I'm drawn to this man.

Did she dare let down her guard? The part of her that craved relationship wanted to fall into his arms. But that wasn't fair. He wasn't her mother and couldn't fill that empty place. Only God could, and He did. If only Quinn could release herself fully, but as the moment proved, she always withheld a part of herself. Even from the God she loved. Knowing that truth, how could she ever hope to love a man the way he deserved?

Gooseflesh prickled on Quinn's arms. She crossed them to ward off the sudden chill. "We should get going."

Quinn avoided Tiago's gaze as they made their way to the interstate and resumed their journey. She didn't want to see the hurt, or more likely, concern in his eyes. But she wasn't worthy of his care, though she didn't know how to explain that without inviting questions she wasn't ready to answer. Best to get on with the real purpose of their cross-country trek and return to Montana where she could eliminate him from her life--for his own good.

CHAPTER 11

Tiago would never understand the woman who sat close enough to touch, yet so far withdrawn he couldn't reach her. Miles had sped by even as his brain spun reasons why Quinn would accept him one minute and reject him the next. He wished the signs proclaiming their imminent arrival in Nashville could point the way toward correcting his own deficiencies. At least show where he could find the elusive *pasión* he sought.

For what seemed the hundredth--or thousandth--time, he glanced at Quinn huddled against the door, staring out her side window. A sigh escaped his lips. Surely the worship music would mask it.

Quinn's glance through a curtain of hair shattered that hope. He'd do anything to ease the hurt etched on her soul. While pain was inevitable, he'd gladly spend his days shielding her from what he could and holding her through what he couldn't. The memory of her in his arms shot a bittersweet ache into his chest that radiated outward, tingling his fingers.

He blinked his eyes in a silent prayer. How odd that he would revert to that habit now after years of disuse.

Traffic increased, requiring most of his attention. The sun overhead glinted off windshields and hoods making sunglasses mandatory. Quinn scooted upright in her seat, the bustle of outer Nashville drawing her from wherever she'd run to after his latest botched attempt at affection.

"It's bigger than I thought." Quinn cleared her throat. "Makes me sound like a backcountry hick, doesn't it?"

Startled by her sudden return to conversation, Tiago fumbled for a reply. "Just because you haven't experienced something doesn't make you a hick. You're one of the most intelligent women I know."

Not to mention compassionate and caring, but he couldn't add that. Bad enough he'd complimented her so openly. The last thing he wanted was for her to return to her silent shell.

Instead, she turned stormy eyes on him, her voice serious. "And you're one of the most compassionate men I know."

She'd turned his thoughts back on him, and they hit with the force of a slap. He made to deny her claim, but her hand closed on his arm.

"Don't you dare tell me I'm wrong. I've watched you try to charm and care for me this entire trip—since you arrived in Montana, really. Even when I rebuff you. Stop thinking the worst of yourself. You're a good person with a huge heart. You work so hard to make me comfortable. You're . . . amazing." She crossed her arms over her chest and shoved her body back in her seat, glaring at him.

The air left his lungs. What could he say? What did it mean? He exited the interstate, then headed east, checking the dashboard clock. Where to go? The restaurant or home?

His stomach issued a long gurgle. "Hungry?"

Quinn placed an open palm against her middle. "I could eat. Do you have a favorite haunt to show me?"

One minute she ran, the next she invited him closer. He was beginning to feel a bit like one of those children's toys with the paddle and attached ball. But even as he considered his bruises, the perfect place came to mind.

Lunch at Melody's Café served two purposes. Sharing a bit of Nashville's musical tradition, and also delaying the reunion with his father, who would be going over numbers from lunch in the lull before dinner. The promise of tasty food delivered yet another plus. Even at this odd hour, he had to park a block away.

Tiago opened the glass door for Quinn who gazed at the vintage décor. The high-backed vinyl booths, checked tile flooring, and retro lighting worked in concert to provide a nostalgic atmosphere. When a dark-haired hostess with "Neve" on her nametag approached in an apron-covered skirt and white button-up blouse, Quinn sent him a smile that shimmied heat up his spine.

They followed Neve to a booth situated at the edge of an open space anchored by an elevated platform. Microphones and other electronic equipment rimmed the edge beneath a pipe railing. A set of steps curved upward allowing entrance via a hinged pipe gate.

Neve handed them each a menu, then glanced behind her. She flashed a warm smile. "You're in luck. Sully's about to sing in the tower."

A tall, young man with dark hair and darker eyes ascended the steps and entered the circle. His black boots gleamed from beneath black jeans, and his pale blue western shirt hung open over a skin-tight, Melody's Café t-shirt that made Tiago self-conscious about his hit-or-miss workout regimen since graduation.

"Annika will be here shortly to take your drink order. Enjoy the melody." Neve left to greet another guest.

As the man--Sully, Tiago supposed--placed a guitar strap over his head and settled his fingers on the strings, Quinn leaned across the booth, eyes wide. "This is the most unique restaurant I've ever been to. It's fabulous."

Tiago tried to see the place through her eyes. Ladies occupied about a quarter of the seats, multi-aged couples another quarter, with eight to ten single men in suits. Leaning toward Quinn, he indicated one of the suited executives and lowered his voice. "That man's likely from music row. Many a current or rising star has been discovered here."

Sully strummed a chord, then began his song. The rich, sorrowful tones turned nearly every eye to the singer. He performed a ballad, perhaps an original, though Tiago didn't keep up on the latest in country music. The waitress arrived at the chorus and took their order. She returned with their drinks, but the song had Quinn enthralled, so he held up five fingers asking for more time.

She nodded and approached another table.

When Sully's song ended, applause erupted from the silence along with a whistle or two.

Sully addressed the patrons in the same warmth with which he sang. "Thank you. I appreciate your enthusiastic welcome. This one might be more familiar." He launched into a popular upbeat tune.

Quinn perused her menu. "He's good, but I prefer the ballad."

Tiago agreed, then pointed out two of his favorite sandwiches.

After they ordered, they listened to a slower cover about searching for love, a better fit for Sully's sultry voice.

"Are places like this common in Nashville?" Quinn's fingers kept time as she swayed to the lyrics.

"Not like this. Melody's is unique. Sully works here. After this song, he'll be back waiting tables while another employee takes over the tower. But lots of clubs hold open mic nights where aspiring singers and songwriters vie for the attention of agents and producers as well as gain experience in front of an audience."

Quinn nodded, her focus on him. "I'm sure it's like rodeo. The practice arena isn't the same as performing in front of hundreds of eyes."

"It certainly isn't."

She cocked her head. "Stage fright? Really? You always seemed so solid, like nothing could touch you."

He raised his brows. "That's the image I wanted to project, but inside, my guts roiled every time I backed Quilombo into the box."

"Huh."

Her reaction had Tiago questioning Quinn's projected confidence, but Sully launched into a chorus, distracting her. He blew out a breath and leaned back, soaking her in. She rested her head on her hand, ebony hair flowing down her arm to puddle on the table. Dark lashes framed large eyes that possessed the power to unravel his thoughts and his emotions. Even in rest, her lithe frame suggested strength and agility, matched by quick intelligence and wit as well as a deep reverence for God.

If she had flaws, he'd not found them. Her sometimes-bossy attitude, the single-minded focus, endeared her to him. He wanted all of her for himself but had no idea how to woo her. So far, everything he'd tried had ultimately ended in failure. The story of his life, it seemed.

But Tiago had long ago learned the value of tenacity and perseverance. He wasn't ready to quit, though he had no idea how to move forward. He'd have to have faith as his mother always admonished him. *"Stop trying to force things. God has his own timing. It is perfect and cannot be hurried."*

Tiago was tired of waiting, but what other choice did he have?

U

Quinn and Tiago left the nostalgia of Melody's to emerge into modern bustle and a blast of heat from the afternoon sun. Her tastebuds tingled from the vinegary perfection of the barbecue burger she'd ordered at Tiago's suggestion. The taste lingered with a hint of vanilla from the fountain Coke.

Cars rushed by even on this smaller street, reminding Quinn she wasn't in Bozeman. When Tiago cupped her elbow, she didn't pull away, needing the anchor in this new environment.

"I'm glad we came here first." She smiled at the handsome cowboy, her stomach clenching around her lunch. Maybe she shouldn't have eaten quite so fast.

He released her elbow to unlock her door and hand her in as if continuing their earlier jest, and she was his lady. If he only knew. She sank into the now-familiar leather and buckled her seatbelt. The click echoed, adding a twist to the tightness in her middle.

She'd soon meet his parents.

Tiago brought sunshine and exhaust into the cab. "Me too. I wasn't ready for my mom's enthusiasm or my father's disappointment."

She narrowed her eyes. "Why would he be disappointed?"

His fingers stalled, and his gaze locked onto hers. "Because I haven't found my passion." He pressed his lips together as if to keep other words from escaping, then started the engine and slipped into traffic with the ease of a born city-dweller.

On the ride to Casa Vargas--the destination Tiago said would take at least fifteen minutes to reach despite being only a mile away--Quinn watched the buildings slide by with only partial attention. Tiago's words played over in her mind. *"I haven't found my passion."*

He'd said something similar before. What did he mean? She wanted to ask, but the tight mask over his features made her hesitate.

Instead, she considered her own life. Horses had once been her passion. One she'd exercised through rodeo. But something had broken inside when she'd been forced to part with her beloved equines. She wasn't sure how to heal the still-raw wound. Seeing Delilah had set it to bleeding again. It hurt, then and now. So she did what she always did--she buried it.

Tiago's offer had prodded the wound. While part of her yearned to be in the saddle again, the other part warned how much pain it would cause. Why she'd even agreed to this crazy journey, she didn't know.

Liar. Spending time alone with Tiago in a happily-ever-after fantasy had sold her. Even though escape was temporary and she'd return to her mess, she'd granted herself this glimpse of what might have been. Likely another wrong choice.

The truck turned onto a side street and arrived at a gate of sorts. Tiago punched in a code that raised the barrier, then navigated a narrow passage leading beneath a large, brick building.

"Private parking for family and staff," he said.

"Wow. This is not what I expected."

Rows of industrial fluorescent bulbs lit the space. Concrete columns supported the building above them, leaving spaces between for parking maybe a dozen vehicles. Only four were parked there now. Quinn knew little about cars, but recognized the Mercedes symbol on a black sedan and the slinking cat on a sleek, sporty two-door.

Tiago inclined his head to the sports car. "The Jag belongs to Casa Vargas' sous chef, Omar. He's enamored with shiny things, but he's a wizard with a knife. The Mercedes is Mom's. Dad insisted she have something reliable and safe." He pointed to a sedate Audi parked in the farthest space along the wall. "That's his."

Quinn frowned. "But?"

Tiago nodded, threading the truck expertly between two columns and shutting off the engine. "He's never been one to spend money on himself. I think it's a hold-over from his Argentinean upbringing."

He opened his door, and she made to follow suit. "Allow me. Please. Argentinean custom dictates utmost respect for women. My father would be disappointed should I fail to open your door and escort you to the elevator. Expect the same deference when we're inside and at home."

Quinn opened her mouth to protest, but he held up a hand. "It isn't that we don't believe women are strong or independent. My mother is both, I assure you. It's a show of respect, even reverence in some cases."

She wrinkled her nose at his sudden formality, then unbuckled her belt. Tiago rounded the truck's hood and opened her door, letting in the stale exhaust and tang of petroleum. When he took her hand to help her down, his unique spicy scent enveloped her. Between the skin-to-skin contact and his intoxicating nearness, Quinn's quaking limbs were glad for his aid. He pressed a hand to the small of her back and guided her to the elevator.

Confronted with the reality of the opened doors inviting her into his world, Quinn's feet refused to move. She glanced at her Bobcat Rodeo tee and worn jeans. Painted toenails peeked from the frayed hems. "Maybe I should change first."

He surveyed her from the toes up, then his eyebrows waggled. "I see nothing I'd change."

She slapped his shoulder, but the tension was broken, her worry allayed--at least for now. "Fine. Be that way. But when your parents give me the stink-eye, I'll say I told you so."

He tugged her forward into the elevator's yawning maw and pushed one, then swiped a card she hadn't seen him retrieve from his wallet. "Security."

Too soon, a ding sounded and the doors slid open to reveal a hallway of old brick on one side and an industrial kitchen on the other. Pans hung from hooks. Long counters stretched between various appliances--stoves, grills, ovens, and others she couldn't name. The smells were a mixture of familiar and not but mouthwatering just the same. She inhaled deeply and surveyed the area in fascination.

A short, thin man in a white apron and cap scurried from one station to another, stirring and muttering to himself. Two women wearing aprons bustled in and disappeared behind the wall to Quinn's right, chatting amongst themselves. Moments later, they reappeared, filled baskets dangling over their arms.

Tiago propelled Quinn forward, then raised his hand in greeting. "Marisol, Anita, *buenos días*. Good to see you again."

The women squealed and rushed forward, depositing their baskets on a cart and taking turns hugging Tiago, then kissing his cheek. The taller of the two put a hand on her hip and slanted her eyebrows accusingly at Tiago. "Does *tú Mamá* know you're here?" Her English held only a hint of accent.

He laughed and reached back for Quinn, pulling her to his side. "Not yet, Marisol. We just came up."

The shorter woman, Anita, nodded to the doorway. "She's in the office."

"Where's *Papá*?"

Marisol swept her hand in a wide circle. "Who knows? He moves like the wind. No one keeps up with him, eh? *Siempre lo mismo*. He'll never change."

Tiago stiffened at Marisol's words. Then he relaxed in a way that felt forced. Or an ingrained habit. She grasped the hand at her waist and squeezed, wanting him to know he had her support. He tugged her tighter against him––a move that set her pulse racing and her nerves on edge. Their fingers interlocked.

Marisol and Anita shared a knowing look Quinn couldn't interpret, then gathered their baskets and flounced away.

Tiago met her gaze. "Ready?"

She scrunched her face. "Should I have brought defensive weapons?"

He laughed as she'd hoped he would, then unwound his arm, transferring hands and leading her past the exceedingly warm kitchen. "Your smile is disarming enough, I assure you."

Quinn wasn't so sure and readied her feet to flee if necessary.

Tiago knocked on an iron-banded wooden door that appeared straight out of the 1600s. "Mom loves medieval artifacts. This is from somewhere in England. They were tearing the building down, and Dad had the door imported. A Christmas gift, or––"

The door opened to reveal a blonde woman with blue eyes and a smile that spread across her face when she registered who stood before her. With arms flung wide, she closed the distance to Tiago, flinging herself into his ready embrace. Her head only reached his chest, and her curves prevented her arms from encircling his trim waist.

Quinn couldn't help the turn of her lips watching the strain his hug put on his shirt seams. She retreated a step to give them what little privacy she could. The brick ended at the doorway. Rough-cut wooden planks lent a rustic look to the rest of the hallway which opened onto the dining area, though only a portion was visible.

"And who is this beauty?" His mother's voice sounded sweet and airy, like birdsong.

Quinn faced mother and son, a tremor prompting her to grip the doorframe. Forcing herself forward, she thrust out a hand. "I'm Quinn. Nice to meet you, Mrs. Vargas."

Tiago's mother bypassed her formality and came in for another hug, only slightly shorter and less exuberant than the one she'd given Tiago. The woman's strength left Quinn a bit breathless when she withdrew. And the sight of Tiago's smirk over his mother's shoulder didn't help.

"I've been looking forward to your arrival since morning. He never said when you'd be here, the rascal." She gave Tiago a playful swat on the bicep.

"He stopped to show me some of the sights." Quinn delivered what she hoped was a winning smile. "I've never been this far east."

"You're from Montana, is that right?"

"Yes, Ma'am."

"Now, don't you go ma'aming me. I'm Laura or Mom to Tiago's friends, and I'll make no exceptions for you. Where are my manners? Come in. You're likely exhausted from all that traveling." Laura ushered them into her spacious office, calling down the hall behind them. "Anita, could I get some tea, please?"

"Of course, Laura," came the reply.

Tiago pulled Quinn onto a low upholstered bench placed strategically below the only window.

"Thank you kindly, dear." Laura closed the door and perched near Tiago on an antique chair. "What are your plans, now you're here?"

To Quinn, the question suggested a certainty he'd have

plans. Would Laura be disappointed if he didn't? Or maybe it was how her husband operated so she assumed Tiago would, too. Or perhaps Quinn's psychoanalyzing brain was on overdrive, and none of it meant anything.

Tiago included her with a look. "We're on assignment to screen a couple of potential scholarship students."

Laura's brows shot up. "Oh, sounds intriguing." She gestured at Quinn. "You work for the university also?"

"Uh?" She glanced at Tiago. "Temporarily."

"Quinn may be rejoining the rodeo team as an athlete this fall. I'm going to let her try Quilombo while we're here." Tiago patted Quinn's shoulder.

"I'm sure he will be grateful for some attention. I've been out a few times, but he misses you." To Quinn, she said, "Are you a roper?"

"Yes, Ma'am––Laura." She amended the title at the woman's grimace.

"She's the best heeler I've seen." Tiago ignored the little shake of her head. "Excellent goat tier and breakaway roper, too. She won silver in the all-around as a junior at the CNFR."

"My, you must be good. My husband insists competing for all-around cowboy or cowgirl is brutal."

Quinn barely kept her jaw from dropping. Tiago hadn't once hinted his father had competed in rodeo. "It requires strong horses and the ability to focus."

"Not an easy task, I'm sure. I have the utmost respect for all the competitors. I loved watching Joaquín compete, but I was terrified the entire time. I didn't know anything about horses or rodeo when he and I met, so it was quite the adjustment for me."

Her eyes softened, relaxing the few lines that marked her face. "I wouldn't trade it for anything, though." Her blue gaze found Quinn's. "You discover a lot about a person by watching them compete."

Quinn blinked, then felt Tiago's attention drawing her to connect. Burnished gold illuminated his pupils. His slow grin crackled across her skin. "I couldn't agree more."

At a light knock on the door Laura called, "Come in, Anita."

A rich Latin voice replied, "I'm no Anita, but I come bearing tea."

Laura rose with an elegance Quinn had already noticed but not put words to. She swept open the door and greeted her husband with girlish delight, pecking his cheek with a kiss, then clearing a space on her tidy desk for the tray.

Joaquín met her first with his eyes and then his embrace as soon as he freed his hands. No one witnessing the scene could doubt the love they felt for one another or the depth of their commitment. Quinn remembered a similar look in Cal's eyes when he looked at Missy, but wasn't sure Missy returned it in kind. Except for Reina, Quinn wasn't sure Missy loved anyone with abandon.

For herself, the day she'd discovered she was pregnant, Quinn had given up on the idea of such a love. In her experience, Cal was the exception, not the rule. Most stepfathers never fully accepted children not born of their blood. The slights her closest friend suffered had solidified her beliefs.

Laura handed Quinn a cup of tea. "Help yourself to cream and sugar, dear." Her elegance was amplified by the touch of Scarlet O'Hara in her speech.

"Son."

Tiago rose to accept his cup, and Quinn felt exposed. He carried the sugar back to her with a reassuring smile. Again, that sense of being cherished and cared for arose in Quinn. She added two spoons and stirred, maintaining her focus on the liquid within the silver-edged porcelain. Exquisite elegance. Even opulence. Quinn felt more out-of-place with each succeeding demonstration of wealth. Never once had she associated Tiago with money––not during their cross-the-arena encounters, nor since he'd appeared in Montana.

Laura reclaimed her seat near Tiago while Tiago's father perched on the corner of his wife's desk. Deep grooves highlighted Joaquín's gaunt cheeks, even filled in with whiskers as they were. The high cheekbones Tiago had inherited cut sharp edges above the neat, gray-dotted beard. His chin remained strong and his eyes dark and brooding beneath thick, well-groomed, brows. His close-cropped, silvered hair added to his overwhelming masculinity.

Joaquín raised his cup toward Quinn. "Welcome to Casa Vargas."

Quinn inclined her head. "Thank you, sir." Did Laura roll her eyes?

Tiago's father dipped his chin in acknowledgement. "My wife tells me you work with Santiago at the university."

"I do." She wanted to add 'for the moment' but decided the less said the better during this interview.

"And you rope?"

"Yes, sir."

"Header or heeler?"

"Most often I heel."

"Ah." He nodded almost to himself and took a sip of tea. Everyone else followed suit as if they were playing a giant game of follow-the-leader.

Quinn breathed in the relaxing mint within the strong flavors. She didn't often drink hot tea, but she needed this one. She studied Joaquín Vargas from beneath her lashes. His presence seemed to fill the room, crushing her and Tiago against the window. Only Laura held her own against him. He projected neither arrogance nor superiority, rather a supreme confidence.

"Santiago, have you decided on the area of research you will pursue?"

Tension stiffened Tiago's arm and thigh muscles where they pressed against hers. She'd felt the same tensing when he'd first seen his mother.

"I have several professors with whom I must consult when we return from this mission. Most are in the field for the summer and unavailable until early August."

Tiago sounded exactly like his father. Quinn pressed closer.

"Very good." Joaquín raised his cup, the others mimicking his movements.

Except for Quinn. She refused, clinking her cup in the saucer and drawing Joaquín's glance. She met it without flinching. Did his lip quirk behind his cup? She couldn't be sure.

This time, he followed her lead in a way, placing his cup and saucer onto the tray before standing. "Would you care for a tour before the restaurant opens for business?"

Quinn stood, secretly delighted when her height exceeded his by an inch or two. She should stop being so petty, but she hadn't liked how he showed so little affection toward Tiago when he had no such compunction with his wife.

"I'd love a tour. Thank you."

Joaquín opened the door and gestured for her to precede him from the office. Laura and Tiago followed like little ducklings.

Despite herself, Quinn couldn't help but be impressed with the rugged elegance of Casa Vargas. Laura's touches were everywhere. Little flourishes in the metalwork on the window shutters, in the electric candelabra lighting the room, and in the photos and art on the mantels above the two working fireplaces.

But the essence of the interior hinted at the machismo Tiago had mentioned. Rough-hewn beams crossed the vaulted, exposed ceiling, the texture reciprocated on the upper walls. Smoother wood graced the lower areas customers were likely to contact, yet blemishes and axe marks remained visible. Cushions in Argentinean patterns padded the numerous booths, the design carried over into the table coverings and trim work.

Men and women could dine comfortably in the space which was somehow both manly and romantic, reflecting with pinpoint accuracy the relationship of the owners. *How intriguing.*

Joaquín quirked a brow. "You are impressed."

"I am. It's a marvel. Truly. Thank you for providing background on the décor. Your narrative enriched the experience." See, she could be elegant and intelligent.

"I see you finally took my suggestion to move the drink refill station out of the server traffic flow." Tiago indicated a short wall, behind which stood a soft drink dispenser, ice tub, and glasses.

His father followed his gaze. "Ah, yes. When your mother explained the waitstaff's lessened workload and the elimination of a traffic pinch point, I had the wall installed. Laura did a fantastic job of making it blend in with the existing space."

Tiago's face darkened. "When *mother* explained? You mean my reasons weren't good enough for you?"

Laura took a step toward Tiago, but Quinn swung to face him, turning her back on Joaquín to create a physical barrier between them. "Tiago, I'm tired. Maybe we can rest before dinner? The last two days have been long ones."

He transferred his gaze from his father to her in an eyeblink, features softened into what she was coming to identify as his Protector Look--fierce around the edges and soft within.

"Of course. I should have realized sooner." His hand settled onto her back as he oriented his body with hers-- their backs to his father. "Excuse us, Mother, Father." His voice grated on the final word. He urged Quinn toward the back hall, but they'd only taken two steps before Laura caught up.

"You'll return for dinner, won't you? I reserved a table in the private dining room for seven o'clock in your names." Her genuine smile lit her face from within.

Quinn read only delight in Laura's eyes each time she looked at her son. Add a bit of curiosity when Quinn was included, along with a healthy dose of welcome kindness, and Quinn couldn't help liking the woman.

They'd reached the office, delicious smells filling the hall- way. Tiago halted and turned to Quinn. "It's up to you."

She drew in a long inhale.

"Omar's Twisted Empanadas are tonight's special." Laura peered up at Tiago as if she knew he'd not be able to resist such a temptation.

"We'll come," Quinn said.

Tiago's mother clapped her hands in an expression of delight. "Wonderful. I can't wait to get to know you better, my dear. I have a feeling we've much in common. Rest well. Tiago, I've readied the Blue Room for her."

Tiago released Quinn to exchange hugs and kisses with his mother who then pulled Quinn into another unexpected embrace. "We're huggers, dear. I hope it doesn't bother you, but if you hang around long enough, I can tell you from experience, you get used to it." She raised up on her toes to whisper in Quinn's ear. "You even begin to enjoy it." Her blue eyes sparkled as they shared a conspiratorial look. "Don't tell.

It's our secret. I'll pray God's protection on your drive across town and for your safe return."

"Thank you, Laura."

"Of course." She entered her office and closed the door, leaving them alone in the hall.

Concern knit Tiago's brows, and he took Quinn's hands in his. "Are you okay?'

Her nose scrunched. "Why wouldn't I be?"

He waved one hand in a general arc. "This. And them. It's all a little much for the uninitiated."

A short burst of laughter erupted from Quinn's lips. She pressed a hand to her mouth to quell another round.

He narrowed his eyes. "What?"

She gave a shake of her head and grabbed his elbow, steering him toward the elevator.

As soon as the door closed, Tiago tried again to apologize, but Quinn stopped him with a finger to his lips. "I'm fine. More than fine. I enjoyed meeting everyone. The restaurant is amazing. It all was. Except I'm sorry your father made you sad, but I loved everything else and can't wait to sample the food."

The door opened to reveal the dim underground garage. Tiago's quizzical expression said he didn't quite know what to make of her reaction, but he led her to the truck, unlocked her door, and helped her in. By the time they'd driven a maze-like route through rush-hour traffic, his brow had smoothed.

They entered an area of large homes spread across a series of hills, the glow of the sinking sun arching to fill the valleys with orange-gold light. The long drive switch-backed up the rather steep hill. "Navigating those curves in snow can't be fun."

Tiago's smile widened. "Remember we're in the South. Snow doesn't pile up here like it does in Montana."

She frowned. "Still."

"Mom insisted we heat the drive."

The house came into view, making Quinn gasp. While not as large as some others she'd seen, it commanded an impressive silhouette against the twilit sky. Rising two stories, the smaller second floor boasted three windows. A large covered front porch added to the main floor with an attached garage off to the right. Farther right stood a single carport. Aesthetic details, like contrasting scalloped trim and fancy scrollwork in the porch railing, revealed themselves as the truck drew nearer.

The house dwarfed any Quinn had ever lived in. "Must have cost a fortune."

"It was expensive, but she wouldn't take no for an answer, knowing Dad would insist on going to the restaurant regardless of the weather. He caved, like he caves to everything she suggests." A note of bitterness rang in the words.

Tiago grew quiet, a pensive look on his face. He parked in the truck-sized carport and killed the ignition but didn't move, his left hand white-knuckling the wheel.

Quinn unfastened her seat belt and slid closer, leaning forward to better see his face. It was far from full dark, but the carport's roof blocked light from entering the cab. Tiago's outline was gray, his features fuzzy. "Talk to me."

He cast her a sideways glance, but his mouth only firmed. "You're tired."

She rested a hand on his arm. "Not so tired I can't listen."

He pulled a huge breath in his nose, then released it. His fist pounded the steering wheel, before he braced his forehead there.

Quinn rested her hand on his back.

"Why couldn't he just take *my* suggestion? Why does he only listen to Mother?"

Not entirely sure what he was referencing, Quinn

remained silent. Her fingers worked slow, calming circles into his tense muscles.

After several minutes, he raised his head and locked gazes with her. The pain in his expression halted her ministrations. He tugged gently until her hand was in his, then found her other one claiming it, too. "Two months before I left for Montana, I presented Father all the numbers proving the very things he said convinced him to relocate the drink refill station. I even drew up plans for the new wall and illustrated ways it could be made to blend into the existing decor." He looked away, a muscle in his jaw jumping.

She kept her words gentle. "But he wouldn't agree."

"Said it wasn't worth the effort. That's the first time he suggested I find my passion. That I couldn't just adopt his."

Tiago's fingers tightened on hers, but she didn't complain. Everyone needed someone to hold on to. If she could be that person for Tiago she would, and not because he'd already been there for her, but because he deserved it in his own right.

"I don't love cooking as much as he does, but I do love the business side of the restaurant."

"And the design side." *Where had that come from?* Then she recalled all the little things he'd mentioned throughout their journey. "Work flow and all that. You pick up on it everywhere we eat."

He hung his head, his hands going slack. "I'm sorry I'm so boring. You probably think I'm a broken record."

"No." She refused to relinquish his hands. Tugged on them a little to draw his gaze back to her face. "I love how you light up whenever you explain your vision to me. Things I would never notice. Your eyes turn golden. Mesmerizing. Like magical stardust or something."

He peered at her, his gaze probing. If only his features were more distinct so she could read the thoughts flitting across his face. Without thinking, she raised a hand and trailed her fingertips across the ridge of his brow, traced his cheekbone to the curve of his jaw, and settled there. The feel of his stubble was pleasant, appealing.

He swallowed, his jaw flexing beneath her palm. She stilled, suddenly aware of their proximity. Her body warmed as if a bonfire had kindled in her abdomen, the flames spreading out and up. Her breaths shallowed, and she was aware of a need she'd never acknowledged.

More than anything, Quinn wanted Tiago to kiss her.

Tiago's skin tingled everywhere Quinn had touched him. Was still touching him. The whisper of her breaths had grown raspy, then shortened into little puffs. He wanted to see her--to peer into the storm. But the shadows had only grown. He could barely distinguish the outline of her face.

The need for her grew and expanded. From low in his belly, it crawled upward, demanding, but he'd never make a move without her permission, and he couldn't read her expression. Her hand had stilled where it cupped his chin.

He wished he could lean in and capture her mouth with his, but that would frighten her. Prove she'd been wrong about his character. Show her all her beliefs about him were a sham.

Oh, but he wanted to be all she'd said he was and more. When they were alone, he half believed he could be. But his father had quickly undermined all her work by reminding him how inadequate his only son was. Surely another child would have measured up. Been able to find his or her passion.

He slammed open the truck door and slid out, pulling her with him. She tried to protest, but he growled low in his throat, then swept her into his arms and carried her to the garage. The motion-sensor light clicked on, bathing them in a harsh glare. She squirmed, and he set her down, certain he'd ruined everything––as usual.

"What was that all about?" Her voice sounded husky, confused.

He punched in the code for the automatic door, then caught his fingers drumming staccato beats on his thigh. He'd failed to break the nervous habit even after his father's repeated lectures on how appearance is an important part of being Argentinean. How in business, image is everything. *"You must always appear strong and proud of your heritage. Even when nervous, an Argentine shows no weakness."*

He'd revealed nothing but weakness and Neanderthal qualities to Quinn today. She'd probably never let him close to her again.

"I'll show you to your room and come back for the luggage later." Tiago didn't look at her as he led the way inside the two-car garage and crossed to the step up into the main level of the house. "Careful here." He unlocked the door using another code and entered the spacious industrial kitchen. Not wanting to linger in his father's domain, he kicked off his boots, sending his mother's cat scurrying, and strode to the stairs.

"Wait for me." Quinn's bare feet padded across the tile, growing quieter as she hit the hardwood.

He almost turned around but forced himself to climb the stairs instead. He couldn't handle the disappointment on her face. The look he'd seen on his father's face more times than he could count. He was nearly running when he reached the top, but he couldn't outrun his feelings. His need for her hadn't lessoned with his flight. If anything, it had grown.

Lord, help me.

The prayer did nothing to relieve his fears or reduce his wanting.

Tiago stopped at the second door, the largest room on the top floor. Still without looking at Quinn, he swept an arm toward the opening. "This is yours." Then he added, "It's Mom's favorite room."

Instead of stepping past him, Quinn stopped outside the doorway. Near enough for him to feel the heat of her body. The scent of ripe apples drifted in the air urging him closer to her hair, but he held himself rigid. He didn't deserve such intimacies. Didn't deserve her. "I'll be back with your bag." He brushed past her and ran down the stairs, fleeing both his thoughts and his desires.

Tiago let himself out the front door and breathed deeply, the loss of the sweet-tart fragrance hit harder than he expected. A light breeze had popped up and ushered in a fresher current of air for which he was glad. He needed to cool off and didn't have time for a shower.

Retrieving their luggage from the truck made him think of all the conversations he and Quinn had shared the past two days. He'd let her see parts of himself he hadn't shared with anyone else, but still he'd held back. Why couldn't he trust her fully?

Likely the same reason he didn't fully trust God.

With a sigh, he hefted the bags and retraced his steps to the porch, kicking at the decorative rocks between the flagstones that made up the path. He plodded up the steps and stopped abruptly, teetering on the top one.

A hand reached out to steady him.

"Quinn. What are you doing out here? You should be resting. We only have two hours before our reservation at Casa Vargas."

Quinn moved in front of him, grabbed his shirt and

pulled him close enough he could feel her breath on his face. She looked into his eyes, so deep it seemed she saw into his soul.

"I'm sorry," he began only to falter when she tugged him closer.

A mere whisper separated their mouths. Her stormy irises swirled in mesmerizing patterns like the kaleidoscope he'd played with as a kid. He sank into them, not caring if he fell and never got out.

"It's not your fault, Tiago."

Was he dreaming? Often someone said those words to him in a dream, only to laugh hysterically and slap their leg in jest.

She jostled him until he focused on her eyes once more, as he'd done to her at Little Big Horn. "Listen to me, Tiago. I don't know what they mean, but I believe you need to hear these words. It's not your fault."

Each word punched into his brain. Forcing him to grapple with their meaning.

"It's not my fault?" His tongue seemed thick, the words foreign.

"No. It isn't. And God isn't punishing you. He loves you. More than anything, He wants you to trust Him."

Tiago closed his eyes and let her words fall on his parched soul like rain. Let the apple scent envelope him. Could he do it? Could he trust God? As if coming out of a daze, Tiago became aware of their location. Of the bags in his hands and the open front door. His heart beat out a complicated rhythm. He needed to sit before he fell.

"Let's . . . go . . . inside." The words were an effort, but he pushed through.

Quinn nodded, and her nose brushed his. The contact set his senses reeling again, but she took hold of his arm and steered them inside the house. Shut the door behind them.

He dropped the bags, looked down, and began to laugh at the dried pine needles and grass clippings adorning his socks.

The laugh turned into a hiccup, which became a sob.

Tiago hadn't cried since he was twelve. His father had called it weak. An Argentine was strong. Tiago wanted to be strong so he'd never cried again.

Quinn maneuvered him to the sofa, and he collapsed onto it. She followed him down, and held him until his tears dried up, then handed him a tissue from the end table.

Tiago pushed himself away from her sweetness and tried to smile. It wavered. Snot dripped from his nose, and his cheeks were wet with tears, but he didn't care. He had to see Quinn's face.

Her teeth were anchored in her lip, her brow furrowed in concern. No hint of condemnation or embarrassment anywhere. Only compassion.

He mopped his face. Then he held her hand and told her about the time he'd asked his mother why they didn't have as big a family as any of his uncles.

"She cried, and Dad came in to comfort her, sending me to my room. I didn't understand of course. I was only eight. But I didn't go to my room, either. Instead, I listened as my father tried to comfort my mother who couldn't stop mumbling, "I'm sorry" over and over. Finally, Dad told her it wasn't her fault. She hadn't done anything wrong. If I hadn't been so big, she might have had more children. It's like the mare––a dystocian birth."

Quinn's other hand curled over his. "You've held yourself responsible all this time for something you had no control over?"

He shrugged. "My eight-year-old-self accepted the blame, and I've never challenged the belief since."

Quinn gave a slow nod. "I understand exactly what you mean. Except my problem was nearly the opposite."

"Do you want to talk about it?"

She shook her head, then nodded, her lower lip trembling.

Tiago smoothed his thumb across the back of her hand, giving her time.

Quinn closed her eyes, then sniffed. "I lied to you. I've lied to myself, clinging to Cal's memory because the truth is too hard. Harder even than I'd thought." She ran her teeth over her lip, meeting his gaze.

Hurt darkened her eyes. He smoothed her hair, then leaned in to kiss her forehead. Her sigh nearly undid him. It took all his will to back away. "What else?"

She wet her lips. "Not only did my father not want me, he didn't want my mother with me inside her. He tried to hurt her. Told her to get rid of me." Her voice cracked. "She . . . she tried to abort me."

Tiago pulled her close and held her, just as she'd done for him. He sank into her hair, the luxurious strands caressing his face. If only he could absorb her pain. "We're a mess, aren't we?"

She nodded but didn't pull away, her body tense as if holding back intense emotion. As if this were new grief.

"Quinn, how long have you known about this?"

She raised one shoulder, the movement shifting her hair so strands caught on his growing scruff.

A coldness seeped into his chest despite her huddled body pressing close. "This is new information."

A nod.

"When?"

Her body shuddered in his arms. Her voice muffled by his dampening shirt. "A week."

Instinct prompted him to rock as mothers soothe their babies. He pressed kisses into her hair and rubbed her back. She didn't heave with grief-laden sobs, only loosed silent tears into his chest. His courageous Queen, even in her sorrow. His heart broke for her.

When she sniffed and shifted within his grasp, he asked, "Do you still want to go?"

A shrug.

"I could make us something here. We'll eat at the restaurant another night."

She hesitated, then pushed away from his chest, wiping her eyes. "Won't your parents be upset?"

"I'll call Mom. She'll smooth it over."

"I need to call Missy."

Tiago frowned. "Are you sure? You might be better off giving yourself time to process."

Quinn hesitated, and Tiago could almost hear the war going on inside her head. At last, she gave him a sad smile. "Missy's still my mother. I can't abandon her, and--" A violent shudder rocked her frame.

Tiago grabbed the rolled blanket Mom kept in a basket beside the sofa and tucked it around Quinn. She rewarded him with a tired smile.

"I'm calling and cancelling our reservation. The empanadas can wait. Take a nap if you like while I rummage around to see what ingredients Dad has on hand."

He tucked the blanket more firmly around her shoulders, then bent to kiss her forehead. Instead, she raised her head, and their lips grazed, sending a shock wave through his body.

She jerked, and they froze, lips hovering a breath apart for what seemed an eternity. Just as he'd decided to straighten and pretend nothing had happened, her arms flew from the blanket to wrap around his neck. They drew him down, but this time, Quinn initiated more than a friendly brush. Her lips were firm and sweet beneath his, challenging him to prove himself.

He slid next to her on the sofa, taking her face between his hands, her skin soft and inviting. She shuddered before her fingers slid into his hair, and her body molded to his. All his desire threatened to burst through his control, but the last thing he wanted to do was frighten her. She'd experienced too much hurt. He only wanted to cherish her and show her how much he cared.

Long minutes later, he pulled away enough to breathe, panting as if he'd run miles. Tiago laid his forehead against hers and closed his eyes, the raggedness of her breaths fueling his courage. "Quinn?"

"Hmm?"

"I've wanted to do that for a long time."

"I think I have too," she admitted.

He let a teasing note slip into his tone. "You think?"

"I've refused to let myself feel." Her voice broke.

Tiago tried to shush her, but she pushed back until their eyes locked.

"Tiago?"

"I'm here, Quinn."

She shook her head. "You shouldn't be."

His voice carried a barely-contained edge. "You just kissed me. Why shouldn't I be here?"

Her lashes fluttered down. "I wanted to see if I––" She swallowed hard. "I shouldn't have kissed you."

"Why in Heaven's name not?"

When she leaned against him but didn't answer, he gently cupped her chin and tilted it upward. "I'm very confused."

Her teeth found her lip. "I know."

CHAPTER 13

Quinn awoke in a strange bed. Where was she? How did she get here? Her pulse skyrocketed. She clutched the blue and silver comforter to her throat. Her gaze swept over sapphire curtains framing a large window. Subtle designs brightened the walls. Her muscles unclenched, and she sank into the soft mattress as last night crowded in.

The kiss.

Warmth fired every nerve as she relived the moment. A moment she'd initiated. Her heart lurched. She'd used Tiago. Oh, she'd wanted to kiss him, but mostly wanted to know if she *could*. Still, it wasn't fair. She hadn't come clean. Instead, his compassion and her need to know distracted her. That, and his irresistible scent. Her bones melted with the memory.

She struggled to sit up. Looked down.

Pajamas?

She scrambled from the bed. Wait, she'd withdrawn into herself after the kiss, like she'd done to survive her attack, but she remembered Tiago carrying her upstairs. Then his mother helping her change clothes and climb into bed.

Last night's conversation with Laura pricked at the edges of her consciousness. She'd been barely processing.

Laura had hugged her and stroked her hair. Why?

With a sinking feeling, echoes of incoherent blubbering words assaulted Quinn. She'd spoken of Missy and Cal. Meeting Tiago. Connecting with him at rodeos and his heroic rescue. Even her failure––her loss of control––before begging for Laura's silence.

But how much more? Her heartrate doubled. Had she mentioned Reina?

Laura's voice sounded in her ears, just like last night. *"Secrets never stay hidden. No matter how much justification we pile atop them to keep them in the shadows, light has a way of drifting in. The best we can do is choose when, and in what way, our secrets are revealed."*

She sank into a wicker-bottomed chair.

Breathe. Calm down. Her mantra in the rodeo arena while being Queen. If it worked then, it could work now.

After several breaths her heart slowed, and her mind cleared.

Her discarded clothing lay atop the desk in front of her. Her phone rode the pile. She picked it up, the device's weight familiar in her hand.

Reina. Missy. She'd never called them.

The screen read 5:42. Minus one hour in Montana equaled too early to call. What kind of mother was she?

Answers tumbled over themselves. Irresponsible. Uncaring. She found her bag on a small antique dressing table and pawed through it. Not uncaring. She loved Reina, though admittedly, she stuffed most of it down. She provided for her needs. That had to count for something.

The tension from her and Missy's strained relationship

pointed an accusing finger. Which of them was selfish? Missy or Quinn?

Quinn stood and crossed to the window, then opened the louvers in the expensive vertical blind. The scene before her came straight out of a dream. Having always lived in valleys peering up at mountains, to be suddenly atop the mountain, looking down into a valley, felt surreal.

Wispy mist decorated the surrounding heights and blanketed the lowlands in lacy splendor, evidence of the night's chill. Soon the rising sun would destroy twilight's handiwork. Already, the sky was lightening, preparing to give way to dawn's brightness.

Something inside Quinn cracked and crumbled, continuing the erosion begun last night when she ushered Tiago into her past--a past that threatened to unravel the tidy puzzle of her present. She didn't know what to do with her new reality.

Tiago didn't fit.

Missy's revelation didn't fit.

Reina doesn't fit.

The whisper swept in as a pale mauve crept over the sky. But not quite a whisper. More like a suggestion. Inside her head.

Lord? Is that You?

Quinn dropped to her knees on the rug, her eyes to the continually morphing heavens. "Reina is my daughter. I saved her." She whispered the words to herself and to Jesus then felt a gentle nudge.

Not true.

She tried again, head bowed. "You saved her. I was merely the vessel."

Yes, that rested easy on her soul.

I saved you first.

A chill began at her toes and worked its way upward to

her scalp. Her whole body trembled beneath the weight of her unworthiness.

Why hide the truth? Do you fear men more than Me that you do not acknowledge the miracles I've wrought in you?

With fumbling fingers Quinn opened her Bible app and searched for 'acknowledge.' Many verses popped up, but she tapped Psalm 91. Her breath caught at God's promise to rescue and protect those who love and acknowledge Him. This was the verse she'd used to justify her--Queen's--flirtation with danger. She navigated to Matthew 10:32 and read aloud, "Whoever acknowledges me before others, I will also acknowledge before my Father in heaven."

"I'm sorry, Lord. Please, forgive me. I need Your help to right this wrong. I need You. Now more than ever. I've been running, Lord, but I'm Yours if You'll have me back."

Mind still spinning with her many mistakes but soul at peace, Quinn sat on the oval rug, knees pulled to her chest and watched God paint light into the sky just for her.

Sometime later, when fluffy clouds drifted lazily across the blue expanse, a voice called from her doorway.

"Quinn? Are you okay?" An edge of panic colored the voice she most wanted, but also most feared, to hear.

She had to find a way to tell him today, regardless of how hard the admission would be or the consequences resulting from her confession. The resolve hardened within her, becoming more--a covenant, a promise between herself and God.

"May I come in?"

Quinn nodded, her bottom numb after sitting still for so long. She couldn't really feel her feet either, but one problem at a time.

He approached as if she were a skittish colt, hand palm out for her to sniff. Not really. But the image made her smile, calming her. She tilted her head upward, seeking his face.

At her smile, his features seemed to relax. The lines on his forehead flattened, and his jaw unclenched. "I hope having my mother help you to bed last night wasn't too stressful. When she and Dad came home, you were asleep on the sofa. She insisted you go up to bed, but you were so out of it, I--" he swallowed and looked away. "I carried you up. She took over from there." He shifted his weight.

Odd. He'd never been nervous around her before. A horrific thought sent her eyes skittering to his. Had his mother relayed their conversation? Quinn dismissed the possibility. Laura wouldn't betray her confidence.

What then? She eyed him anew. Maybe he needed boldness from her.

"Sit down, you're making me antsy with all your . . ." She flicked her hand at his feet. "Whatever that is."

With the grace of an athlete, he folded his long limbs and joined her on the floor, not touching but not separated, either.

The Siamese cat she'd glimpsed last night strutted into the room, tail tip flicking. His sapphire gaze settled on Quinn's before he padded over and rubbed against her thigh.

Her smile broadened. "Now what's on your mind?"

He exhaled. "Fifteen minutes to breakfast according to Chef Vargas." He dipped his chin toward the cat. "Meet Nero."

She stroked the cat and sniffed, suddenly aware of the tempting aromas wafting up the stairs, and the rumble of her empty stomach. "Great, I'm famished. And . . ?" she prompted.

"We should visit the Alliegro twins today. I've a friend who said they practice every weekday at an arena west of the city from nine to eleven."

Grabbing her abandoned phone from the floor, Quinn

checked the time. Nearly eight. "We'll have to hurry if you want to get there when they do."

"It might be better to arrive later. See them in action first before we chat. What do you think?"

"We'd have a clearer picture of their skills before they discover we're scouting them." She raised her fist. "Way to go, Coach. Good decision."

Her praise relaxed his features. He bumped knuckles, then rose. "We'd best get downstairs. I'll leave so you can dress."

"Uh, Tiger?"

He frowned at her use of the silly nickname.

"I may need help getting up. I can't feel my legs."

His eyes shone gold. "Any time."

Ten minutes later, she sat at a table tucked into an intimate nook overlooking the back yard. The view through the many windows included both corners of the house, a porch hugging one and an herb garden off the other. Tiago's dad served first his wife, who sat to Quinn's right, then her before placing the casserole dish in the center for himself and Tiago to help themselves. Had she time traveled into the past? While the attention unnerved her, she felt oddly valued--honored even.

Quinn indicated the small garden. "Do you grow your own herbs, Mr. Vargas?"

"Please, I am Joaquín." He placed his cloth napkin on his lap. "But yes. As many as I can. Let us pray."

They bowed, and he blessed the food, the company, and the home, asking for guidance and protection as each of them went about their day. Quinn chorused "amen" with the others and some of the morning's peace returned.

The uniquely-spiced egg and brisket dish made her mouth happy. Tidbits of conversation passed around the table, cut through by the clink of utensils. She chewed the final bite and laid down her fork. As she straightened her back, a niggle of worry over her unladylike posture and lack of refined table manners overshadowed her peace until she dismissed it out-of-hand. No sense bothering with trivialities.

Glancing to her left, she found Joaquín studying her. She tensed, then met his gaze and smiled. "Let me apologize for causing Tiago to miss last night's dinner reservation. It seems I was more worn out by the travel than I realized."

His lips twitched beneath his moustache. "So my wife tells me. No worries, I believe you young people say. All is well. You may come any evening you wish."

"I'm looking forward to a traditional Argentinean meal, especially after sampling your breakfast fare." She gestured at the nearly-empty serving dish, then at the framed photos gracing the nook. "Forgive me, but I wasn't aware you were *the* Joaquín Vargas, champion heeler and breakaway roper."

Tiago sent her a look she couldn't decipher, but she'd committed to the topic.

Joaquín stroked his short beard and glanced at the captured scenes. "That was another life many years past. How do you know of me?"

"My father,"--she winced--"taught me roping techniques using videos. He called you the greatest college heeler in recent history."

She'd thought Joaquín might preen a bit at Cal's title for him, but he waved it away. "I never set out to win anything, only do my best. Rodeo was a means to an end. Cooking, starting Casa Vargas, and, later, my family, have always been my passions."

His shared look with Laura reflected the love Quinn had witnessed at the restaurant. The long glance between father and son, however, overflowed with a complex mixture of longing, challenge, love and hurt--more than Quinn had the context to sort out. What silent struggle raged between them? Whatever it was, she wished to help.

She connected gazes with Laura and recognized an ally. Perhaps together, they could ease the strain.

Tiago gripped the steering wheel in frustration. He'd wanted to jump across the table and snatch Quinn's words out of the air when she mentioned his father's rodeo career. But instead, he'd been forced to listen to the woman he loved idolize the man who knotted his insides. The disappointment evident in his father's face when they'd connected afterwards had spoken volumes.

He and Dad didn't lack love for each other. They lacked respect or maybe trust. Whatever it was, the gap had grown larger over time until it seemed as though a giant chasm lay between them, unbridgeable, uncrossable, and unreconcilable.

Quinn's attention seemed glued to the landscape when he glanced across the cab at her. Good. He'd sensed an unsettling vibe between her and his father. Maybe he could get his mother to take Quinn shopping or sightseeing. Surely their positive connection would offset his dad's negative one.

"The views are spectacular outside the city." Quinn squirmed with eagerness. "I never knew mountains could look so different."

Tiago shed his morose thoughts by concentrating on Quinn's excitement. "I was blown away the first time I traveled west, so I get what you mean." He flipped his turn signal and steered onto an off ramp. "You'd love the ocean with all the waves and sand."

She raised her foot toward the dash, then changed her mind, chuckling. "Boots."

He nodded. "Boots stay on the floor."

"Aye, aye, Tiger."

"Don't get sassy. Technically, I'm your boss."

She snorted. "Not yet. I haven't agreed to come back."

Quinn's face clouded as soon as the words left her mouth. She'd killed the easy banter and light camaraderie they'd shared. Tiago missed it already. If only he had her gift of putting others at ease, he could smooth it over. Fortunately, the arena they sought was only three miles ahead, so they only had to endure a few minutes of silence.

He parked next to several farm trucks, a couple with trailers attached. Movement in the open arena caught his attention. His glance collided with Quinn's, assuring him all contention could wait. With a nod, they exited the truck, closing their doors with minimal sound.

Using the other vehicles as cover, they approached the action. Two riders, each wearing a flat-topped hat with a narrow brim, swung ropes above their heads. A steer raced ahead of the galloping horse only to be caught by the first rider's loop over his horns and turned. The second rider missed, the loop landing empty in the dirt.

Tiago gauged the second rider's response to her mistake. A long, black braid was the only thing giving away her gender. She slowed and quieted her horse, a rangy bay. Without looking at the header who was presumably her brother, Abelardo, she recoiled her lariat.

In contrast, Abelardo's face twisted in an expression of anger or disgust. He released the steer who ran across the arena then jerked the reins. When his horse's head slammed upward, the cowboy's rigid posture slumped. He set to soothing the sorrel and white paint gelding until it calmed.

"Looks like he can control himself when he wants to." Quinn spoke softly so the handful of men gathered around the area wouldn't hear her.

"They're loading another steer." Tiago pointed.

Two men moved a spotted animal from the holding pen to the chute. Someone handed Abelardo his rope, and the twins maneuvered their horses into position on each side of the steer.

"*Presta atención, esta vez*, Yoani." Abelardo glared at his sister who stiffened in her saddle but continued to face forward, loop at the ready.

Quinn elbowed Tiago's ribs. "What did he say?"

"He wants her to pay attention."

The chute opened, and the steer burst free. A second later, Abelardo's horse raced after it. The cowboy sent the loop sailing over the animal's head for a clean catch. Yoani's loop slid harmlessly off the beast's hindquarters and landed in the dirt. She rolled her hips in the saddle, her horse sliding to a stop on its haunches, dirt spraying up from the hooves.

The move sparked Tiago's appreciation of the horse's talent, and the rider's control. Her reins hadn't moved. The cue had all been in her change of seat.

"Impressive."

Quinn's assessment mirrored his own. He used his chin to indicate Abelardo's stormy countenance. "He's not happy. Maybe we should intervene before he blows his top and makes a fool of himself."

"Yes. Let's."

As one, they strode toward the arena. Tiago scanned each person as they approached, an eye out for trouble. Yoani noticed them first but contained her reaction. When Abelardo rode up to her dragging his lariat in the dirt and spouting a string of Spanish obscenities, she gave the slightest tilt of her head. He pivoted his horse and glared a challenge.

The men began a slow, almost menacing, walk toward them as well. Tiago hoped this interview wouldn't come to blows. He might not be able to protect Quinn against so many. Rolling his shoulders reflexively, he reached for Quinn's hand to keep her close, catching air. His heart lurched as she climbed the arena fence, perched on the top board for a moment, then landed on the other side.

She shoved her hands in her front pockets and closed the distance between herself and the young Cuban-American rider. Her clear voice projected loud enough to be heard over the backdrop of mooing from the stock pens beyond the arena. "Yoani, I'm Quinn Mulroney."

A look of curiosity, maybe even recognition, crossed the girl's face.

Quinn continued, "How'd you train your mare to slide without a visible cue? I've tried, but my mare always needed pressure on the reins."

Yoani patted her horse, then dismounted despite her brother's menacing countenance. Tiago didn't think his face could get any more maroon without exploding. He urged his gelding forward, but Yoani held up a hand and he halted, glowering at his sister and Quinn as they walked together, heads bent in animated discussion.

Several hours later Tiago seated Quinn in Casa Vargas' private dining room. With her ebony hair shining in the ambient light from the candelabras, she appeared radiant and held herself with queenly bearing, back straight and chin high. She made him proud to be at her side, though thus far he'd been little more than an observer.

He seated himself as the Alliegro twins settled in across the table, their presence a feat Quinn had managed via her unique gift of connection and God's grace. His heart swelled over her accomplishment. Not because of the success it portended, but because of the confidence it seemed to have lent Quinn herself.

"Isn't the craftsmanship magnificent?" Quinn joined

Yoani and Abelardo in admiring the intricate woodwork and detail of the room's interior.

Abelardo inclined his head toward a backlit woodcut depicting a working cow horse cutting a calf from a herd. *"Es un original, no? Como el otro?"* His light brown eyes nearly matched his tanned skin, and he peered with interest at a similar woodcut featured on the opposite wall.

Quinn looked to Tiago, brow questioning.

"My father knew the artist in Argentina and commissioned the works specifically for Casa Vargas. They are quite unique."

"Is it the art or the subject matter you enjoy, Abelardo?" Quinn focused her attention on the younger twin whose eyes roved over the walls instead of meeting her gaze.

Yoani softly cleared her throat. "My brother enjoys working with wood as well as horses." Her smile deepened. "He is very good at both. Though he'd never tell you himself."

Abelardo shot her a scowl that softened as soon as he took in her earnest expression.

A sense of wonder radiated from Quinn as she glanced between them, settling on Yoani. "It's obvious you care deeply about each other. I can see why you'd not want to be separated, Yoani."

"He's all the family I have. It may sound childish, but I wish to be near him as long as I can."

Tiago added to his mental notes the ways in which Quinn put others at ease. He was eager to discuss them with her to better understand her methods.

Their waiter arrived with menus and water goblets and took their drink orders. Quinn thanked him, her gratitude expressed in the way she moved, the tilt of her head, the set of her chin. He observed as the three of them perused their menus.

Thoughts had been percolating in the back of his brain

since Quinn charmed Terri, grumpy waitress and proud football mom. He'd spent the silent stretches of their drive organizing his thinking around a business plan that was only now beginning to crystalize.

When the waiter returned with their drinks and to ask for their choice of entrée, the twins still couldn't make up their minds. Tiago leaned forward. "If I might make a suggestion?"

Quinn turned her brilliant smile on him. "Please, everything looks phenomenal."

Abelardo deferred to Yoani who nodded, a shy smile gracing her full lips. "We would also like your help."

"Berto, if you'd be so kind as to bring a full sampler platter, *por favor*. We will give our guests a taste of Casa Vargas, eh?" He easily fell into the speech rhythms he'd learned from his youth spent working with the restaurant's mainly bilingual employees.

Berto gave him a little bow, grinning from ear-to-ear. "*Sí, señor*. Your dish, right away."

"Your dish?"

Quinn clearly expected an explanation. The twins too, from Yoani's interest and Abelardo's smirk. The kid breathed attitude.

He exhaled sharply. Fine. "Casa Vargas maintains a limited menu, something unique in this area. The platter sets us apart and offers a varied Argentinean dining experience. Since we began offering it three years ago, it has become one of our customer favorites." Yet another idea his father hadn't acted on until his mother took up the cause after Tiago had gone away to college.

Quinn squeezed his arm, a momentary frown creasing her lovely face. Was she thinking of the refill station? Without missing a beat, she transferred her attention to their recruits, smiling and chatting until they ventured from their respective shells.

"Yoani, you mentioned earlier that UT Martin recruited only you and then only if you could transition to team roping. Is that right?"

The girl nodded, her long braid barely moving. "They refused to consider Lalo." She traced a pattern on her napkin. "He insists I take the chance for an education, though education is his dream. Not mine."

"What is your dream, Yoani?" The gentleness in Quinn's voice pierced Tiago's soul but lit fireworks in both his chest and head. This. This was her secret.

The girl's head snapped up. "My dream? No one has ever asked me." She peered around the room as if the answer hid in a corner for her to find. "I want to be near Lalo." She hesitated, then glanced from Quinn to Tiago and back. "Someday, a family of my own--a big one." Her smile peeked out.

Quinn found Tiago's hand and squeezed.

Yoani's words hit Tiago with double impact. The old hurt stabbed, but hope bandaged the wound. He hadn't imagined his dream either until Quinn came along with her hero talk, but for the first time, he seemed on the road to finding it, just like Yoani.

"Are you willing to rodeo for MSU while awaiting the man of your dreams as long as Abelardo is with you?" Quinn's smile faded, her expression hardening. "You'll have to prove you can remain academically eligible, and you'll have to work hard. No complaining or whining that rodeo isn't your favorite or wasn't your first choice. Once you commit, you're expected to pull your weight. Do you understand?"

Yoani's frown deepened. "What about Lalo? Won't they reject him like UT Martin? Nothing has changed since he applied there."

Tiago took the lead at another squeeze from Quinn, speaking to the surly young man. "Your grades and rodeo skills are good, so why did they reject you?" His jaw clenched in anticipation of the cowboy's response.

Abelardo didn't flinch. "I nearly killed a man. Beat him so bad they had to reconstruct his face. Did time in juvie because of it. My record's sealed, but the guy's dad knows some bigshot at UT, and they found out." A fierce intensity dared Tiago to doubt his word.

"Why'd you beat him?"

The young man blinked. "No one's ever asked or cared to hear my answer."

"I'm asking."

He glanced at his sister. Shrugged. "The guy attacked Yoani. I dragged him off. Beat him ugly. Didn't want no chance he'd try it again."

"You ever in a gang?"

"Once. We moved, and I got out. Stayed out." Abelardo pressed his lips together as if battling strong emotions.

Quinn tapped a finger on her lips, then addressed Yoani. "How'd you get your horses? They're expensive to acquire and to keep. You were orphans in the foster care system. What's your story?"

Yoani brightened. "They were gifts. We went to a rodeo camp with our foster brother, and a lot of people saw us ride. An organization of Latin Americans helped us. You saw some of them today at the arena. They've been almost like family."

Abelardo nodded.

Their food arrived and between bites, Tiago explained the scholarship, and Quinn shared details about boarding, practice, and competitions. By the end of the night, Tiago considered the two his friends––found he liked them. They were survivors, like Quinn.

Hearty embraces and kissed cheeks reinforced Tiago's notion of friendship. The twins' former foster dad collected them, though they'd technically aged out of the system several months ago when they turned eighteen.

Their conversation had warmed his insides. Being able to offer them another step up was the seasoning on the steak to use his father's expression.

Quinn clutched Tiago's arm as the car pulled into traffic. "If we could do stuff like this every day, I'd be all in."

He pretended to be confused. "What? Hang out with me in fancy restaurants and eat delectable food?"

She rolled her eyes, something he'd never seen her do before. "You know what I mean." Her expression turned wistful. "I could embrace Yoani's dream, though I have no idea what having a big family feels like. It sounds nice, doesn't it?"

Tiago's skin prickled. A cold chill spread to his bones, the accusation pinging inside his skull. *His fault.*

Her mouth pinched while her eyes widened. "Tiago. Don't you want kids?"

He worked to draw breath, but his throat seemed so small. Strangled, like her voice. He wanted to comfort her, but his own pain wouldn't relent. Leaning over, he pressed his hands to his thighs.

Moments later, Quinn's fingers found his back, their pressure unlocking the grip on his lungs and throat.

She eased him into an embrace. "I'm so sorry. I shouldn't have said that. I didn't think."

The regret in Quinn's voice pulled Tiago back from his own precipice--one he thought he'd walked away from already. "No, Quinn. I need to beat this. Every mention of family shouldn't push me to the edge. Without you here, I'd likely have tumbled over and spent the next week wallowing."

He pulled back enough to see her fully. Tears. He hadn't expected that. Placing one hand on each side of her face, he thumbed away the drops. Her eyes remained closed, but her fingers gripped his arms. Leaning in, he placed a lingering kiss on her forehead. Then realizing they were on a busy sidewalk in downtown Nashville, he whispered, "Come on."

Emotions swelled within him as Quinn let him tuck her against him and lead her through the door toward the back hall. Diners followed their progress, but Tiago didn't care. He loved this woman and needed to fix whatever was hurting her, if he could.

Lord, You know what she needs. Use me to give it to her, please. Or if I can't, make another way.

The prayer seemed weightier than any he'd prayed in the past. Like a renewal of his original confession of faith. Tiago felt the change of heart to his bones. Renewed trust. Something he hadn't fully done since he was eight.

They reached the office, and Tiago escorted Quinn inside. His mom wasn't there. Likely off tending to one of her many hostess duties. She loved interacting with the customers, just like he believed Quinn would. If he could ever get his business idea off the ground, she'd be the perfect partner.

First, he had to figure out what had affected her so profoundly.

CHAPTER 14

Quinn was weary. Maybe not physically, but mentally and emotionally. Once again, her thoughtlessness had hurt someone she loved.

Wait! *Loved?*

Her conditioned response to such an emotion-welling word was to shove it down, force it away, embrace distraction, or hit the denial button and hold it until she'd convinced herself she didn't feel anything.

This time, she refused to gloss over or ignore the full impact of her admission.

The door opened, startling both her and Tiago based on his shoving her behind him. When Laura appeared, they each deflated, twin exhales loud despite the buzz of voices from the dining room and the seemingly constant clatter and clang from the kitchen.

Tiago's mother jerked rounded eyes from a stack of papers. They softened when she glanced between their faces. "Your dinner meeting must be over. Good results, I expect." Her brows lifted, inviting a response as she stepped forward and eased the door closed with her hip.

"Quinn was brilliant. Had them eating out of her hand. They'll be headed to Bozeman in August for an official try-out."

Tiago's praise plopped Quinn into the antique chair. After the hurt she'd just caused, she'd expected bitterness and withdrawal, not enthusiasm. Had it been hurt he'd felt earlier? Or something else? Her emotional resistance had not given her a good foundation for reading others.

Laura deposited the papers on the desk. She took Quinn's hand in hers, their height difference putting their eyes nearly level. "My dear, you must let me take you on a proper Nashville tour tomorrow. We could leave around ten, have lunch and be back by two, so I have time to complete my work here." Her disarming smile made it impossible to say no.

Not that Quinn wanted to. "I'd love that."

Tiago cleared his throat. "Then maybe I could introduce you to Quilombo when it cools off a little around five or so? If you still want to."

The vulnerability in his tone sent her back to her thoughtless words. She *had* hurt him. Denial rose to her lips, but something stopped her. A breath of air stirred the hairs at her nape. She inhaled deeply, her response a breathy, "Yes." She couldn't say more.

Luckily, he seemed to understand and tipped his head. Something shot between them, fluttering her stomach.

Laura faced her son. "I nearly forgot. Your father would like to speak with you if you can bear to part with the lovely Quinn for a few moments. He's in his office." She patted Quinn's hand. "I'll keep her company."

Tiago's expression darkened, but he stepped toward the hall. He glanced back once before exiting, resistance telegraphed in his pinched mouth and lined forehead.

The click of the closing door sounded ominous to Quinn; Tiago's unease bleeding into her. Quinn stood, prepared to abdicate her seat for Laura, who dismissed the attempt with a regal wave of her hand.

Laura lowered herself onto the bench beneath the window. "He's smitten with you, you know. And I can see why." She folded her hands in her lap and stared at them for a long moment before her softened gaze reconnected with Quinn's. "He's always tried so hard to please everyone, even when he was a little boy. He'd put aside his own wants if he thought he could make someone else happy or give them a moment of joy. We often had to forbid him from giving away his possessions to the poor children he found in random places."

Quinn swallowed. Why was Laura telling her this? But she had no trouble picturing a young Tiago regifting his toys, games, books, even electronics, to a less fortunate boy or girl he came across. "It seems he's always giving but has a hard time receiving."

Laura's expressive eyes lit at Quinn's description. "You've noticed. It's a flaw as well as an asset. He may not know how to accept your gifts either. I hope you'll be the one who gets through to him." She stood, dipping her chin and smiling. "You've the gift of hospitality and work to make others feel at ease around you. Quite evident during yesterday's visit and again tonight with those youngsters."

Quinn stood as well, sliding away from the desk to give Laura access. "Thank you for your kind words. I'm looking forward to seeing more of Nashville with you."

"We will have the best time. It's been so long since I've been out just for fun with someone other than my husband." She busied herself with organizing her work, then paused and stopped Quinn's attempt to slip away. "That came out harsher than I intended. My husband is fun and spontaneous. He gives me adventures and romance and time to connect. I prefer his company, in fact. But you are authentic and unpretentious. Exactly the kind of person I could become friends with."

Quinn's head reeled with Laura's matter-of-fact pronouncement. But Quinn agreed. She liked Laura as a person, not just because she was Tiago's mom. She stood outside the office door, pressed on one side by the wall of sound emanating from the dining room and on the other by the delicious smells crowding in from the kitchen. Her taste buds still tingled from the savory flavors of the dishes she'd sampled.

Where was Joaquín's office? She hadn't thought to ask. Was there a matching alcove on the kitchen's other side? Before she'd taken two steps, Tiago emerged, hair rumpled and expression darker than when he'd left.

Oh, dear. What had his father said now?

Quinn rushed to his side, determined to undo whatever damage she could. She laid a gentle hand on his arm, trying not to startle him since he seemed oblivious to his surroundings. His skin appeared chalky beneath his perpetual tan.

"Tiger?"

She touched his cheek.

He surprised her by kissing her palm. The feather-light touch of his lips shot shivers through her stomach, and she gasped. His hand slid down her arm, creating more delicious thrills. Was this love? If so, she wanted more.

U

Tiago delighted in the look that came over Quinn's face as he brushed his fingers against the soft skin of her arm. That his touch could elicit such a reaction boded well. Maybe he hadn't completely scared her away with his pity party earlier. His heart begged for him to pull her into his embrace and kiss her with all the passion heating his blood, but his head settled for tucking her hair behind her ear and a quick kiss on her forehead. If only he had the words to explain to Joaquín Vargas that he'd sought and found his passion, not in any worldly pursuit, but in one woman.

His gruff tone reflected the rough ride his emotions had endured. "Let's get out of here."

Quinn turned with him and tucked her hand in the crook of his elbow as if it were as natural as breathing. He shouldn't be surprised. They'd been in synch since they'd found each other's gaze over the arena fence four years earlier. If only he could convince her they belonged together permanently.

They'd left the city proper before Quinn broke the comfortable silence between them. "I thought Joaquín might have said something to upset you, but you seem oddly calm."

He glanced over, but the shadow of the mountain masked her features. "He gave me the same tired speech about needing to find my passion."

But the sense of unease that had vibrated his chest in his father's office returned. He pictured the vibrant man he remembered and compared it to the haggard version he'd sat with tonight. Hair grayer. Face more lined and cheeks hollower.

"Talk to me."

He shook his head. "Dad looked older. And, maybe . . ." He couldn't put his worries to words else they gain the weight of truth, and regardless of their inability to communicate, Tiago loved his father, valued him. "Likely my imagination and too much active avoidance."

"I think all children avoid really looking at their parents until something happens that forces us to see them, or *try* to see them, as people rather than only caregivers and authority figures." She released a mirthless chuckle. "Or maybe that's just the two of us because trauma entered our lives early."

Tiago navigated the turn into his family's driveway. "You

think we're that unique? Look at the Alliegro twins. Look at our own parents. I'm guessing growing up with trauma is more common than escaping it." When he reached for her hand, she met him halfway, her touch electrified silk. He killed the engine and quiet invaded the carport. Dim light shadowed Quinn's knitted brow and flattened mouth, but she returned his pulse of pressure. Hard to believe how reassuring a reciprocated gesture could be.

He was about to release her when she spoke.

"Ellee once told me shadows exist everywhere, in every home, every school, every town and city. Even for those who embrace God's light and carry it with them, sometimes our most difficult challenge is letting the light shine to illuminate the surrounding darkness."

Quinn's gaze rose to meet his, and the tension there tugged at his compassion.

"I've been guilty of adding to the shadow, of hoarding light for myself instead of releasing it into the world."

He wanted to protest, but her look silenced him.

"I've let a time that began in deep shadow block the light that came out of that darkness. But it's time I release the light and let it be seen by others regardless of what that means for me. I hope you'll understand."

Why was she being so cryptic? His heart rhythm changed gaits, from a trot to a canter.

"My darkest time has nothing to do with my parents or my being unwanted. I was attacked because of my stubborn refusal to heed warnings––my arrogance even when it came to faith." She hesitated. "I'll understand if discovering the truth of who I am changes the way you feel." She pulled her hand away and slid from his truck in a flash.

Mind whirling, he couldn't keep up. In a daze, he followed her and let them into the house, planning to sit her down at the table over a cup of coffee and figure out the cipher she'd just handed him, but she raced up the stairs before he could even call her name.

His mother and father stepped in from the garage several hours later, laughing and joking with each other as they often did.

Tiago acknowledged them with a nod but didn't move from his spot at the breakfast bar, hands wrapped loosely around a room temperature cup of coffee. His mother whispered into his father's ear and squeezed his arm. Dad placed a fleeting caress on her cheek before exiting through the hall leading to their bedroom.

Even exhausted, Laura Vargas moved with elegance. She approached, wrinkled her nose at the contents of his cup, and pulled juice glasses from a cupboard. She filled them with an orange-mango concoction and placed one before him as she settled into a stool across the bar.

"What has wriggled its way between you two, son?" Her pale eyes took on an iridescent glow in the reflection of undercounter lights off the tile backsplash.

At first, he assumed she meant him and his father, but as he considered, he realized she'd surmised the depth of the relationship between Quinn and himself. Her sharp mind missed little, and her extraordinary mediation skills had served both his Uncle Vasili and his father well as they negotiated contracts and business deals for the restaurant.

When he didn't respond to her question, she took a swallow of juice and studied him. He couldn't maintain her gaze, shifting to peer into cold, dark coffee.

"Tiago."

His name on her lips held a mother's love, pure and freely given. More than he deserved. His fingers clenched on porcelain. After a moment's hesitation, she pried it from his hand and replaced it with the chilled juice glass.

"It seems you've inherited more than a little of Joaquín's

amazing ability to misread, misinterpret, and miscommunicate." She softened her words with a toasting motion of her glass and a wink.

The indignation that had fired at her pronouncement fizzled as he raised his own juice to clink with hers. She loved him. He let the thought settle. She wanted what was best for him. Even though he'd shattered her dreams. His brows drew together, and he met her scrutiny over their still-raised glasses. "How?"

She abandoned the juice and clasped her hands where they rested on the bar. "How what?"

"How can you still love me when I . . ." His voice faltered.

"When you what?" Her tone remained even, calm, in control.

He grimaced. She'd always been controlled, whether during his father's passionate rants or his own petty tantrums. "I'm the reason our family is small. I broke you."

Her hands grasped his, and she leaned forward, breaking decorum. "You did not break me. Where did you get such a ridiculous notion?"

In halting words, he recounted the conversation he'd overheard as an eight-year-old and what he'd believed it meant. When he finished, their tears mingled on the bar's marble surface.

"Come here."

Tiago rounded the bar into her arms. He was that boy again, hurt and afraid of what he'd done, however unintentionally.

Arms squeezed tight around his frame, she whispered into his ear. "God gave me the perfect family. He granted me my heart's desire: your father and you. I needed no one else."

After a moment, she grasped each forearm and locked her eyes on his. "My son, I remember that night. We'd received word earlier that day that Vasili's daughter had miscarried for the third time and the doctor said she'd never be able to carry a child full-term. I grieved for her--with her--because I'd also suffered miscarriages. Five lost children.

"When you asked about a big family, the news hit me hard. I realized how blessed I was to have you, healthy and whole. That's why I cried." She sniffed, and Tiago handed her a tissue.

She dabbed at her nose, then went on. "My husband, bless his heart, took my reaction just as you did. He only sent you to your room to keep you from witnessing him cry. An ingrained reaction from his Argentinean upbringing. Men are not supposed to cry, you see. It goes against the *machismo.*"

Her pronunciation sounded so like Father Tiago couldn't help but crack a smile. Her explanation soothed the hurt, but he'd need time to process a lifetime of guilt.

His mother swiped hair from his forehead as she'd done when he was little. "You had nothing to do with the size of our family, Tiago. Only God controls such things." She brushed a kiss across his temple.

"Now. I must get some sleep. I've an important morning planned with the woman who's won my son's heart." She slid from the stool and disappeared down the hall.

Feeling lighter, he downed the juice and carried the glasses to the sink. Quinn had indeed won his heart. If only he could win hers.

CHAPTER 15

Quinn stared at her meager clothing choices. What did one wear to a morning on the town with a woman as elegant and refined as Laura Vargas? Plucking a flowy, turquoise top from the bag of mostly t-shirts, she held it up. Not too many wrinkles. She slid it over her head, enjoying the softness of the fabric.

Pairing it with black capris, she looked a little less back-country and a bit more feminine. Popping a hand onto her hip, she stole a glance in the mirror. When she tossed her head like one of those shampoo models, her long hair swung in a shiny arc. Quinn giggled.

A knock had her spinning toward the door, heart beating a frantic pace.

Laura stuck her head in, then clapped her hands in apparent delight. "How lovely you look, Quinn. That color brings out the softness in your eyes."

"Thank you." If God was merciful, Laura hadn't witnessed her lapse into fantasy. Neck and ears burning, Quinn couldn't form words. To cover, she retrieved her handbag and slid the long strap over her head and shoulder.

Nero serpentined his sleek body around her bare legs. When she stooped to pet him, he jumped onto her bed and curled into a ball.

"It appears he's coopting your bed for his morning nap. You look ready." Laura's smile relieved some of her embarrassment.

"I am."

"Perfect. Today's forecast calls for record temperatures these next few days. I propose we get our walking in early then do the driving tour afterward, with air conditioning." She tossed Quinn a conspiratorial grin, then breezed from the room, leaving Quinn to follow.

Laura waved at Tiago who lounged at the bar with coffee, scrolling through his phone. He rose and crossed the space, pecking his mother on the cheek. Then he pulled Quinn into a side hug and whispered, "I've never seen her bite, but if she does, I guarantee she's got her shots."

She giggle-snorted into his shoulder.

His arms came around her, aligning and pressing her into his muscled frame. He felt good. Safe. Smelled good, too. Something woodsy with that hint of spice. She relaxed into his touch until last night's conversation dropped into the pit of her stomach. If only she'd been brave enough to tell him the whole truth. Would he even want to touch her if he knew about Reina? She wiggled to loosen his hold, but his arms were like steel.

The trapped, helpless feeling she'd experienced in the arms of her attacker returned. Panic surged up her throat. She shoved her palms against his chest. Hard.

He released her like she'd burned him.

Hot tears filled her eyes. Muscles tensed to run.

"Quinn, wait!" His fingers grazed her elbow. "I'm sorry. I didn't think. Forgive me."

Forgive him? She was the one with baggage. Pivoting, she

took in his outstretched hand and those sincere, pleading eyes. They dragged her toward him. One step, then two. She couldn't keep her finger from tracing the curve of his cheek. "There's nothing to forgive." In fact, she should be asking for his forgiveness for letting him believe something could come from their friendship. The admission, even to herself, cut deep into her heart. The same heart she'd thought immune to love.

He cupped her cheek and his eyes softened, then grew darker. Was he going to kiss her? No. She couldn't let him. But, oh, how she wanted his lips on hers. She compressed the thought, squashed it down.

"You'd better go." His voice was huskier than she remembered.

All she could do was nod, then run to the relative safety of the white Mercedes where Laura waited, a broad smile on her face. Had she seen their intimate exchange? Quinn's panicked flight? Likely not all of it by the contented look on her face.

Quinn's stomach tumbled with uncertainty. Why continue her farce? Her past would never go away. Another thing she couldn't control. Yet she couldn't bring herself to admit her failure. To let everyone see the Arena Queen wasn't invincible or even courageous, but a bald-faced lie.

So she did what she was best at——she swallowed her feelings and smiled. "Where are we headed first?"

U

Around one that afternoon Laura blotted her mouth with the paper napkin and smiled at the waiter who'd delivered their check, sharing some insight about the brisket dish she'd eaten.

Quinn sat across from her in the cushioned booth,

savoring the lingering flavors of cayenne and buttery biscuit from her own delicious meal. She swallowed the last of her peach tea and reflected on the morning.

As it turned out, Laura was an excellent private guide. They'd walked down lower Broadway, lined with honky-tonks and bars where many a country music legend had been discovered. Then they'd driven around music row, Laura extolling the history of the recording studios, record labels, and upscale shops and restaurants occupying the area.

They'd toured the Grand Ole Opry and seen the Opry-land Theme Park, as well as a few of the many distilleries, and some beautiful old mansions and hotels preserved from the colonial era. Between descriptions of the passing scenes or tidbits of history, Laura told Quinn about her days as a legal aide working for Joaquín's Uncle Vasili, and her first meeting with her husband. Romance and happily-ever-after filled her tale, something Quinn would never experience. A pinprick of jealousy stabbed her heart, but her growing love for this kind, vivacious woman easily uprooted it.

The waiter moved away, a jaunt to his step. Quinn smiled, recognizing the kinship Tiago had hinted at growing between them. She would miss this woman when she returned to Montana. Another stab. Reina and Missy. Quinn hadn't spared them much thought with so many distractions. She'd called last night after running from Tiago, and Missy had assured her they were both more than fine, and she shouldn't worry.

"Our beginning wasn't all sunshine and roses either, you know." Laura's thoughtful expression made Quinn wonder how long she'd been observing while Quinn drifted through her thoughts.

"Either?" What was Laura hinting at?

"Yes, dear, either. Whether you're willing to admit it or not, you and Tiago are falling in love." She slanted her head and pursed her lips. "Perhaps you've already fallen. I can't say for sure. Regardless, you each have issues to be dealt with for your relationship to work."

Quinn bristled at her comment. "Tiago has wonderful ideas for restaurant design and recognizes hidden possibility in both spaces and people. I don't understand why his father insists he pursue something other than the restaurant business."

"You misread my meaning, but I'll address your concern first." She fingered a filigreed cross dangling from a fine silver chain. "My son craves acceptance by his father and others. By insisting Tiago find his passion, Joaquín believes he's protecting Tiago from the fate his father tried to push on him before he left Argentina. And machismo prevents them from discussing their varying interpretations of events. So nothing is ever resolved."

"You're saying it's not that Joaquín doesn't want Tiago to work in the restaurant, rather he doesn't want to force him into it because of loyalty?" She examined Joaquín's interactions with Tiago from this new perspective. Could what she assumed was disdain or lack of love actually be regret?

"He wants to give Tiago a choice, something Joaquín almost didn't get for himself."

"And Tiago thinks his father is pushing him away because he's not good enough."

"Quite the dilemma, isn't it?" Laura leaned her chin on her hand and leveled Quinn with a sorrowful look. "I can't fix it because I'm too close. Each would feel betrayed. You, on the other hand, might be able to reach beyond their pride and help them see reason."

"You like me because you think I can reconcile your family." Quinn was only half teasing.

Laura's eyes narrowed. "I like you because you're a remarkable young woman. Beautiful, talented, kind, unselfish, and, unless my keen observation skills have grown dull over the past few days, persistent enough to love my son through difficult times. I wanted you to know the power you could wield in this situation. Woman to woman. I believe you're the one God sent to bridge their differences."

"Oh, Laura." Quinn deflated. "I'm not worthy of your praise. Or your confidence."

"I disagree. I can't see your heart or read your thoughts, Quinn Mulroney, but I can judge your actions, and you've shown yourself to be gentle and compassionate. You're able to communicate on a deeper level than most--read tells and the direction a person is leaning. It's one of your gifts."

"You don't understand. I've lied to Tiago, to you, to every-one. I've denied"--she swiped a hand through the air--"so much. It's inexcusable. Especially to someone as wonderful as Tiago. He deserves more. Better." A rising sense of hysteria shrilled Quinn's voice. She had to make Laura understand.

"By that standard, no one would marry." Laura paused to let her words sink in. "Each of us is flawed. We've all made mistakes, bear the regrets of our pasts, but the wonderful thing is we don't have to let those define our futures. Jesus promised that in this world we will have trouble, but He has overcome the world. Let Jesus' victory wash your past clean."

Quinn could barely breathe. Hadn't she done that? Even in the aftermath of the attack, her faith had faltered but never broken. She'd claimed her faith as the reason to keep her unborn child when everyone said she would regret her decision. Blackness swirled around Quinn's vision. She swayed.

Laura reached out and caught her hand. "Quinn!"

Quinn sucked in a breath. Then another. The world returned to focus, fuzzy at first, then clearer.

Laura clutched her hand across the table, eyes wide, mouth pinched in concern.

A quiet thought filtered between the clatter of utensils and muted conversations of other diners. Quinn's gaze flickered to Laura's then away with the speed of a hummingbird. She couldn't.

The thought refused to be dismissed.

Laura's fingers tightened as if in encouragement.

A gulping swallow. A quick breath. She couldn't do it. "Tiago's my hero, the one God sent to rescue me when I needed him most, but I can't let him be anything more. He'll hate me for the secrets I've kept or at least doubt me. I'd just hold him back. Better to push him away so he can find happiness with someone else than suffer for my cowardice."

Rather than snatch her hand away as Quinn expected Laura to do, the woman's knowing gaze never faltered until Quinn squirmed under her perusal.

Laura's phone beeped. She sighed. "I'm afraid we must be getting back. Today is ordering and delivery day at Casa Vargas, and I need to be there in case there's a problem." She patted Quinn's hand before releasing it. "Keep praying, dear one. I believe you're close to a breakthrough."

Whatever did she mean? Quinn tried to smile, but it fell flat. Unsurprisingly, she couldn't read Laura when the lawyer-turned-accountant shuttered her expression. But the feeling Tiago's mother hadn't accepted Quinn's line of reasoning, seemed certain.

Laura continued her guide service on the return drive giving Quinn's churning thoughts little time to process. She managed to nod and comment when needed, but retained none of the information.

They parked and entered the house, Laura's smile as unaffected by Quinn's revelations as if they'd discussed the weather. They parted in the kitchen. Quinn meandered toward the living room then stopped short in the doorway. She hugged the wall trying to make sense of the scene.

Tiago perched in one of the overstuffed chairs, body hunched over what appeared to be a tablet, scribbling furiously with a stylus. On the television one of those restaurant make-over shows played with subtitles even though the audio blared. As the expert advised the owner of all the changes he recommended be made, Tiago checked lines on his document. At the commercial, he put down the stylus, leaned back, and crossed his arms over his chest, bunching his muscles beneath the fabric.

Quinn's heart wavered. She abandoned caution and approached, getting close enough to touch before Tiago noticed her. His startled movement sent the stylus careening off the tablet to bounce off the edge of the coffee table and roll beneath the chair. They both bent to retrieve it, foreheads colliding.

Quinn came up holding the stylus in one hand and her head in the other. "Ow. You have a hard skull." She held out his pen.

His grin disarmed her. "So I've been told. Mostly by my father."

The grimace she expected didn't appear. She nodded at his now-dark tablet. "Whatcha working on?"

The grin grew, and he waggled his eyebrows. "I'm not ready to divulge that information. Yet." He thumbed the remote and the T.V. clicked off. "Still game to try Quilombo? Clouds are supposed to roll in around three. Should help with the heat."

The prospect of riding both accelerated her pulse and dried her mouth. She hadn't been on a horse since she'd been forced to sell hers months after Reina's birth. Best she stay grounded. The thought swelled disappointment through her chest. Swallowing gathered enough moisture to turn him down. "Yes." Traitorous tongue.

"Good." Tiago stood. "Let's change into riding clothes and meet back here."

Smiling despite her thwarted intentions, Quinn raced up the stairs, excitement urging her feet faster. She was going to ride a horse. More than that, as the possibility loomed, she was ready to ride. *Wanted* to ride. Something she'd not been sure would ever happen.

After the devastation of losing Delilah--her truest friend--and her father in the span of months, she'd closed off that chapter in her life. Did this mean she could consider returning to rodeo, too? To the team where Tiago would be acting as a coach.

She allowed a tiny bit of the dream where she competed again and connected with Tiago over the arena rails to animate in her mind. Those moments had been some of the best of her life. Moments when she'd felt truly seen and cherished as a woman.

While pulling on her favorite riding tank--one she'd tossed in at the last second--the feeling swelled within her chest. She wanted Tiago. Wanted to fall in love and have him love her back. Wanted the cozy little family with the house and the land and the animals grazing in the pasture. But how could she consider the possibility?

With God all things are possible. The verse bubbled up from her memory. And its conclusion: *for those who call upon his name.* What a fantastic promise. Quinn dropped to her knees and prayed for courage and strength. In order to get what she wanted, she'd first have to become the person Tiago needed.

CHAPTER 16

Who knew changing clothes could make his heart race? The juxtaposition of restaurant and rodeo clashed on the walls of his bedroom, and for the first time, Tiago realized his father was right. All his life, he'd chased after the things Joaquín Vargas valued. Time now for Tiago to pursue his own passions. Quinn first. Business second.

Today's ride on Quilombo weighed critically in the plan. He agreed with Coach McCloud. If Quinn got back in the saddle, she'd agree to return to the team. Her resistance would crumble, and then he'd have a reason to see her every day. A low heat simmered at the thought. He slid on his boots and snagged his white Stetson.

Hesitating for a moment at the top of the stairs, he recalled the first time his and Quinn's eyes had met and locked. The same sense of connection and responsibility he'd been struck with then pulsed in cadence with his heartbeat. He wouldn't give up until her rhythm synched with his.

Thank you, Lord, for these revelations. Be with me as I pursue the path you've mapped out for me.

Tiago jogged down the stairs only to be stopped dead at the bottom, all thought knocked from his head. Quinn faced away from him as she pulled two bottles of water from the fridge. The sight of her bare shoulders in a form-fitting black tank, with her hair a dark plait down her back pointing out the well-fitted jeans, nearly unraveled him. Made him want to toss away the plan and kiss her until she couldn't deny her feelings for him.

Only a lifetime worth of training in public forums kept his wild desires under control. He cleared his throat and entered the room.

Quinn greeted him over her very attractive shoulder with a wide smile that brought her gray eyes to life. "Ready."

Tiago nudged her toward the door with a hand at her back. The zing from the touch choked off his reply.

Quinn balked, tilting her head toward the counter and her black Stetson.

Sweeping it up with his free hand, Tiago plopped it onto her head, the action releasing some of his tension. She nudged the brim upward and grinned while he relieved her of one bottle and opened the front door, closing it after himself and setting the alarm.

They were settled in his truck and heading to the nearby boarding facility when Quinn glanced at him. "Your mother is truly a wonder. She reminds me of Ellee, perceptive and wise. Strong. Ellee is a tiny spitfire and Laura a lioness."

Navigating one of several hairpin turns down the mountain, Tiago nodded, but kept his eyes on the road. "I'd love to meet your Ellee. She sounds like an amazing woman. And you're right about Mom. She had to be strong in her own right to handle a man like my father. To hear her tell it, he's always been driven and single-minded, pouring all his passion into building up his restaurant and securing their relationship. She had to learn early the art of give and take. They fought a lot at the beginning, according to her. Dad would never admit such a thing. He'd consider it a betrayal of trust."

The road straightened, and Tiago glanced over as Quinn cocked her head in her "thinking posture." Her tendency to examine an idea before offering her opinion or questioning it was one more reason he loved her.

"But it's not a betrayal if Laura discusses their history with you?"

"There's a double standard at play in machismo. Men are held to different rules than women. And before you get offended, it isn't because they––or at least my father, I guess I shouldn't speak for all Argentines––consider women inferior. In fact, women are to be revered and treasured. Women may speak of their husbands to trusted others in private, while men would be considered weak if they voiced complaints. In public, women are expected to show the utmost support of their husbands."

"Do some men take this to extremes, lording their superiority over their women?"

"Probably, but this has never been the case in my home, nor have I noticed such attitudes whenever we've visited family in Argentina."

Quinn cocked her head and stared out the side window, making it impossible to read her eyes. Was she thinking about her attackers? On the way to the hospital, she'd mentioned one of the men had spoken with an accent. Could this fear be holding her back from fully accepting him?

He drove through the gate to the boarding facility and along a wide lane flanked on each side by small green pastures dotted with fenced-off clumps of trees. A few horses and ponies grazed. Those closer to the drive raised their heads for a quick perusal, then returned to their meals. In the background, mountains rose to meet the sky where clouds gathered to block the brightness and heat of the afternoon sun.

Parking in the near-empty lot, Tiago turned to Quinn before killing the engine and the air-conditioning. "I treasure you, Quinn. I'll never do anything to hurt you if I can prevent it."

At his words, her face crumpled. Tears glassed her eyes, and her fingers clenched. He'd been going for reassurance, not to freak her out.

When he reached for her face, she flinched. He jerked back at her reaction, helpless as she fumbled with the seat belt release and then the door handle. She scrambled from the cab and half-ran, half-stumbled across the asphalt toward a grazing pony in a pasture. A brown and white horse pricked his ears in the adjoining paddock, tracking her approach.

Quilombo. He'd recognize the distinctive swirl pattern on his gelding's face anywhere. An unexpected surge of affection mixed with his confusion over Quinn's response. The swirl of emotions sharpened his interest in the meeting between an important part of his past and the woman he hoped would be an important part of his future.

Quinn seemed oblivious except for whatever was going on in her own head. Crossing her arms over the top board of the fence, she lowered her forehead and stood, feet apart, shoulders shaking.

Billowing clouds reminded Tiago of Quinn's eyes. Eyes he imagined soaked in tears for whatever ill he'd inadvertently caused. Quilombo tossed his head, as if indignant he'd been ignored, and ambled toward the woman near his territory. The pony also raised his head coming closer. Quilombo bobbed his nose with each step.

The three converged, and Quinn inched her head

upward. Quilombo snuffed and blew a trumpet of air through his nose, apparently gaining her full attention, for her slumped body straightened. The pony trotted the final distance, not to be outdone. Quinn extended one hand, palm up for Quilombo to examine, the other extended toward the dappled pony.

"Attaboy, Qui. You too, pony." Tiago whispered, though he remained inside the warming oven of his cab.

The gelding snuffled her fingers, then rubbed his forehead up and down against her hand the way he'd always done on Tiago's body.

She withdrew her arm from his overly enthusiastic rubbing but remained at the fence, patting the pony's neck.

From the direction of the barn, a screen door slapped against the frame. Tiago followed Quinn's reoriented attention to where a scarecrow in a cowboy hat sauntered toward the paddock. With his thumbs hooked in his belt behind a large buckle, and his exaggerated gait, his elbows flapped like chicken wings––or so Tiago had always thought. Whipping off the safety belt, Tiago stepped from the truck intent on intervening. One thought restrained him from slamming his door and intercepting the barn manager.

Would Quinn want him to rescue her?

Maybe she'd rethought his "hero" label since she'd gotten to know him better. Her jerk away from his offer of comfort stayed his feet as well. Best let this play out. She knew he was here if she needed or wanted his help. Besides, Tiago could best Elvis in a head-to-head comparison.

Couldn't he?

Quinn's stampeding thoughts refused her mental corral as she stumbled across terrain she barely noticed. Tiago tried so hard to put her at ease, to comfort, to make sense of her mess. All the things Laura said Quinn did naturally. But he couldn't because of his inflated and unrealistic opinion of her--and she wouldn't tell him the truth. And now, after they'd spent so many days together, wouldn't hearing her story be even more difficult to accept? Wouldn't he be hurt she hadn't told him before they left Montana, or at the very least, that first day on the road?

She'd fall to her death from the pedestal he'd elevated her onto. Their relationship couldn't survive the fallout. Her body collided with a board fence, and she lowered her head to her arms.

A paint horse bobbed his head as if to underscore her cowardice and stupidity. Cowardice because she'd let fear seal her mouth. Stupidity because she would alienate the one person who could have made her happily-ever-after dream a reality when she eventually handed him her secret. She *would* tell him, hang the consequences. The lies had gone on long enough.

A gorgeous gray pony approached from the pasture, dapples shining as he trotted toward her.

The slap of a screen door swiveled her head toward the large barn and the dandy tromping her way with his wannabe cowboy walk. She glanced at the horse, whose ears flicked between them with interest, and extended her hand. The gelding sniffed and raised his lip--smirk or laugh, she didn't know.

Whatever. She wasn't in the mental state to deal with anyone right now. The pony nuzzled her fingers, and she patted his sleek neck. The jealous paint rubbed his forehead violently against her forearm. She withdrew before he gave her a bruise.

"Howdy there, ma'am. I'm Elvis, the manager here. Are you looking to ride or for a place to board? Or perhaps a nice pony? This one's for sale."

Elvis? Really? Quinn surveyed his eager smile, fancy boots, and cowboy hat. Even if he'd just polished his boots and recently purchased a new hat, the overlarge belt buckle guaranteed he'd be doing little work. As skinny as he was, she'd be afraid for him if he bent over. Its weight might over-balance him.

Perhaps this was a way to get out of Tiago's trap. Not that he'd intended it in a harmful way. After all, he was right. If she fell in love with his horse, she'd never be able to say no to returning to the rodeo, especially with the monetary bait they'd dangled.

But if she rode a different horse, she could satisfy her itch without forcing a choice. Mr. Dunn's offer remained on the table if she ignored the loss of time spent with Reina, not to mention her education. She gritted her teeth. No way she could work with Tiago every day after she shattered his image of her with reality.

"I'm here to ride. What about this horse?" She pointed to the brown and white animal. "Is he available?"

Elvis paled and swallowed several times before turning his head toward Tiago's truck.

"Is something wrong?" Her concern grew as his skin went from chalky to pink, then scarlet. Afraid he was having a heart attack, she stepped closer, but halted when he raised a hand.

"He tricked me again, didn't he? Humiliating me once wasn't enough. Had to make fun of poor, gullible Elvis."

Wondering if the man was all there, she tried once more to approach.

He jumped back, looking as though he might bolt at any second. White ringed his eyes.

Tiago appeared at her side from nowhere. His hand out in a calming gesture, exactly what she'd been about to do.

"It's okay, Elvis. This wasn't a set-up, and I've told you

before, I didn't think that prank up. I tried to stop them."

"Uh-huh. I didn't believe you the first time, and I don't believe you this time, either." He darted wild-eyed looks between them. Why would she ask to ride your horse if you weren't trying to prank me?"

"She didn't know––"

"This is your horse?" Quinn hooked a thumb at the paint who'd returned to his hay.

Tiago nodded. "Quinn, meet Quilombo."

Quinn could almost hear God laughing at her. Not because he was petty, but because she'd tried so hard to ignore the Spirit's nudges and even in her defiance, she'd ended up where He'd pointed her all along.

Fine, Jesus. You win. I'll take up my cross and trust you for the outcome. I'm sorry I kept trying to change lanes. Tiago's expectations are in Your hands.

"Elvis, I truly didn't know. I had no intention of pranking you, and I doubt very much that Tiago was responsible for whatever prank you referenced earlier. He's as serious as they come and pranking someone wouldn't have been on his radar, even in high school. But for the record, I'm sorry you suffered. It wasn't a very kind or considerate thing to do."

Elvis's color was returning to normal, as was his breathing and swallowing. He eyed Quinn, then Tiago.

Beside her, Tiago offered his hand in friendship. "I'm also sorry for what happened. No one chooses his name and it wasn't fair to use it against you. I should have tried harder to talk the others out of their scheme."

Elvis accepted Tiago's olive branch with a skeptical hesitation. "I'll leave you to your business. If you need anything, I'll be in my office." He pivoted on his heel, teetered while he regained his balance, then walked with stiff strides toward the barn.

Her gaze trailed to the pony who'd returned to munching

grass.

"You like him?" Tiago asked.

A memory swelled, broadening Quinn's smile. It demanded to be shared. "Cal bought me a pony when I was five against Missy's wishes."

"Oh? Why didn't she want you to have a horse?

Quinn shrugged. "She never said, but likely she was afraid I'd get hurt."

"Was the pony gray like this one?"

"Chestnut with a flaxen mane and tail. Beautiful but quite the stinker." She flashed a smile, then sobered. "I knew for certain Cal loved me that day. It was the happiest day of my life. Every time I rode, I felt that love all over again. Cal did something just for me. I felt special because of that gift. Seen. Accepted."

Tiago squeezed her shoulder. Something other than gold flickered in his eyes. "Still want to ride?"

Quinn couldn't have denied her desire if she'd wanted to, but that flicker bothered her enough she attempted to divert his thoughts. "I've come thousands of miles to sit on this horse's back. Are you kidding?"

His smile woke the sparkle in his eyes. "Let's get 'er done then." He strode toward the barn on Elvis' heels, tossing over his shoulder, "Better catch up. I'm no mule. I'm expecting your help to tote the tack out here."

She marveled at the return of their easy banter, despite her despicable treatment of Tiago not ten minutes before. Was that what it looked like when you loved someone? You forgave easier? Or was it he simply believed she could do no wrong? She shrugged off her speculation and hurried after her hero.

Fifteen minutes later, they'd caught, brushed, and saddled Quilombo, working together like a seasoned team with that same sense of synchronicity Quinn had noticed for three years of intersecting rodeos. Though come to think of it, the only rodeo both their universities competed in was the CNFR in Casper.

Why had she never wondered how he came to be at so many of her competitions?

"I think it's best if he lunges a bit before you mount up." Tiago held up the long, flat nylon tether. "He's always been a character with a strong personality, and he's been holed up without any forced exercise for nearly a year." He winced. "Once I graduated and Dad gave me the "find your true pasión" speech, I couldn't bring myself to ride again. It reminded me of my motivation for joining rodeo in the first place."

They stood near the center of the small paddock. Quinn stroked along the horse's neck where white changed to brown. "You followed your father into rodeo."

"Dad was a star. You've seen the photos. A four-year qualifier and multiple gold medals in the CNFR. Your dad used videos of him to train you for crying out loud. I barely qualified in one event over my career, made the short go once as a senior. No medals."

A large dose of Joaquín's pasión welled up, leading her to act. Something she'd have done during her rodeo days without a second thought. With one hand on his tensed shoulder and the other on his reddening cheek, she compelled him to meet her gaze. "Santiago Vargas, you cannot base your worth on a comparison of physical rewards. You did something more important than winning, though you deserve a medal. You rescued me—chose to save me. You were my hero. You still are."

Tiago stilled, not a twitch, barely a breath. So still, Quinn feared she'd sent him into shock. If those words had such a chilling effect, what would dispelling his Queen myth do?

Quilombo rather violently rubbed his head on Tiago's

back, nearly causing him to faceplant in the dirt at her feet.

"Any commands I should know?" Quinn took the line from Tiago's hand after he'd recovered and turned the horse in a circle. Quilombo's bit clinked, his tongue working the roller.

"He used to know walk, trot, canter, and whoa, but who knows how much he'll pretend to 'forget.' He'd try that on me after the break between the fall and spring rodeo seasons every year."

"A trickster, huh?" She patted his shoulder and scratched his withers beneath the saddle pad. "If you do a good job, I can mount up sooner. That'll be more fun. I promise."

They survived the lunging with minimal difficulty. At one point when she asked the horse to speed up, he humped his back to buck but ended his rebellion after three crow hops. She reeled in the line once he stood still with his head lowered in submission. Though a glint in his eyes warned her to be on guard.

"Ready?"

She dipped her hat brim. Tiago held the horse's head while she gathered the sweat-slicked reins and put her left foot in the stirrup. A sense of déjà vu shifted her back to a time when Cal held her horse, and she used a bucket to reach the stirrup. When her bottom hit the padded seat, her perspective shifted to the present. Her right foot found the off-side stirrup, and she settled into the familiar positions: toes in, heels down, calves against the horse's ribs, back straight, elbows in, head up.

"I'll go with you for a round."

Quinn gritted her teeth. She'd been riding on her own since Cal turned her loose at ten years old. Right after the Bobby incident. Just because the horse was new . . .

She pulled a long breath through her nose and let it out through pursed lips, imagining the grousing flowing away with her breath. No sense wasting her moments in anger and negativity. Besides, the day was too hot to add emotional heat to the mix.

She focused her mental energy on the animal beneath her. Power pulsed through every step. Power he wanted to unleash if the prancing was any indication. "Did Quilombo ever run barrels?"

Tiago shrugged. "I don't think so. He's straight off the pampas of Argentina."

"Oh?"

"Yep. Dad bought him on one of his restaurant beef contract trips. Quilombo was only green broke at the time—still mostly wild. I spent months taming him before I ever tried to ride."

"You trained him yourself?"

"Not really, but I got him acclimated enough a professional could work with him."

"Sounds a lot like Delilah." The words were out before Quinn could consider the emotional impact they'd have. The horse noticed and danced beneath her, head bobbing, foam slinging, hooves tattooing a lively beat.

"Let me have him." The strain of Delilah's loss cracked her voice.

Tiago glanced back, concern flashing across his face, replaced by understanding, then stoic control. With a nod, he stepped away, fading into the center and relinquishing the rail to her and the horse.

Quilombo strained at the bit, and Quinn wanted what he wanted. He broke into a canter, head bowed like a racehorse. "I wish we had a cow to chase," she told him. "Then we could really fly."

He shook his head as if in agreement.

Quinn steered the gelding into a figure eight pattern, his stride smooth, transitions quick and responsive. Next, she mimicked a header's path, then a heeler's. The horse accelerated and maneuvered on cue, but disliked slowing, fighting her attempts to curb his speed. "Easy boy. This area's too small for your taste, isn't it?"

Quilombo finally stopped but stood in the center of the paddock trembling and fidgeting.

Tiago hopped over the fence where he'd withdrawn and approached, keeping his steps slow and steady for the horse's sake. Quinn could read his desire to run to their side, questions spilling from his lips. She refused to smile or smirk. Maybe she could keep him in suspense a bit longer as to whether she'd fallen for his ruse.

Or was that cruel? Their eyes caught and a shiver shook her body.

Quilombo's feet left the ground, catching her with her guard down. Distracted. Her left foot lost the stirrup and slammed his side. Ever responsive, the horse spun to the right.

Quinn made a wild grab for the saddle horn, her fingertips brushing leather before sliding past without purchase. Her body listed left, momentum carrying her beyond her center of gravity.

In a blink, her shoulder exploded with a jarring crunch. Pain lightninged through her chest and down her arm. She may have cried out before black edged her vision.

Then Tiago was there, on the ground beside her, cradling her head in his hands. His frantic voice tunneled through the thick buzzing in her ears. "Are you hurt? Quinn, speak to me!"

She managed a moan.

His eyes darkened and fear etched lines in his forehead, around his eyes.

He was so handsome. And so kissable. Quinn hooked his neck with her good arm and pulled his head toward hers until their lips touched. He hesitated, then pleasure overcame the pain when he deepened the kiss. A thrill wended its way from her belly up into her chest, piercing her heart.

She loved this man. She'd do anything for a future with him. Would he accept her and her mistakes, or was it the perfect Queen he wanted?

When Tiago broke the kiss, Quinn's swollen lips curved upward. She smoothed an unruly curl near his ear. "I need to tell you some--."

"Later." His hand covered hers. "First you need to be seen. You could have broken your shoulder. Or sustained a concussion. Or worse." He didn't iterate the "worse."

Quilombo snuffled at Tiago's back, then latched onto his shirt, teeth tugging.

"Not now!"

The horse jerked backward.

Quinn squeezed Tiago's fingers, forcing words out between sharp pauses to breathe. "Not his fault, Tiger. Don't blame him for his nature. I knew better."

"So did he."

"Delilah would have dumped me quicker than Quilombo. I fell off. An accident, nothing more."

Tiago's mouth worked, as if chewing on her words. She tried to reach for him, but a stabbing pain convinced her to stay still. Her cry seemed to zap Tiago from his internal conflict.

He held her good shoulder down. "Relax a moment. Let me get Quilombo secured so he doesn't step on us in his concern. Then we'll get you checked out."

"I'm fine." Her attempt to keep her voice strong only halfway succeeded. And was completely undermined by the wince that followed.

"I know you're tough but don't run off. I'll be right back."

"Ha." Quinn shoved out the syllable, then clenched her

teeth, breathing through the pulsing pain. She heard voices. Saw Elvis and Tiago shake hands. Then Elvis led a still-prancing Quilombo toward the paddock gate. By the way the man handled the antsy horse, it seemed she'd misjudged him. Imagine. Another apology owed.

Tiago returned to her, imitating the birthing mother breathing they always described in movies. Embarrassing, but it helped. He held her good hand, his thumb caressing her knuckles. Even through her discomfort, tiny thrills spiderwebbed her core.

"What are we waiting on?" she pushed out between breaths.

"EMTs. Elvis called them, and they're en route."

"Don't need––"

"Hush. You don't get to decide what you need until your head is looked at. Then we'll see."

Tiago sounded so much like his father at that moment–– confident, in charge, brooking no argument. Quinn found herself––her, the independent loner––enjoying his care. Feeling cherished rather than squashed.

Sirens announced the ambulance's arrival. Tiago shifted, but didn't rise or leave her side.

"Elvis met them." Relief tinged Tiago's tone. "Seems we've overcome our previous difficulties. Finally."

Quinn would be happy for them once she got off the ground, and her shoulder stopped screaming.

Three hours later Tiago helped Quinn from the passenger seat in his truck. A sling and Velcro wrap secured her left shoulder to her side preventing movement and making maneuvering difficult. Pain meds scrambled her thinking and her balance, so she leaned heavily on Tiago inhaling his spicy, hard-working scent. When he deposited her on the living room sofa, she acutely missed his warmth.

"Come back. I need you." Her med-slurred speech gave

her a drunken sailor vibe, and she began to giggle while extending her good hand toward Tiago.

He hesitated, then gave in, returning to intertwine his fingers with hers.

Still giggling, she gazed at his handsome face. The only semi-coherent thought in her brain involved dinner with her two favorite people. She couldn't get her lips or tongue to cooperate, so she smiled up at him. Her overflowing emotions produced chuckles and sighs now and again, along with a yawn or two.

At some point she must have stretched out on the sofa because she woke an undetermined amount of time later, on her back with drool running down one cheek, and her injured arm propped up with pillows and blankets, aided by a sleeping Nero. Her eyes refused to open more than thin slits, which made seeing across the shadowy room difficult. When she attempted to speak, her tongue seemed glued to the roof of her mouth.

Shifting brought a dull ache from her left arm and a moan low in her throat. She closed her eyes, intent on focusing her thoughts, though her brain seemed clearer than before. No spinning, at least.

A rustle of cloth and footsteps announced Tiago's approach. He looked a bit haggard. Had she done that? Before she could think, she smoothed her fingers over his forehead, down the bridge of his nose and across his roughened cheek and chin, stopping short of his lips. Her neck and ears heated when she recalled their last kiss––the one she'd initiated.

Oh, my. She had to tell him. She wasn't being fair, leading him on when he didn't know the real her. She jerked her hand from his stubble and wiggled in an attempt to sit up. Nero hopped off with an indignant meow.

"Let me help." He snapped into action, moving pillows

and supporting her injured arm. His other hand at her back applying just the right amount of pressure to ease her up. Helping her swivel and get her feet on the floor. A complicated process Tiago handled without error.

His actions nudged her spirit. Drew connection. Urged her to speak.

A buzz came from the garage as the mechanism raised one of the overhead doors.

The sound compounded the urgency inside Quinn. "Thank you. You're a Godsend. Truly. Now please, sit down. I have something I need to tell you."

He lowered himself onto the sofa leaving some space between them. Tension radiated off him, but she had no time to soothe his nerves.

A muffled slam preceded another buzz, lowering the door.

Quinn latched on to Tiago's hand, gaining his attention. "I have a--"

"Tiago? Where's Quinn? Is she all right? What happened?" Laura burst through the door, questions spewing from her mouth like candy from a busted piñata.

Quinn deflated. *Why God? I'm trying to do as you've asked. A little help, please?*

Tiago met Quinn's eyes with a sort of apology, then rose from the sofa. "Quinn's right here, recovering. Need help, Mom?"

"As long as she's okay, then yes, son, that would be nice. I've brought your favorite dishes for supper. I hope you're hungry."

Laura's chatter continued as savory spiciness circulated throughout the space. Quinn's stomach growled. What time was it? How was Laura here? Wouldn't Joaquín need her at the restaurant? The endless questions flagged Quinn's energy. And she wasn't any nearer to her revelation than before.

A phone vibrated on the coffee table. Quinn's phone. How odd. She didn't remember putting it there. Of course, she didn't remember much, so who knew. Scooting out to the edge, she snagged it with her right hand and glanced at the screen. Missy. Six missed calls! She slid to answer and held it to her ear.

"Missy, what's wrong?"

"Are you watching the news? You need to watch the news. It's . . . There's . . ." A huff came through the phone. "Just watch it. You need to see for yourself."

Quinn's pulse kicked up. "Missy, calm down. Which network?"

"What? Um, I don't know. ABC, I think. It's one of those streaming ones. They replay all day."

"Okay. Hold on. I have to find the remote." She moved the phone away. "Tiago? Missy wants me to watch ABC's streaming news program. Can you turn on the T.V.?" Hearty Argentinean roasted beef and vegetables permeated the living room, prompting another jungle-like growl from Quinn's complaining stomach.

Tiago grabbed the remote from an end table and flipped through the channels until he found what she asked for. A commercial played.

"Do you have it yet?" Missy's voice sounded strained. In the background a wail rose. "Reina's awake. I have to go. Call me after you've watched." A click sounded, then the hum of dead air.

Quinn stared at the phone a moment before placing it beside her on the mauve and gray patterned cushion. What had riled Missy up enough to prompt seven calls?'

On the large screen, the pretty anchor woman said something about a professional basketball player returning to his hometown to stage a fundraiser. The video cut to a fire ravaging a large building, then lingered on the sign for a community center.

Quinn's phone vibrated. She narrowed her eyes. "Give me a chance, will ya?" She focused on the story playing out on the larger screen. "I'd love helping those kids get a new community center."

Tiago glanced at the T.V before placing a loaded plate of food on the coffee table. "Planning the fundraiser set-up would be fun."

Inhaling to another long stomach gurgle, she glanced between the fork and her phone on its third ring.

Tiago chuckled. "Want me to answer? I can stall while you take a bite."

"Would you? Missy's being impatient."

She shoveled food into her mouth while he muted the anchor woman and picked up her cell still grinning. "Hello?"

Chewing, she savored the perfect blend of spices as a man wearing a Denver Nuggets blazer spoke with the anchor woman. She'd taken another bite when two mug shots came onto the screen with the caption: Two suspects arrested in Casper, Wyoming rape and murder case.

The fork clattered to the hardwood floor. Her shoulder screamed as her body jerked taut, her right hand flying to her mouth. Her focus narrowed to the faces in the photos––faces she'd seen before.

"Quinn?" She barely recognized Tiago's voice through the ringing in her ears. "There's a Detective Bolen from Wyoming asking to speak to you."

She swallowed, heart pounding, then looked into the creased worry on Tiago's face. Heat flooded her body as she mechanically reached for the phone. "I'm Quinn Mulroney. May I help you?"

Tiago glanced at her and raised his brows.

She gave a shake of her head, then focused on the matter-of-fact tone in the officer's voice. Tiago retreated to the kitchen. The cowardly part of her sighed--craved more time as his Queen before she destroyed that image with the ugly truth.

CHAPTER 17

"Everything okay?"

Tiago took a seat at the breakfast bar, eyes fixed on Quinn, even as he'd distanced himself to give her privacy. What he really wanted was the right to be at her side. The right to demand what business the police had with his wife.

"Tiago?" His mom paused in her plating of the dishes and peered at him with the clear blue gaze he remembered from childhood. The one that rooted out his secrets.

"I guess so. Quinn wanted to watch something on the news, then she was interrupted with another phone call. I hope it isn't serious." Tiago watched Quinn seem to curl in on herself the longer she talked to the officer. His inner alarm bells clanged. Something was definitely wrong.

He'd about decided to barge into the living room demanding to know what was going on when his mom laid a hand on his shoulder. The knot in his stomach twisted tighter. Twice today Quinn had tried to tell him something. Each time they'd been interrupted before she could.

Was she trying to let him down gently? Tell him thanks, but no thanks, she'd go about her life without him? He didn't think he could do that. He wouldn't do that. He'd be patient and win her over. He had to.

But what did that have to do with the police? Or Wyoming? Her battered, bleeding face invaded his mind.

Quinn lowered her phone in slow motion. The news anchor introduced another story. Tiago pushed off the bar and strode to Quinn. Her pupils had dilated, and she seemed to be staring at nothing. Was she in shock?

Tiago grabbed the blanket and wrapped it around her good shoulder and across her chest and back, tucking it beneath her leg. Then he knelt on the floor in front of her and covered her hands where they rested on her knees. "Quinn?" No response.

He cradled her cheeks and tried again. "Quinn, tell me what's happened."

From behind him, the light shifted on the screen, revealing Quinn's dull eyes and set jaw. Tiago grabbed the remote and twisted to shut off the T.V. A familiar scene met his gaze. He clicked the sound on. "Let's go to Casper, Wyoming and hear from Donovan Davis who's interviewed several eye witnesses to today's arrests."

Tiago turned back to Quinn. She'd lost all vibrancy. A surge of panic rose into his throat. He swallowed it down. No time. "Quinn, look at me. Look right here in my eyes."

A tiny spark lit the gray depths––too far away. He had to bring her back.

"Good, that's good. Now breathe with me." He put her hand on his chest. "Ready? In. Out. Again."

She followed his instructions, then her gaze strayed to the television. "It's him, them." She barely whispered the words, and Tiago had no idea what she meant. She pointed.

Tiago turned in time to see a mug shot of a large Hispanic man. In profile, his nose bore signs of having been broken, perhaps more than once. Then another mug shot of a smaller

Caucasian male appeared. He tuned in to the reporter's words.

"--arrested in connection with a series of brutal assaults and the recent murder of a young woman. That woman's friend remains in a coma after the brutal beating and rape, suffered, police allege, at the hands of these two men who are in custody tonight in the Natrona County Detention Center."

"I have to go."

Tiago's attention spun back to Quinn. Lines ridged her forehead. "Where?"

She blinked. Licked her lips. "To Casper. Right away. I have to identify those men. or they'll get released. The other girl . . . can't. Unless she wakes up. The detective said that's unlikely to happen soon."

"I'll drive you." Tiago made to stand, but Quinn laid her good hand on his shoulder.

"You have a horse to bring back. It's crucial I'm there by tomorrow. I can't let them escape again."

Her lips trembled, though her voice projected the strength he always associated with her.

He understood her desire to see justice done and the need for urgency, but letting her go alone would break his heart. "I'll book your flight." This time when he pushed to his feet, she didn't stop him.

"Thank you."

"Anytime." He jogged up the stairs for his laptop.

U

Tiago should be going with her. His muscles tensed, but for the hundredth time he forced himself to stand down. She'd chosen to do this without him. Pain blazed a trail from his head to his chest.

"Here you are Miss Mulroney. Your flight is on time and

departs today at seven fifty-seven from Gate A2." The United agent handed Quinn her boarding passes with a smile. "May I be of further assistance today?"

"No. Thank you." Quinn accepted her ID and the two passes, one from Nashville to Denver, the other Denver to Casper, Wyoming, and met Tiago's gaze where he waited a few steps behind her.

Anger churned in his belly at the look of desolation on her lovely face. He placed a hand at the small of her back and guided her through the people mingling around the various check-in counters. The airport was a hive of sound and motion. Announcements droned above vocal and instrumental accompaniments. Passengers and families scurried here and there. Carts transported baggage. People zipped past as working dogs and TSA officers keenly observed.

As Tiago escorted Quinn toward security, his mind spun with the sudden change in direction. Yesterday, he'd been sharing in her joy as she rode his horse. Her smile, her confident seat and gentle hands, the way she communicated with a headstrong animal had made him almost giddy. Excitement had grown because he'd known she'd agree to return to the rodeo team and to school. They'd see each other every day, and he'd woo her even after they became inseparable.

Then she'd fallen, and he'd comforted her through her pain.

Today they'd risen early to his father's scrambled eggs and leftover *bife*, eaten in near silence, and loaded her bag in his truck for the short drive to the airport. Dark circles underscored the dullness of her eyes and the tense set of her jaw. The sling and Velcro strap securing her shoulder were visible reminders of yesterday's disaster. One of yesterday's disasters. The phone calls had been exponentially worse than the fall because they'd taken her away from him––both physically and emotionally, it seemed.

The simple press of his hand to her back wasn't enough. Tiago wanted to pull her to him and kiss her until they were both breathless. No matter they were amid a crowd of speed-walking travelers at Nashville's International Airport.

He didn't care. He loved Quinn, and everyone, especially Quinn, should know it.

With difficulty, he reined in his runaway desires. The last thing he wanted was to scare her when they would be separated for a time. Not long, he vowed. Only as long as it took to gather his things and drive. Of course, the horse trailer would slow him down a bit, but still.

Stanchions filled with passengers and their carry-ons appeared before them. Tiago steered Quinn to a wall out of the flow of traffic and faced her. "Quinn, I--"

"I have a daughter." Quinn's strong voice interrupted his words and coldcocked him.

He swallowed and worked to remove the shock from his expression. "It doesn't--"

Again, she stopped him, her fingers pressed to his lips. He engulfed them with his, kissing her palm before lowering their hands between them. He stepped as close as he dared with her injured arm. Her eyes roiled with stormy emotion.

His heart withered at the thought of her loving another man, but there'd never been mention of anyone in all their time together. "But you're not with anyone?" He couldn't help the hopeful note punctuating his question.

The flicker of a smile curved one corner of her mouth, begging Tiago to kiss it.

She shook her head. "I've never been *with* anyone the way you mean."

A frown drew his brows together. "But?" His eyes went wide, scouring her face for a denial of the horrific possibility his mind had conjured.

Her chin dipped a fraction, eyes turned to steel. "I know

it's a lot to take in. I'm sorry I didn't tell you from the beginning. I meant to, but . . . things kept getting in the way. A poor excuse. I should have--" She huffed in exasperation. "Too late for regrets. It is what it is." She glanced at the growing line. "And now I have to go."

"To identify the men who attacked you? Who--" The word stuck in his throat.

Her gaze shifted back to his and locked on. "Tiago, I don't expect your feelings for me to survive the secrets I've kept from you. I wasn't being fair when I came with you on this trip. I'm sorry, for what that's worth." She heaved a breath, then gripped his hand with ferocity. "I'm not the perfect Queen you believe you know. She never existed. If you came with me now, you'd regret your choice when you realized how flawed I am. Regret having to care for a child that's not your own."

He gripped her back in determination. "I do know you. You showed me the true Queen, even when you hid her from others. You're strong and courageous--"

"No." Her sharp tone drew the stares of passersby.

She lowered her voice, but its edge continued to slice through his heart. "I'm a coward and a liar. I lost control. Let Queen's arrogance make me helpless. Nearly get me killed. I can't live under the weight of your expectations for me. I'll crumple, and you'll wonder where your strong Queen disappeared to. She's gone, Tiago, and I don't want her back. Ever. She's too dangerous."

"What about your expectations of me?" He couldn't help his harsh response. Desperation drove him. "You call me "hero" and "Tiger," but I'm neither of those. I'm meek and so lacking, my own father doesn't want me--his only son--to take over the family business."

"Is everything all right here?" A TSA officer closed in, suspicion in the angles of his body.

"Fine," both Tiago and Quinn nearly shouted at the intruder.

His frown prompted Quinn to continue, her voice insistent, but calmer. "Really, Officer, everything is okay. We're having a minor disagreement. That's all."

He didn't look convinced, but he motioned to the security check point. "There's help if you need it, ma'am." Then he continued his rounds.

Quinn laid her hand on Tiago's arm. "Did you know your father almost didn't get to come to the United States?"

Tiago furrowed his brow. "What are you getting at?"

"Laura said your grandfather wanted him to be a rancher, continue the family tradition. If his brother hadn't needed medical treatment here, he'd never have been allowed to come. He watched over his brother, then applied to university and was accepted on a rodeo scholarship. Your grandfather couldn't deny him, and when his brother returned to Argentina, he stayed."

"I knew some of that, but"--he shook his head--"what does that have to do with his not thinking I'm good enough?"

"Oh, Tiago. Joaquín is so proud of you. Your mother said he tells everyone about the improvements you've made to Casa Vargas."

"Everyone but me. And why was I never told that story?" Bitterness colored Tiago's tone and years of hurt flooded in.

She nodded. "Machismo."

"I hate that word."

"Which is why you don't embrace it. You're approachable and kind. You openly care about others and their welfare. It's why people love you."

"Doesn't make me worthy."

"Your dad wants nothing more than for you to partner with him, but he understands the pain of being forced to conform to someone else's vision of your future. He won't do that to you, so until he's sure you're doing it for yourself and not to please him, he'll push you to find your pasión."

"Doesn't mean I'm worthy to be labeled a hero. Talk about unrealistic expectations." Tiago dropped his head, didn't want to read the truth in her eyes.

"You didn't know me at all when you decided I was strong and fit to be the queen everyone called me. But when I chose your name, you'd already proven yourself a hero by rescuing me."

"Sure, I got you to the hospital, but--" He threw up his hands, dislodging her touch and immediately regretted his frustration. Felt a bit like the tiger she'd likened him to. He wanted to pace and stalk, but the traffic just outside their circle kept him caged. A growl rose in his throat, along with the desire to drop to his knees and beg her to stay or let him come. He didn't care which.

She put half a step between them.

"It took a hero to step into my situation." She sighed. "I'm a big girl. I can get home from Casper once the police are through with me. In some ways your father is right. You need to follow your passion. You're so talented, Tiago. Don't give up on your dreams for anyone's sake. Especially for an imposter queen."

She retreated another step. "Please tell your parents again how grateful I am they paid for my flight. I'll find a way to repay them." Her teeth found her bottom lip.

Tiago wanted to shout that the flight was a gift, like his love for her. That he didn't care she had a child. They'd be a family. But she'd pushed him away. If he declared himself now, she'd turn him down flat. Doubts seeped into his mind. What if she was right? What if he didn't know her? Couldn't handle loving another man's child?

"I'll tell them, but rest assured, they expect nothing in return." He had to make her understand not everything was done out of obligation. He dug into his pocket and held out the little blue box. "No matter what happens, this is for you. From me." He unslung her bag from his shoulder and stuffed the box into a pocket.

"Be safe, Quinn." Stepping forward, he placed a lingering kiss on her cheek. When he straightened, he offered her the bag along with her wish for freedom.

She took it and sent him a last watery smile, then walked away to join the queue.

Tiago's arms felt empty, and his heart ached, but he didn't leave until she disappeared beyond the scanners. It hurt that she hadn't looked back, not even once, but it underscored the strength she didn't recognize she had. Her determination to free him from any obligation towards her held, and in a way, he respected her more for it.

Time for him to become worthy of her title. Heart aching and head spinning, he located his truck in the parking lot. As if her harsh truths had brought order to his brain, scattered ideas, plans, and to-do lists coalesced. First, he had to tackle his father. Then he could consider how best to set his other ideas into motion.

For the first time since he'd been sent to find his passion, Tiago understood why the idea held such importance. Now he had to convince his father his plans were valid. He felt a little like Jacob, disguising himself to steal the blessing from his older brother, but he had no siblings.

It's not your fault. Quinn's words washed over his skin like a gentle rain.

"It's not my fault." He repeated the words. Then again, louder. "It's not my fault. God is in control." The declaration released something inside him—a stronghold he'd harbored for too long. "Thank you, Jesus."

Was this why Quinn had been sent? Had he read the situation all wrong?

Tiago flicked the unlock button on his fob, opened the door, and climbed in. The cab seemed empty without Quinn. "Hang on," he told his reflection in the rearview mirror. His heart wasn't sure it could.

Only one person knew for sure. A Person he hadn't called on nearly enough.

He folded his arms over the steering wheel and bowed his head. "Lord, I know You hear me. That You want to hear me. Quinn has taught me what it means to be special and loved. You are the source of her light. I want that, too. The ability to see others with Your eyes and love them even when it's difficult. Help me, Lord, to learn to love as You first loved me. Help me to trust You with everything: with Quinn and the future, with my plans and my heart. My very life is in Your hands."

A peace settled over Tiago, dulling the lingering pain of Quinn's rejection and helping him understand the wisdom of her words. He started the truck and made his way out of the lot to take hold of his passion and lay it all out for his Lord to bless as He saw fit.

CHAPTER 18

Quinn's stomach protested the rush of power as the plane took off from Denver International Airport on the final leg of her journey. The bright nearly-noon sun glared through the tiny window. She sat in the third row--she'd refused to allow Tiago's parents to purchase first class tickets for her. It was enough they'd shucked out the money for the extra legroom row. She was tall but not pro athlete tall. Like the guy beside her wearing a blazer with "University of Tennessee Basketball" embroidered on his left chest and his legs extended beneath the seat in front of them.

She tried not to worry about what lay before her or obsess over Tiago's responses. *I trust You, Lord. At least, I'm trying.*

The basketball player shifted in his seat, appraising her boots. "Say, you wouldn't be a rodeo star, would you?"

"I used to be on a college rodeo team, but I wasn't a star." She craned her neck to see his face. Even sitting, he was a head taller.

"What college?"

"Montana State, but that was two years ago." Quinn fiddled with the delicate silver charm bracelet concealed by the sling, wishing she'd gotten one of those passengers who ignored the existence of seatmates. Silence drew out, heaping guilt on her for shutting down the conversation. "Are you going to Wyoming in an official capacity?"

He smiled, showing straight, white teeth. "Nah, I'm hoping to be drafted by the Nuggets later this month. Several guys from the team are doing a fund-raiser next weekend for some kids whose community center burned down. They invited me, so I thought, why not go and help set everything up? It's for a good cause, right?"

Quinn nodded. "Sounds like it. That's a pretty cool thing to do."

He shrugged. "It's some kind of cook-out. Folks come and donate to eat at a celebrity's table, get pictures, autographs, and chat with the athletes. I'm not expecting many fans, because I'm just getting started, but, hey, should be fun." He nudged her. "That's why I was hoping you were a rodeo star."

"It's good to use your success to help others." She extended her hand. "I'm Quinn. If I *were* a rodeo star, I'd join you."

His hand was easily two of hers when they shook. "My momma would tan my hide if she knew I didn't introduce myself first thing. Franklin Williams the Fourth, but my friends call me Willy."

Quinn leaned closer and stage whispered, "I promise not to tell her." She hesitated, then asked, "Why Willy?"

His grin widened. He let go so he could talk as that seemed to involve numerous gestures. "Because when you're the fifth generation Franklin, nicknames get used up. And Momma refused to call me Fourth. Something about it being too close to some white guy in a sci fi flick."

The laugh bubbled out of Quinn, surprising and relaxing

her. Worry and tension melted into the background. *Thank you, Jesus.* "You, Willy, are an answer to prayer."

"I am? I mean, Momma's told me that a few times, but then, she's also claimed I came straight from the devil, so I'm not sure which to believe." He winked at her, a shared joke among friends.

"And you played for--"

"UT, of course. I grew up in a little town east of Nashville. Always dreamed of playing ball for them. God granted my wish."

Uh, God, is this Your doing? Quinn settled in. "I have a friend who rodeoed for UT Martin. His family owns the Casa Vargas restaurant."

Willy's eyes widened. "Now that place has some good food. The team ate there once for a celebration dinner. I've never been so satisfied in my life." He elbowed her good shoulder. "Another thing I'd appreciate you not tell my momma." His gaze landed on her sling. "What happened to you, if you don't mind talking about it?"

"I fell off a horse."

"Ouch."

She nodded. "Very ouch. Thankfully, the shoulder's only partially dislocated. Could have been much worse. The doctor said I can remove the sling after a few days, but it'll take a while before I can raise my arm over my head. No tossing my daughter for airplane rides until it heals."

"You look too young to have a child, pardon my presumptions."

"It's fine." And it was. No quickened pulse. No tightness in her chest. She'd just shared about Reina--granted she'd likely never see Willy again--without any qualms. Perhaps she was making progress. "I didn't choose to become pregnant, but I did choose to keep her." She grimaced. "Sorry if that's too much sharing."

Willy's dark eyes softened with compassion. "I'm sorry you had to go through that. You didn't have to deal with it alone, I hope."

"My parents were there for me. Nobody thought I should keep her, though. Everyone said I'd resent the baby because of the circumstances of her conception. But I couldn't. And she's so beautiful and sweet. Truly a gift, you know?"

"The good that comes out of the trouble."

Quinn narrowed her eyes. "Exactly. How did you know?"

"I'm a Jesus man. The Bible's words are good for the soul, my mom always tells me. I read it every day, and I believe she's right. When things go wrong, like that fire or your situation, where else can we turn? The world doesn't have the answer, though it thinks it does. Jesus. He's the answer."

"Amen."

"Quinn, do you mind me asking you something personal?"

"We've already gone way beyond that question. Ask away."

He laughed, the sound rich and soothing. "I sense something's troubling you right now. There's a tension in you, despite your lighthearted words. If I can help, I'll do what I can. If you need a listening ear, I've got that, too. Even though my mom insists I talk her ears off sometimes."

Before Quinn knew it, certainly before she was ready, the plane touched down at Casper-Natrona County International Airport.

Willy concluded his prayer, gave her hand a final squeeze, then let go. "You've got my number if you need to talk or anything else for that matter. If it's in my power to help, I'll do it."

"I know I've said this already, but you remind me so much of Tiago and his heart for easing others' burdens."

He nodded, a teasing grin on his lips. "Only about a

213

million times." He sobered, unfastening his seatbelt as the light blinked out. "I guarantee, unless your guy's blind and an idiot, he knows how fortunate he is to have met a woman like you. He won't leave you hanging--daughter or no daughter he didn't know about. If he loves you, he won't care you kept secrets from him or pushed him away. He'll show up in God's timing. That's how you'll know if he's the one intended for you."

Quinn rubbed moisture from her eyes. "I hope you're right. I laid some heavy words on him."

"Sometimes it takes another person to see to our core. He may understand you better than you think. Trust me. Don't be afraid to fight for him when he does come around. He might need a hero as much as you do."

All through the disembarking process Quinn turned Willy's words over in her mind and heart. She prayed and considered, then prayed some more.

The detective she'd spoken with last night when she'd confirmed her travel plans met her in the arrivals area. His jeans and maroon pullover hugged his trim build while his balding head and the salt in his remaining hair attested to his experience.

The sun glared from nearly overhead, baking her in the back seat while he drove her to the station. She hadn't eaten since breakfast but refused his offer to stop for sandwiches.

"I'd rather get this over with." Besides, her knotted stomach couldn't handle food. Quinn peered out the window but didn't recognize much of the city. She'd only ever been at the fairgrounds to care for her horses, and a few restaurants near the Ford Wyoming Center where the CNFR performances were held. Her stomach curdled with the flash of memory from the last time she'd gone to the horse barns and her ill-fated decision to cut through the stock pens.

"Did you have any questions before we arrive, Miss Mulroney?"

She pressed the bracelet's charms against her wrist, Tiago's gift a precious lifeline. "I don't know what to expect."

Detective Bolen steered onto a side street and then into a parking lot behind a multi-story, two-tone beige, block building. "We're at the back entrance. A few reporters have staked out the front snapping photos since the story aired about the men you're here to identify. We had no idea it would hit the national news, but we don't want your picture getting out since we're tracking another suspect."

"Thank you."

"That's also why you rode in the back. It's less conspicuous." The detective killed the engine and exited, opening her door since it didn't open from the inside.

Quinn's lungs expanded fully the second her boot hit pavement. "Trapped in a police car" hadn't been on her bucket list.

Bolen motioned her beside him. "There'll be several photo line-ups. You'll point out anyone you recognize. We'll ask you to describe the third attacker if you can to help us apprehend him more quickly. Our officer only saw his back as he fled the scene."

Quinn nodded and concentrated on moving forward, relief flooding in at hearing she wouldn't face the actual men. She could do this. Focusing her inner attention on Reina and Tiago helped calm her ratcheting heartbeat. As did imagining her hand on Tiago's chest as he breathed with her.

Soon they were inside and navigating a maze of desk-filled offices, some occupied and others not, all with computers, stacks of papers, and discarded coffee cups littering their surfaces. They entered a different part of the station, this one geared more for the public based on the effort at décor and lighting.

For the next few minutes, she listened to another officer explain the process, sat in a poorly-padded chair, and stared at photos of men projecting some level of animosity or boredom. In the first photo set, none of the choices stood out, though two sparked a hint of recognition. She couldn't see their hands, so no help there.

Her raised head drew the officer to her. "Would it be possible to hear them speak? It was dark, and I mostly remember their voices. Also seeing their hands would help tremendously."

Her officer consulted another in low tones, then the second disappeared.

"We'll see what we can do about voices and hands. In the meantime, take a look at the next lineup, if you would." She slid the first aside and placed a new set of headshots before her.

The fourth man's face shoved her upright and back as far as the chair would allow. Her gaze darted over the swarthy complexion, the wild, springy hair, and prominent forehead. In her mind, his full lips repeated the accented taunts used to goad the others into beating her. The fear and pain––the utter helplessness of being under his control––flooded back. She shrank away from his cruel eyes, mouth dry as if she'd been screaming. Her breath came in short gasps.

The officer was beside her in a moment, offering water and a warm hand on her back. Quinn closed her eyes and drank. Her bracelet jingled, and she was glad she'd awakened with the presence of mind to straighten her clothing before Tiago ran into her in the dark. Glad the men had left her for dead before he came because he would have played the hero. At three to one he could have been hurt or even killed. The warm metal reminded her that just because she couldn't see or touch the one she loved, didn't mean she was alone.

Besides Tiago, God had been with her that night. The knowledge gave her courage.

She slid upright in the chair and pointed at the image. "That man directed his buddies to beat me up, then . . ." her voice faltered. She couldn't say the violent word––couldn't associate Reina's conception with such a vile act. She swallowed. "He'll have missing fingers on his right hand. There's a photograph of the hand print on my cheek from when I arrived at the hospital. It will match."

The officer picked up the lineup then wrote in a notebook. "It's all right. You won't have to see him again until the trial."

"The trial." Quinn hadn't considered they'd want her to testify. *Oh, Lord, must I?*

"All that comes later. You're doing what's required, now. Are you up to looking at the final lineup while we wait for word on the voices?"

Quinn shrugged.

Half an hour later, a sketch artist arrived, and she related all she could remember of the third man's face. During another long wait, Quinn strode laps around the tiny room.

Finally, the woman returned. Behind her, Detective Bolen entered and set a small recording device on the table. "Miss Mulroney, let's see if any of these voices sparks something." At her nod, he pushed play.

A gruff voice she didn't recognize spoke what was obviously a scripted reading. A second higher-pitched voice did the same. The third began. Its timbre weakened Quinn's knees, and she sat hard in one of the chairs, jarring her shoulder. Memories of the man's rank scent while he punched and slapped her hollowed her blessedly-empty stomach. She turned away from the staring officers, grasping for control. The fourth voice spoke the passage in a nasally drone she dismissed after the first sentence.

"Three. I remember his voice." Her own came out thin, the sickening scene replaying in her head. Again her helplessness threatened to collapse her will––steal her hope.

"Do you need a moment?" The detective's words cut through her fear.

Willy's words rushed in. *"I'm a Jesus man."* She was a Jesus girl. Tiago's face, then Reina's, came into focus. She could do this. Her stomach settled, and her breathing eased. "What's next?"

The officer spoke. "We've confirmed the hand prints match. We still have some questions, but then you'll be free to go. You'll receive word of trial appearances at the address you gave us in Bozeman if the prosecutor believes we've enough evidence to charge the suspects."

Her hands clutched the chair arm. "You mean they could be released?"

Detective Bolen shook his head. "From what I see, that's unlikely."

After reanswering the questions from two years ago, Quinn rode with Detective Bolen to the hotel where the Vargas's had booked her a room through Saturday.

She called Missy, thinking how terrible a mother she'd been the last few days and how much she'd relied on Missy to care for Reina. Was she any different from the young mothers who bore children only to let their own parents raise them? She'd fought so hard to keep Reina––to bring her into the world––when everyone had said she should reject her. And now, wasn't Quinn essentially rejecting the responsibility she'd signed on for?

Laying back on the king-sized bed, she waited for Missy to answer. On the seventh ring, a breathless "hello" sounded through the speaker.

Quinn sat up, straining her shoulder in the process and

letting out a little squeak before she could silence it. "Is everything okay? You sound like you've been running."

A girlish giggle rose in the background. "We're fine. Just having a tickle fest. I've been laughing too hard is all. What about you? Shoulder hurting?"

"Only when I move too fast. I'll be over it in a few days."

"Hmm."

"What's 'hmm,' mean? You don't believe me?"

"Whoa, there. Don't get so defensive." Missy's voice softened. "Q, tell me the truth. How are you, really?"

"Today was hard. Harder than I thought it would be." Quinn swiped at the silent tears flowing onto the bedcovering. "She has his hair and skin tone." The sobs came then, ripping at Quinn's throat. She almost didn't hear the notification for a FaceTime call and then almost didn't answer it.

When she did, Reina's sweet face filled the screen. Missy's voice in the background was soothing in its calm assurance. "Look at this beautiful child, and tell me she's anything like that villain who assaulted you."

Reina's chubby fingers pressed against Missy's screen. "Mama. Cry." Then her rosebud lips smashed against the glass. "Kiss Mama. All better."

"Reina." The name emerged on a half choke, half sob. Quinn pulled in a deep breath, her hand pressed to her chest. She felt Tiago's strength beneath her fingers. Her daughter was the true queen, and if he never came, it would be her fault. She shook off the thought and focused on her daughter's caring heart. "Reina, my sweet girl. Mama's all better, now. Thank you."

As long as she had Jesus and Reina, she'd survive. She could live without Tiago. The ache in her chest called her a liar.

"How's that hunk of a cowboy doing?" Missy's features replaced Reina's.

Quinn frowned. "You know he's not here."

Missy rolled her eyes. "Of course, he's not there." Her eyebrows slanted upward in her "oh no you didn't" look. "Haven't you called him? Texted? Anything?"

Quinn looked away as a stab of guilt battled with desire. She steeled herself. She'd done the right thing by rejecting Tiago. He had his future to sort out and expectations to adjust. If Willy was right, she'd know if they belonged together by whether or not he came looking for her. "I'm not calling or texting. He knows where I am and where I'll be. If he wants me and Reina, he'll find me. I trust this to God's hands. Please say no more about it."

Shock spread over Missy's face, then turned into something like . . . delight? "By golly, that's what I've been waiting for. You've grown a backbone. All those years of bulldozing ahead without thinking because you were too scared to stop and take a gander at the situation and finally, you're taking charge." She wiped a stray tear from her face. "Cal would be so proud. Not only for what you just said to me but also for what you did today. Two years ago, you didn't have the courage to pursue justice. Even if they'd been caught, I believe you'd have let them get away. But now, you're doing the right thing, and I'm so happy for you."

"But it took one girl's death and another in a coma she might not wake from for me to step up. If I'd done more earlier, maybe those girls wouldn't have been attacked."

"Oh, Quinn, darling. Always so hard on yourself. For being so close to Jesus, you don't always claim his forgiveness and grace. Everything good is from God, but rain falls on the righteous and the wicked. Back then, the men escaped. The police had no one to charge. Now they've been caught, and you're there to be sure they stay that way."

"I guess."

"It's true. Now Reina needs her supper and a bath before

bedtime. Call again tomorrow and let us know the plan. I love you, Quinn."

"I love you, too." The call ended, leaving Quinn with only her thoughts for company. She didn't dare let herself hope Tiago would come for her soon. Or ever. Because hoping led to disappointment and her responsibilities removed the luxury of breakdown and recovery time.

Still.

Jesus, I've given this to You, and You know my heart.

A sob ripped the rest of the prayer to shreds. If she was doing the right thing, why was it so hard?

CHAPTER 19

Tiago's hand shook, poised in midair inches from the polished wood of his father's closed office door. He inhaled, the remembered pressure of Quinn's hand on his chest hitching the breath. Squeezing his eyes shut, he basked in her encouraging gaze branded on the inside of his eyelids.

He could do this. He would do this because if he failed, he failed them all.

His knuckles met wood twice.

"Enter."

His father's strong, commanding voice stiffened Tiago's spine. He opened the door and strode inside with purposeful steps, peering across the neat oak expanse into alert eyes bordered by life lines. The salt seemed more prevalent in his immaculate hair and beard. His shoulders not quite as rigid, nor his mouth as set. Was he seeing Joaquín Vargas differently because of Quinn's revelation? Had he been so blind, he'd missed the sparkle of humor that lurked in his onyx irises? Or the twitch of his lips?

"What may I do for you, son?"

Was that hope in his tone? Tiago cleared his throat. "I've discovered my passion."

"Please sit. I'm eager to hear."

When Tiago had outlined his plan to start a restaurant revitalization business and answered all of his father's questions, he folded his hands in his lap and waited for the verdict. Odd that his palms were dry, his pulse relaxed. He still valued his father's blessing, but he would go ahead with his plans regardless. Quinn's opinion mattered more, and he would seek it as soon as possible.

Joaquín steepled his fingers. "I'm curious how you arrived at this idea."

Tiago's smile unfurled. "Quinn. Her unique way of interacting with waitstaff made me consider how I could use my love of flow and design to help others by improving their work experiences. This is the result."

"Your ideas work. Casa Vargas is an example despite my reluctance to listen. I'd be happy to write a recommendation and endorse your work once you are ready to market your business." His father's expression softened into the look usually reserved for Mom, constricting Tiago's chest. "Your mother says I cling too much to my pride, and it has pushed you away. You should know I've always believed in your talents and only wanted to shield you from the fate I nearly suffered because of my father's desire to protect the family business. It seems I've gone to the opposite extreme."

His dad's attempt at reconciliation tasted sweet on Tiago's tongue. Not an apology, but close enough to begin mending the chasm between them.

"Don't make the same mistake I did, son," Joaquín continued. "When I met Laura, she had a promising career. Because of my single-mindedness and maybe my short-sightedness, she gave that up. Don't assume that your passion and your wife's are the same. Give her the freedom to be who God made her to be, just as you pursue your gifts."

Later, when Tiago visited his mother in her office, she agreed. "I gave up being a practicing lawyer because Joaquín needed me to become an accountant. I did it out of love and haven't resented the change, but sometimes I wonder what I could have become, what good I missed out on doing, because I didn't pursue my calling."

That night gathered at the kitchen bar, he and his parents shared a meal and a connection Tiago hadn't felt in years. It grounded him and gave him hope for the future, but he still had questions. "Why didn't you tell me you came with Tío Felipe for his surgery? I always thought your first time in the States was when you and Mom met."

When Joaquín looked away, his mother covered Tiago's hand with hers. "I'm glad you two have made peace. I tried to convince your father to talk about his relationship with your grandfather and the difficulties they went through before he met me, but you know how stubborn he can be. Machismo demanded he remain silent." His mother couldn't maintain her sternness when she looked at her husband. Love showed through every glance and touch.

That's what Tiago wanted with Quinn. A love so deep nothing could hide it.

"And don't worry about your conniving Uncle Bertram or that son of his," his father said. "We've made sure they won't touch the restaurant or any of our assets if something should happen to your mother and me. You are my heir. The best man for the job."

The acceptance Tiago had craved all his life felt wonderful, but next to what he wanted from Quinn, it fell flat.

Tiago couldn't help imagining Quinn in her hotel room thinking about him. In his fantasy, she wished he were there with her. He wished he had been there when she'd faced her memories alone. His heart squeezed at the emotional pain it must have caused her. One of them may have been the father of Quinn's daughter. It was enough to make him sick. He acknowledged his errant ideals where Quinn was concerned. She wasn't perfect. She made mistakes because she was human.

But Quinn *was* strong and resilient. She'd bounced back from every hardship in her life so far. She'd bounce back from this one as well and be stronger than ever. Now, with God's help, he hoped to make the right choices––to listen to her and be willing to meet her where she was.

U

Oh, how she wished for Tiago's leather seats. The bus droned onward, pausing in yet another town to shift passengers and luggage, then lumber on. Quinn seemed the only passenger to have signed up for the long haul from Casper to Bozeman. She curled up against her window and tried to sleep, but the constant vibration of rubber on concrete jarred her brain. Funny how it hadn't bothered her while riding with Tiago.

Transferring her knees to the back of the seat in front of her, she thought of the events of the past week when she'd been stuck in Wyoming waiting for the Monday bus to transport her to Billings, then on to Bozeman.

She'd just gotten off the phone with the only bus service she could afford, shaken by the news she'd missed the weekly departure by minutes when she'd taken a call from Willy. He chided her about actually being a rodeo star and invited her to help with the fundraiser after she explained her situation. He even drove the fifty some miles one way to pick her up and found her a place to stay.

She reveled in helping plan for the barbecue, setting up tables, and meeting the kids whose center had burned. The work was mentally and physically challenging, but the praise, worship, and prayer led by local churches was spiritually uplifting. A few fans even asked for autographs.

She called Missy and Reina multiple times to share the progress and managed to keep Tiago from hijacking her thoughts until she lay down each night, dreaming of kisses and tigers prowling through shadows.

When the announcement declared they'd raised over the amount needed to rebuild the community center, she whooped with the crew, dancing and popping balloons. She even talked several of the Nuggets into dumping water on the director. Afterward, Willy drove her back to Casper.

He glanced her way, dark eyes serious. "I've been praying about your dilemma. Tiago's father insisted he find his passion, but what about you? What's yours?"

When she didn't answer, he continued. "All this is from an outsider perspective, but it seems to me you're not happy in your own skin. You say you're not strong like Queen. But it takes bravery to face your past then jump in *with* strangers working *for* strangers this past week."

Quinn crossed her arms protectively across her chest. "Queen was too rash. She rushed headlong into danger without thinking. People got hurt."

"Have you considered the need to embrace both halves of yourself? God doesn't make mistakes. He made you strong and stubborn but also kind and giving. We're all meant to feel deeply, not stuff our feelings away and forbid them to show." The car stopped in front of her hotel. "I'll be praying you learn to accept yourself as God sees you. Not a separate Queen and Quinn, but His child--brave and cautious, kind and spontaneous. Blessings, my friend."

Her body swayed with the change in direction.

Learn to accept yourself.

What a hard thing.

The bus pulled into yet another town, rocking her back to the now. Perhaps she should have looked for a llama expedition or an elephant caravan traveling her route. Certainly either would have been quicker than this infernal bus.

Then again, maybe slower was better. She had lots of praying to do.

She sucked a sharp breath and dropped her feet to the floor with a plop loud enough to resurrect the snoring man across the aisle.

"Sorry." She gave a little wave.

He snorted and returned to his deeper-than-should-be-allowed slumber.

She settled her head against the seatback and conversed with her Creator.

During the layover in Billings, Quinn withdrew her phone. Had she saved the contact? *Please, Lord.* "Yes." She raised a closed fist over her head and pulled it down in a power arm gesture, then glanced around self-consciously. Not a single head looked up from books, phones, or newspapers in the sparsely-populated waiting area, so she pressed call before she could change her mind.

When she said goodbye, a glimmer of purpose flickered to life. She found the next person she needed to call. And the next. When she slid her dying phone into her pocket, a satisfied smile crept onto her face. Hours later, when the bus arrived, she climbed on and slept until something jolted her awake. She peered out the window into darkness, then sat up in the seat and stretched her good shoulder. The shadow of mountains rose ahead, fanning out like arms to embrace the valley and the city of Bozeman.

She rose as a loud burst of air announced engagement of the bus's airbrakes. At least Missy had agreed to wake Reina and meet her at this ungodly hour. Bag in hand, she stepped from the bus, peering about the well-lit, Walmart parking lot for Cal's old truck. There, under the light pole. She jogged toward it, relief and exhaustion playing havoc with her coordination.

A siren split the quiet. Then another. A glow lit the sky quite a way off.

Lord, please be in that disaster as you were in mine and rework it for good. She mouthed the quick prayer as she neared the truck.

Missy exited the driver's door as Quinn approached, arms wide in the welcoming hug she'd always longed for as a child, but never received. Quinn shoved away the bitterness, another byproduct of her exhaustion and hunger, and enjoyed the newfound affection from her mother. Unable to withstand another delay, Quinn broke away to peer in at a sleeping Reina. Dark eyes concealed by heavy lashes and curls subdued in the padding of her car seat, this cherub looked nothing like the evil she'd revisited at the police station.

Missy opened the passenger door. "Let's go home."

Never had a suggestion sounded so perfect.

The next morning, Quinn groaned and turned over in her bed. Why was Missy making so much racket? It wasn't like her to be so loud. She fumbled for her phone on the night stand. Eight a.m.? "Mis-sy." Her meow-like complaint did her about as much good as a begging feline at a guard dog convention.

"Ah, you're awake. Great. You'll have Reina this morning. I have an appointment."

"An app . . . what?" Quinn struggled to push herself up while her eyes kept drifting closed. "Reina?" She accepted Missy's help to find an upright position, legs off the bed and feet on the floor. Her head spun a little, and she clutched the mattress to stay oriented. Four hours of sleep was not enough. She should have delayed her appointments until the afternoon.

The thought woke her fully. How was she to attend meetings with Reina in tow? A lump formed in her throat. But the memory of two kisses—-one through a phone screen and one on her cheek—-pushed her to accept what she needed to do. But with only one vehicle, how could they both leave?

Missy straightened the comforter and then some books on Quinn's desk. She cleared her throat. "A friend is picking me up in a few minutes. You can have the truck."

Quinn paused mid-stretch. A friend? Missy?

"I've laid out all Reina's things and packed her diaper bag, so you can enjoy each other without having to worry about details." Missy embraced Quinn in a suspiciously-enthusiastic hug and spoke into her hair. "I love you so much. I'm thankful you've let me experience some of what I missed out on. I'm sorry I let myself be caught in blame and guilt when I should have been mothering you."

Missy sighed and held Quinn at arm's length as if fixing Quinn's face in her memory.

A tremor crawled across Quinn's shoulder blades. "You're scaring me."

Dropping her hands to her sides, she gave a slow shake of her head. "I've missed you. That's all. And something about you is . . . different. I can't put my finger on it, but I can feel it. You're more like you were in your rodeo days but without the recklessness." She tipped up Quinn's chin and peered down her nose like she used to do when Quinn had done something especially inscrutable. "It's a good change, I think."

She glanced at the microwave and bustled around the kitchen gathering her overlarge handbag and a Walmart bag Quinn hadn't noticed. "Time for me to go." Her voice was almost a sing-song—-very un-Missy-like.

Able to do nothing more than stand with her mouth gaping as her mother practically waltzed from the house, Quinn was propelled into motion by the slap of the screen door and the subsequent cooing noises that meant Reina was awake and playing. What a good baby she was. Quinn had been separated from her daughter way too much in recent months.

That needed to stop. Quinn's plans, if all went well, would ensure she had more time to be a mother to her child.

CHAPTER 20

Quinn's daughter had made a splash at each of their morning stops. With a prayer of thanksgiving and a satisfied smile, she tucked Reina and her sparkly blue Pegasus outfit into her car seat.

Reina waved a stuffed horse Doc Liza had given her when they visited Two Sisters Vet Clinic.

"That's a pretty horsey."

Reina mimicked the words, delighting Quinn, who grinned as she closed the back door and opened her own. Her cell phone pinged. Quinn climbed in and checked the screen. A text from Missy. Odd. Quinn's stomach rumbled as she scanned the message.

> Could you meet me at that place you used to board your horses around noon? I've discovered something I think you should see for yourself. It's rather urgent.

Quinn frowned and tension gripped her chest and throat. Missy rarely texted. She preferred to call and to include the word "urgent" sent Quinn's morning elation into a tailspin. She hit call next to Missy's name in her favorites. Straight to voicemail.

Now she was officially worried. She composed a reply:

Of course. On our way.

Quinn motored away from Dunhorse Ranch toward the Logan and Marshond Rodeo Facility driving as quickly as she dared with her precious backseat cargo. Her thoughts raced about as fast as Reina's babbling as she put her stuffed horse through its paces. Would this "discovery"––as Missy had termed it––unravel all the positive outcomes from her morning meetings?

The thought sent a chill through Quinn's body. She'd been so proud of the choices she'd made and the negotiations she'd accomplished. Too proud?

God, have I jumped ahead of your plans? I thought I was following your will, but was I trying to manipulate Your whispers into what I wanted them to be?

What she really wanted was Tiago, though he had little to do with the events she'd set in motion this morning. Not that he wouldn't fit into them if he chose to find her.

Her mouth pinched. She wasn't being fair. Couldn't expect Tiago to fit into *her* plans. He had plans of his own. Big dreams, though he hadn't seemed to recognize them yet. He dripped with talent and the desire to improve the world and people's lives. He would have loved helping with the fundraiser. The food wouldn't have known what hit it.

Love for him swelled inside her, bursting to escape. Automatically, she started to tamp it down, then stopped.

Why should she keep it a secret? Wasn't she done with secrets? So what if she left him the next move? Maybe Willy was right, and it was time for her to fight for what she loved.

The sign for the rodeo facility loomed ahead, but Quinn pulled to the narrow shoulder and dialed Tiago's number. It rang. *Please let him answer.* Her hand trembled where it held the phone to her ear. Her entire body shook. It rang again. She waited.

A fifth ring. Then a sixth. His voicemail picked up. "Hey, you've reached Tiago Vargas. Leave me a mess––"

She hit the red button and tossed the phone in the passenger seat. Tears blurred her vision. Hope. She'd let herself succumb to hope when she'd already pledged to wait on his answer. Well, maybe she didn't have to wait. Maybe that was it.

Tiago didn't want to talk to her. He wasn't coming.

He didn't love her enough to be saddled with a child that was not his own.

"Mama ouch." Reina's high little-girl voice broke through Quinn's descent into self-pity.

She was loved. With or without Tiago. She had Reina, the best gift in the world. And Missy. And Jesus, who'd saved her more times than she could count.

Quinn hit her blinker and checked her mirror, then pulled back onto the road. "It's okay, sweet girl. Mommy's okay."

"Mama okay." Reina giggled and bounced her horse through the air.

Despite the hurt lingering in the pit of her stomach, Quinn smiled.

"I'm sorry, Lord. You are Adonai and El Shaddai. There is nothing you can't do. Even heal my broken heart. I trust You. My life and plans are in Your capable hands."

Quinn turned into the long drive to begin the slow work of living without the man she loved beyond anything except her God and the little girl seated behind her.

One of the hardest things Tiago had ever done was send Quinn's call to voicemail, but he'd invested too much into this surprise, and it was too important to ruin now. Missy said she was on her way. He'd wait a little longer. *Give me strength.*

A little guilt dogged him for not swinging through Wyoming from Nashville, but only a little. Mostly, hope and anticipation leap frogged through his body riding a steady current of love.

"She's in the drive!"

A wave of Missy's excitement poured over him, along with several other emotions he didn't care to name. Would Quinn think him too pushy? Too invasive? Too--

He didn't want to be "too" anything. He wanted to be "just right" like all the things Goldilocks prized. Maybe not the best analogy since she got frightened away in the end.

Tiago's hands clenched, then the verse he'd heard in this morning's devotion floated into his mind as on a gentle breeze--a nudge. *Wait for the Lord; be strong and take heart and wait for the Lord.* He could be patient. He could be flexible. He was a new man with a new heart. He planned to declare his heart for Quinn in front of the crowd of witnesses he'd gathered and later, before Quinn in private, if she didn't volley his heart back over the net.

He should have prepared her. His confidence shriveled. This was a bad idea.

"She's here. Everybody hush." Missy darted away from the barn's half-closed sliding door, her command effective as all conversations ceased and only the horses' snuffling and shuffling filled the expectant silence.

Tiago forced his fists to unclench, beseeching for his heart's desire.

Slender fingers grasped the edge of the door.

Tiago's throat clenched. His breathing ceased. He stared at her hand, even that small part of her inciting a surge of emotion within his chest.

"'Orse."

What had to be Quinn's daughter's voice changed the surge to a tidal wave. He already loved her, remembered the glimpse of tight curls and dark eyes huddled in Missy's arms.

"Yes, Reina. Horses live here. Do you want to see them?"

"'orsey!" An adorable giggle followed.

Battling a tsunami that threatened to burst from his pores, Tiago stepped forward just as Quinn entered carrying Reina. The aisle lights popped on and arms flew into the air along with, "Surprise!"

Everyone except Tiago. He could only stare at the beauty before him. Close enough to touch. His courage faltered. He could never be worthy of their love or their time. His feet refused to move, either toward or away from the woman who could break him with a look.

Quinn's eyes were impossibly round. It had been too much. His lips struggled to form words. "Quinn," was all he could force out.

She found him then. Came full circle of those gathered at his behest.

Take courage, for I have overcome the world.

Tiago drew a shaky breath. Took a step toward her. "Quinn, I--"

She rushed forward, wrapping one arm around his neck and pulling his lips to hers in a kiss that was not sweet, but demanding--desperate even--and yet, welcoming, reassuring, filled with a cascade of love he'd hoped for, but not expected.

"Mama kiss."

With a laugh, Quinn broke the contact but kept her hand

on his shoulder as if she was afraid to let go. At least, Tiago hoped her thinking ran along those lines because those were his intentions.

Her eyes found his, the gray velvety soft and swirling with a sparkle he'd only dreamed of seeing. "This is what living with a toddler is like. Think you can handle it?"

Tiago frowned, and Quinn stilled, her fingers digging into his shoulder. She sighted along the rows of her friends--most of whose faces he couldn't match with names.

Dori stepped forward and offered a hand for Reina's high five, smiling at Quinn. "Thank you for introducing us earlier today. She's beautiful."

Quinn released Tiago to hike Reina higher on her hip then move in full view of the gathered crowd. "For those I've not been able to tell, I have a daughter. God's gift to me."

Reina tugged at a lock of Quinn's hair and laughed, the sound sweet and innocent.

Quinn expertly removed the strand from baby fingers and handed her the stuffed horse she'd dropped and Dori had retrieved. "Having this child taught me love can come from the darkest places, but I'd denied love's existence for so long--fought it back with daring and bravado--I wasn't ready to acknowledge it or her. Until I ran away from the next gift God tried to give me."

She glanced at Tiago, and his heart raced. He wanted to hug her, to protect her from this scrutiny, but he knew she needed to do this on her own.

"And then sent him to find me in my stupidity. Praise God and thank you, Tiago, for understanding me more than I understood myself."

He stepped up and fitted a hand to the small of her back.

"Everyone, meet my daughter Reina."

When the applause and whistles died down, Tiago blinked. "You aren't wearing your sling."

"My shoulder's fine unless I try to raise my arm. As long as it's low, there's no pain."

"That's great, Quinn. I'm--"

Missy stalked up to the three of them stopping him midsentence and holding out her arms for the baby. "We're on toadstools and pinecones here." She gestured at the dozen or more people lining the aisle. "You promised a surprise."

Quinn frowned, but seemed reluctant to give Reina up. "Reina, this is Tiago. Tiago, my daughter, Reina." It was as if each time Quinn repeated the declaration, it became stronger.

"Hello, Reina." He smiled at the little girl.

She grinned at him. Then lifted a chubby hand and waved. Her other hand clutched the stuffed horse.

"That's a pretty horse you have there. Do you like horses?"

She lifted the stuffed animal and shoved it toward him. "'Orse."

"Would you like to see a real horse?"

The girl nodded, dark curls bouncing with her enthusiasm. "'Orse."

He smiled at Quinn. "With your permission, I have a gift for Reina."

"A gift?" Her mouth puckered and Tiago held himself back from claiming another kiss.

"She'll have to grow into it a little, but we can help her until she's ready to go on her own." He couldn't resist arching one brow at her.

"Stop talking in riddles." Her face was a mask of consternation. "Show us."

"May I?" He held out his arms to Reina, who giggled and held out her arms too, the horse dangling by its tail. Quinn stepped closer and transferred the child to his care. Hope wound tight in his chest. Surely this was a good sign. Taking

Quinn's hand, he stilled at the silver sparkle. "You're wearing the bracelet."

She smiled, nodded. "I hoped."

Pressure threatened to burst his ribcage. He led her past the waiting guests to the next-to-last stall in the row. *Please let this show her my heart.*

He let go of Quinn so he could open the stall door and step inside. Behind him, Quinn gasped. "Look, Reina." He pointed to the dapple gray pony munching hay in the corner.

Reina clapped her hands. The stuffed horse fell to the shavings.

Tiago squatted to retrieve the toy, then handed it to Quinn who'd followed them into the stall. He carried the child to meet the pony who'd raised his head to investigate the intrusion. Taking one of Reina's hands in his, he held it toward the gelding who snuffed warm air into her palm, making her giggle in delight. "This is Prince. He's your pony. So you can learn to ride as well as your mom."

The pony left his hay to snuffle the toddler's toes. She giggled and kicked, but Prince only backed up a step and raised his lip in a laugh.

"You bought him? For my daughter?" Quinn's breath warmed his ear, she stood so close.

"I'm hoping to change that pronoun——one day soon."

She swallowed, angling away from him.

Tiago shifted, catching the shadow cross her face. "What's wrong?"

She flicked her gaze from the pony to Reina. "We can't afford to keep him." She met his eyes, tears glassing hers. "The heart behind this touches the happy place inside, but——"

Tiago cupped Quinn's cheek. "Be patient. You'll see. I have a plan."

A smile flickered, then died. "So did I."

Tiago's hope wavered with her smile, but he held on. "Trust me. Play this out to the end. I promise I won't hurt you or Reina. I'd never ask more than you're willing to give."

She managed a small smile, then a nod. "I trust God's plan, but I believe God works through people. Show me what you've got, Tiger."

CHAPTER 21

pony. Gathering everyone who mattered to her. Missy's complicity. How had Tiago managed it all in such a short time? Quinn cradled a sleepy Reina on her shoulder and shook her head.

"Close your eyes."

She complied, the smile in Tiago's voice finding its way onto her face.

The stall door next to the pony's opened. Quinn almost peeked but forced herself to wait. Hoofbeats came towards her, their rhythm oddly familiar. Her heart swelled with possibility she rushed to deny. Genevieve would never——

"Open your eyes, Quinn."

The words were so soft and gentle, they melted her fear. She opened her eyes. The black animal before her gave a soft whicker of recognition, then chuffed into her hair. Delilah's breath of affection brought instant tears. Quinn wrapped an arm around the mare's neck, ignoring the protest from her injured shoulder. "I've missed you so much."

Tiago's hand on her back produced a shiver of delight and his whisper another. "I think she's missed you, too."

Keeping her hand on Delilah's neck, she faced Tiago and found him so near, she forgot to breathe.

He answered her unspoken request. "Apparently, Genevieve doesn't have the touch required to manage this 'dangerous and uncooperative' animal. Her father was more than happy to trade for a gelding who is 'better-trained and more experienced.'"

Quinn rocked back a step. Reina swayed, and she steadied the girl. "You traded Quilombo for Delilah?"

Tiago's arm snagged her waist and eased her toward him until they were as close as possible with the baby between them. His gaze anchored hers, the gold ring sparking in their depths mesmerizing her. "I did this for all of us. You and Delilah need to be together. You're a team that's broken when you're apart. Kind of like how I want us to be."

Her heart stuttered at his words. She wanted that too, but . . . "What about you and Quilombo? You're a team."

"We were, but he's part of my past. Delilah belongs in your present. Quilombo loves rodeo. He hated not working. This is best for him and for you. Haven't you figured out I'd do anything to be your hero?"

She opened her mouth to respond, but his lips touched hers, silencing her. The kiss was too quick, and she chased after him, only to be halted by Reina's warm body. His arm slid upward from her waist, shifting her to his side. His forehead lowered to hers, his breaths quick and uneven. Had she done that? A little thrill coursed through her.

"I spoke to my father."

"Yeah?" She wanted to squeal as his fingers pressed heat into her back, but she forced her attention to his words.

"He agrees I've found my pasión."

"You have?" When he didn't respond, she asked, "What is it?"

"My pair of queens." He chuckled low in his throat, then

cleared it at her raised eyebrow. "You and Reina. And a new business I want to start. One designed to rescue and revitalize failing restaurants and eateries."

Love swelled into her chest, and she didn't stuff it down. "It's perfect!"

"I'd love for you to join me."

A sinking feeling dragged her gaze from his and opened up a pit in her stomach, diluting the thrill of a moment before. Was this the choice Laura had had to make? Her career or her love? Could she make the same choice?

Tiago tipped her chin up to regain connection with her eyes. "But not before and until you're ready. Not ever if you don't want to. You're entitled to your own dreams. I won't steal them from you. Instead, I'll help and support you any way I can."

"Really?"

"Really." Then he kissed her again until raucous clapping roared in the confined space.

Reina squirmed and released a string of nonsense words into the dying applause.

Heat warmed Quinn's ears, but a smile curved her swollen lips when Tiago finally released her. She needed to thank those who'd taken time from their busy lives at a virtual stranger's request.

She found Tiago watching her. "These were my plans. Each of them. How did you know?"

"I didn't--don't--really. I asked Missy to give me the numbers of those who might be part of your future. These were the people she put me in contact with."

Quinn blew out a breath. "Let me take you on a tour of my morning with Reina."

A beaming Rhiann stepped forward to take Delilah's lead and return her to her stall. The girl practically glowed, obviously in favor of Tiago's public display of love. Quinn hoped they'd become friends, smiling her thanks before tugging Tiago forward.

"Meet the two sisters, Doc Liza and Doc Macie." The trio exchanged handshakes and hellos. "They agreed to hold a job for me until I earn my vet tech certification."

She crossed the aisle to stand before MSU's rodeo coach and his assistant. "I think you're familiar with Coach McCloud and Coach Dori?"

Tiago nodded. "I had a long chat with them over a late dinner yesterday." He sobered. "I'm no longer employed as a coach because I'm no longer pursuing a graduate degree from MSU or anywhere. I plan to focus on building a family and a business. I think that's enough for any man, besides my Heavenly relationship, which thanks to you, has vastly improved."

"Tiago, that's fantastic." Why did his announcement fall flat? She should be rejoicing. To cover the awkward moment, she shifted to the coaches. "Apparently I'm taking over some of your former duties. I'll be the . . . How did you put it, Coach McCloud?"

"Meet MSU rodeo's newest scholarship athlete and acclimation point person. Which, once she graduates, could turn into a paid, part-time position."

Dori grinned. "Quinn will be helping our freshmen recruits learn the ropes, ensuring they maintain eligibility by connecting them to the resources they need to succeed and giving them someone to talk to about any difficulties in adjustment they might have."

Tiago pursed his lips. "She's a perfect fit."

Quinn's ears warmed at his approval, but she persisted, nodding at former teammates, before moving back across the aisle to a late arrival. "Mr. Dunn. You had to know about this scheme when I spoke with you just before coming here."

His smile gave him away, wiping years from his weathered face. "I hid it well, don't you agree?"

"Indeed you did." She raised her eyes to Tiago's once more, drawn as always to the dancing gold. "Mr. Dunn has agreed to modify the terms of his employment contract to make it a part-time position. During the rodeo season, his oldest daughter will monitor the mares."

Mr. Dunn scratched his head. "Turns out she was always interested in the foaling side of the business. I never took the time to ask, I guess."

"The Docs say the experience will be good for when I get my vet tech license and can help them in an official capacity. Plus, since I'll be monitoring rather than intervening with the mares, I can bring Reina."

The child roused with a huge yawn and stretch then wiggled to get down. She toddled toward the pony's stall and waved. The way her little fingers opened and closed had Quinn sighing. Her hand closed over her heart to prevent the swell of love from erupting. Prince met the toddler with a snuffle before Tiago scooped her up.

Reina's little nose wrinkled in her attempt to look stern. "Down."

Quinn's laugh was almost a sob. She connected with Missy who looked on from nearby, and then with Tiago as he held the wriggling toddler. "Sometimes I can't believe she's mine. Her cuteness is over-the-top, but I suppose all mothers feel that way." She nearly choked on her own words, her gaze flying to Missy, who winced and joined them.

"When you were little, I was lost in a world of grief--a world I'd locked myself in needlessly." Her look encompassed all three of them. "Don't be like me and run from love. Embrace it, because no matter how hard or winding the path appears, I guarantee taking any other road will only gain you one thing: a lifetime of regret."

Reina extended her arms to Missy. "GeeGee."

Missy arched her brow at Quinn who nodded. Tiago handed her daughter over.

Missy kissed Reina's curls. "She's tired. I'll get her home. You take all the time you need." With another meaning-filled look, she tickled Reina until she giggled then headed toward the parking lot, promising stories and treats.

Tiago seemed subdued after he and Quinn finished thanking everyone who'd gathered for his big surprise. People drifted toward the parking area, chatting in small groups.

She grabbed two brushes and tugged Tiago into Delilah's stall. Something was bothering him now the grand gestures were revealed and his heart had been laid bare. Actually, something was bothering her too, but she couldn't dredge up words to describe what it was.

Delilah met Quinn with a nudge on her pockets. "No Oreos, girl. Next time, I promise."

The horse blew another breath of affection into her hair, the ready acceptance misting Quinn's eyes.

Through the open windows a warm breeze wafted, stirring the leaves in a clump of nearby trees. Birds chirped. The straw rustled as Tiago stepped up behind her. Handed her a cookie.

She met his gaze over her shoulder, read the resignation on his face. Delilah snatched the Oreo and crunched, leaving Quinn to face the man she loved.

With her right hand, she traced the worry lines radiating from the corners of his devastating brown eyes. "Talk to me."

He caressed her cheek, then lowered his hand. "I'm impressed at how well you've organized your future, Quinn, but I don't see where I fit into it."

"Oh, Tiago. I was caught between hoping"--she raised the beautiful charm bracelet--"and fear. Too afraid of getting hurt to include you in case you didn't come. But you did. Not only that, you brought my daughter--a child you'd barely met--a pony. Nothing could have shown me your heart more clearly. Your willingness to accept her, even factor her into your bid for . . ."

She patted the black horse who was searching for more sweets. "Even without Delilah, I'd have known the depths of . . ."

She huffed and dropped her hand. "Seems I can't finish a sentence."

"Quinn." Tiago pulled her against him. "I love you. I've learned people let us down, but God never will. He was always there, reaching out, even when I'd failed Him, but I was too afraid to take His hand. You showed me the truth, and as long as I'm able, I'll seek to be what you need. If you need me to return to rodeo for a season, I will. My plans can wait. I'll be wherever you are, holding your hand through whatever trouble comes. I want to walk into the future with you."

Quinn closed her eyes and pressed her cheek to Tiago's strong chest. Inhaled his spice and the horsey scent that clung to his clothing. Relished the feel of his strong arms around her. What must those words have cost him? She wanted nothing more than to sink into him and offer her lips and heart, but she couldn't. Not yet.

She flattened her hands on his chest and pushed, needing space for her brain to function. When he loosened his hold, the hurt in his eyes stabbed her heart. She willed him to understand. "I showed you all my plans because I wanted you to know I could stand on my own. I don't need you to make my way in the world."

Beneath her hand, his muscles tensed. "But don't you see, Tiago? I don't want to make my own way. I want to make it with you. I don't know what that looks like or how the pieces will fit, but I guarantee God does. Only He can join our separate paths into one."

Tiago cradled her face in his hands. His eyes bored into hers as if drilling down to read her heart or her soul. She relinquished all control of her emotions, letting them flow upward into her eyes. All her love and the respect she harbored for this man, her hope and her fears. She let them all go because she didn't need to hide anymore.

The Bobbys of the world couldn't control her. The bad men couldn't harm her. "I love you, Santiago Vargas. I'm with you for the long haul, no matter what comes, as long as you'll have me and Reina. I trust God to reveal what that will look like as we go."

"Quinn Mulroney, you've stolen every word I wanted to say." His low, husky laugh made her insides ache and her body yearn to press closer. "I guess my actions will have to speak for me."

His lips came down to meet hers with a gentleness that seared her core. Her body responded with a will of its own. Her injured arm encircled his waist while her good arm stretched upward, fingers twining in the silky strands of his hair. When he deepened the kiss, she opened to him, a tiny moan escaping. Pleasure tingled everywhere his hands explored--her waist and back, upward to stroke her hair, cupping the back of her head. She never wanted him to let her go.

When at last they separated, she felt as though she'd completed one of Coach's workouts. Her breaths came in short gasps, and her side ached from lack of oxygen. But her heart was full, and she felt cherished--alive. Her fears melted away.

"I was afraid you'd equate my touch with the man who used you." Tiago whispered his confession into her neck.

"Never. Heroes protect those they love. And you'll always be my hero."

"Was it him?"

She nodded, her cheek on his hair.

Tiago created some space between them, so they could see each other. "Are you hungry? I haven't had any food since . . ." He shrugged. "Time was tight once I arrived, and I wasn't thinking about my stomach.

"Oh? What were you thinking of?"

"My two queens. Both noble and each possessing my heart." He picked her up and twirled her around, returning her to the ground breathless. Again.

Delilah pranced in the corner.

"Sorry." They both apologized at once and laughed. Quinn stepped out of his arms long enough to soothe the mare, then met him outside the stall.

"I'm starving." She patted her stomach. "Let's go to Kelsey's"

"Where it all began?"

She flipped her hair behind her shoulder and sent him a saucy look. "It did not all begin at Kelsey's. It began four years ago across the arena fence in Casper, Wyoming with a single meeting of our eyes. I had a feeling about you, even then. Hero material. Turns out I was right."

Tiago laughed and caught her hand, spinning her against him and waggling his eyebrows. "I knew you were a true Queen, strong and compassionate, not the 'off with her head,' type the media portrayed you to be. I coveted that knowledge because you let me in when you kept everyone else out."

"Queen began as Cal's nickname for me. He yelled it at every rodeo. I hated what it came to represent, but I couldn't seem to buck the image. One day, I sort of became her, and deep down I resented that shift, knew I was hiding, taking the easier road. When Cal died and I was so broken up, I blamed the attack on Queen."

"Yet, you named your daughter the Spanish translation."

Quinn nodded, pressing close to hear his heartbeat.

"Queen and Quinn are not separate entities. They are both you. You're not an imposter, nor do your mistakes make you less than. They make you human."

Tiago's voice rumbled into what was left of the wall she'd created, breaking it down to mere rubble. Love roared to life like a flame, warming her all over.

She nodded, still clinging to Tiago's strength. When their gazes connected once more, his flared gold. "I've accepted that I'm not one or the other, but a mixture of both, like a child is a mixture of both parents. That mixture can be trained and shaped to look like the child God envisioned when he molded it in the mother's womb. No mistakes."

Tiago smiled and brushed his lips against hers, then sobered. "Are you worried about the third attacker, the one they haven't caught?"

"Not really. The one that . . ."--heat tingled the tips of her ears--"*contributed* to Reina called the shots. The other won't be dangerous without him, and the police had leads. I'm confident they'll catch him soon."

He tightened his hold and whispered against her lips. "I'll keep my queens safe."

"I'm counting on that, Tiger." The exquisite pleasure coursing through her as his mouth claimed hers was enough to transform her into the queen he proclaimed her to be--to make her believe in miracles. After all, love was the biggest miracle of all.

A final realization clicked as her body heated under Tiago's kiss. Tigers might be protective, but they weren't entirely safe. She looked forward to discovering how dangerous hers could be and opened her heart to the love flowing through her.

A vague melody sang inside her head. Perhaps Heaven rejoiced as two of God's children found their way to each other through Him.

ABOUT THE AUTHOR

Rebecca Reed loves adventure. Writing romantic tales filled with discovery, hope, and horses springs from a lifetime of similar journeys and fulfills a lifelong calling as a storyteller. From riding race horses to welding to teaching Spanish to traveling, she sees obstacles as challenges.

A lover of Jesus, animals, music, and nature, you might find her listening to audiobooks on her rural Indiana farm. As a wife, mother, and grandmother, she's learned to embrace joy where she can find it--in life's unexpected moments and inside a good story.

Find out more and connect with Rebecca on her website and social media. Use the QR code to subscribe to her newsletter.

Author Website: https://rebeccareedwrites.com

Do you like bookish podcasts and videos? Check out Rebecca and Rebecca on Spotify and YouTube. I co-host with the amazing Rebecca Yauger, and we review books in a plethora of genres and chat with their authors.

If you enjoyed this story, consider posting a review to help other readers find fun, uplifting novels. Thank you for reading! I'd love to connect with you because you, reader friends, bring my words to life with your imaginations. You make them more than simply a collection of words. In your hands, they gain substance and fulfill their purpose.

¡Que te vaya con Dios!

amazon.com/author/rebeccareed

instagram.com/rebeccareedwrites

bookbub.com/profile/rebecca-reed

youtube.com/@RebeccaandRebecca

facebook.com/RebeccaReedWrites

PREVIEW OF BOOK 2

Ready for another college rodeo adventure?

Winning the Twin's Heart, Book 2 in the *Love Overshadows* series, will be available in early 2025!

When contentment brings disaster and legacy trumps desire, can two people from different worlds hope to build a future together?

College rodeo roper Yoani Alliegro can't stop looking over her shoulder despite, or maybe because of, her recent success. She longs for family––the one she lost, and the one she hopes to have.

When rejection shatters Yoani's sense of belonging and sends her running in search of truth, will it lead to the family she's dreamed of and freedom from her past, or will she discover she's left all that behind in Montana?

Bull rider Chantz Nannenga is caught between following his dream of teaching and upholding tradition by managing the family ranch. Should he settle for less than his dream when conquering his regrets could prevent him from winning Yoani's heart?

A closed-door, friends-to-more, contemporary rodeo romance that takes you from Montana to Miami on a journey of discovery and faith and leaves you filled with hope and happily-ever-after.

Continue reading for a preview of Chapter 1.

CHAPTER 1 - WINNING THE TWIN'S HEART

Waiting twisted coiled knots in Yoani's stomach. Anchoring her gloved fingers in Bonita Flor's mane, she tried to ignore everything but her horse's solid body beneath her.

She flinched as the announcer's tinny voice blared from the speakers at Rodeo Grounds Arena. "It's time for the team roping short-go here at the Trapper Stampede. Let's give a big Wyoming welcome to our first pair: header Bonnie Yelnick from the University of Montana, and heeler Allen Conroy from Montana State Northern.

Yoani glanced at her partner Quinn sitting statue still aboard a bit-chomping Delilah and empathized with the mare's nervous habit that flecked her black muzzle and chest with foam. "I'll never survive eight pairs either, girl." Her pat on the damp neck left a white handprint.

Quinn caught Yoani's eye, smiled, and winked.

She tried to smile back but couldn't force her taut lips to move.

The crowd clapped. Too politely for the performance to

have been more than adequate. The heeler exited the arena with hunched shoulders.

Breathe, Quinn mouthed.

Breathe. Right. Yoani pushed air out her mouth, then pulled it slowly through her nose. The crowd reacted to each new pair of riders with varying degrees of enthusiasm.

"And now, from Montana State University, header Yoani Alliegro and heeler Quinn Mulroney." The announcer's voice ignited the crowd's anticipation listing their previous times. He'd made her name two syllables instead of using the Spanish "ah" sound in the middle and completely butchered her last name, but the wrenching in her gut didn't let her care.

Why had Quinn insisted on working with her when she could have had her pick of headers? What if she missed the catch? Let everyone down?

Moisture pooled inside the thin leather of Yoani's glove. She stood in the saddle to stretch tense leg muscles. Wiggled her toes in her black boots. Her heart pounded harder, trying to move nonexistent oxygen to her limbs. Sounds came from far away. Her vision fuzzed.

Pressure on her calf, just above her boot, brought her panicked gaze to bear on a huge cowboy wearing a blue and gold vest. His navy blue, long-sleeved button down bore the words Montana State Rodeo and the bobcat symbol on the left shoulder, same as hers. He looked up at her with eyes so clear and blue, they stilled her instinct to kick out and gallop away.

Her heart pounded for something other than the threat of his proximity.

"Hey." His rich baritone melted her fear like chocolate in the sun. The pressure on her calf increased, then disappeared. "It's no different than any practice. You've got great instincts and your mare reads cues like none I've ever seen.

Don't let the crowd or the competition get in your way. Do what you know. Ignore everything else."

The words sank in, soothing as they went. She blinked, unsure what to say.

The cowboy flashed a brilliant smile then backed away.

She drew her first deep breath and glanced over to find Quinn studying her. Yoani sent a tight-lipped smile and urged Bonita into the arena, rolling her hips deeper into the saddle until the bay mare backed tight into the timing box's padded corner.

Yoani shook out her loop with a trembling hand, then tucked it under her right arm. The lariat lay coiled alongside her reins opposite. She waited, legs gripping her horse's sides, feet planted firmly in the stirrups, eyes and ears alert.

The chute opened. The calf ran out, Bonita leaping after him, hitting the barrier as the steer pulled it free. Yoani's heart sped up to synch with the pounding of her mare's hooves as they shadowed the racing animal. The loop circled her head, the ridges familiar in her gloved fingers. She breathed deep as Quinn had taught her, dismissing her nerves. Centering her focus. Sent the loop flying toward the target. Four heartbeats later it settled over the horns. She dallied the rope and sat tall, knees cueing her horse to pivot and tighten the slack so Quinn could snag the animal's back legs and turn Delilah to stop the timer.

For a long second, the steer hung suspended between the two ropes balancing on his front hooves. Then Quinn urged her black mare forward until the cow kicked loose. With a flip of her rope, Yoani sent the animal jogging unharmed toward the stock pens at the far end of the arena. She followed it in. The crowd's cheer became a roar, the chant "MSU" echoing off the walls.

The announcer's voice cut through the din. "And that's how it's done, folks."

The sound enveloped her with the acceptance and adoration of a group hug, curving her lips upward. She accepted her rope with a nod of thanks. Their time brought more applause. Their fastest yet with one team still to compete. Accomplishment spawned a tightening band of conflicting emotions.

After a moment they eased, and she expelled a long breath. The pressure hadn't cooked her. She'd survived. Quinn nudged Delilah close. Yoani slapped her raised palm with a satisfying *crack*. Maybe she'd even done well.

"Whoo hoo!" Quinn's skin, only a shade lighter than Yoani's island hue, sported a pink tinge. "Thanks for the prime target."

"Just doing my job." Yoani ran a thumb over the worn stitching on her saddle and swallowed another wave of emotion. Quinn's praise soothed a raw place from years of Abuela's silence and gruff instructions followed by over-crowded foster homes too chaotic to allow the acknowledgement of individual achievements. Not that Yoani had done anything praiseworthy. She'd been too busy keeping her twin and herself alive and out of trouble.

They dismounted and Quinn gripped Yoani's hand while the final team took their run. When the header's loop landed short, Quinn whooped and pulled her into a tight hug. At her lack of response, Quinn pulled back and squinted at her. "Come on, chica! Celebrate!"

She choked out a laugh, then latched on as Quinn hopped up and down, turning them in circles. This must be what having a friend was like.

Quinn's boyfriend Tiago jogged toward them with her daughter Reina perched on his shoulders. The little girl was decked out in blue and gold, her springy curls bouncing in adorable short pigtails tied with ribbon. She waved her stuffed horse who sported a Bobcat logo around its middle. A wave of joy rippled through Yoani at the child's giggles. If only she could fill her arms with laughing children one day. But first, she had to be clear of the Maloperros because she'd never intentionally put innocent children in their crosshairs or force a child to grow up without their parents as she and her twin had done.

An hour later curls of excitement unfurled in Yoani's stomach as she fell into step with the rest of her Bobcat Rodeo teammates. They followed Coaches Chet McCloud and Dori Walstra outside the arena, away from the tromping feet of the dispersing crowd. The team jostled each other, high fiving, fist bumping, backslapping. Flashing toothy smiles all around.

Except for Yoani's twin, Lalo. He'd missed a leg in the tie down competition and finished last in the short go, a decent showing, but out of the points. He shuffled along, head down, hands in his pockets, occasionally sending a dirt clod zinging away from the force of his boot.

Couldn't he at least acknowledge her win? The flash of annoyance tugged at Yoani's conscience. Apparently, his ultra-competitive nature couldn't see past his own mistakes. None of this surprised her. She'd just hoped he'd mature from the times she'd had to head off multiple near suspensions for his unsportsmanlike behavior during their high school rodeo competitions.

The group fanned out in several arcs around the coaches, wedging Yoani between two cowboys. One was the huge, blonde man who'd spoken to her before she entered the arena. He shifted, inviting her to step in front of him so she could see. Though relatively tall for a woman, these over-sized men dwarfed her. She sent him a tentative smile, and he beamed back, warming her under his perusal.

Coach cleared his throat, providing a welcome distraction.

"Congratulations, Bobcats!" Coach McCloud turned until he'd met every eye.

Another tingle of acceptance wound through Yoani before she doused the spark. She couldn't deal with upheaval right now, so best to tamp down her feelings of belonging and comfort before they brought disaster upon her. As Coach continued to speak, her attempts grew feebler until they fizzled out altogether.

"You've done something this weekend no Bobcat team has done in more than a decade. We've won plenty of rodeos. Garnered attention and awards. But this year is our year to win a double championship. Top the standings in the men's and women's divisions in the Big Sky Conference *and* at the CNFR. That's our goal and we've set the bar with our performances tonight and over the past days." He paused, connecting once more with everyone in the circle.

"Accomplishing this feat requires an extreme extended effort from each member of this team. It'll take dedication and practice, encouragement and learning from our mistakes. We'll need to grow as athletes, students, and people. Each individual is vital to the success of our team as a whole." He looked to Dori who took up the speech.

"That means supporting each other during practice and preparation for events, while studying for academic success, in personal behavior and integrity. Are we prepared to meet these challenges?"

A few called, "yes" and "we're ready."

Coach Dori frowned. "Is that all you've got? Can we meet these challenges? What say you, Bobcats?"

A collective roar shook the walls of the alcove and vibrated Yoani's eardrums. She joined in, a bit late, but with more enthusiasm than she'd shown since she was eight. The cry released something inside Yoani that had been locked away when Abuela had whisked Lalo and her off into the night from their Miami home.

The coaches joined the ranks and gripped hands, instigating a chain reaction around the circle. Yoani found her hands entwined with the lightning-smiled cowboy and a beautiful blonde barrel racer whose name she couldn't remember. As one, they raised their joined hands overhead and chanted "MSU".

When the chant died down, hugs and high fives made it impossible to spot Lalo. Maybe in addition to working hard to be the best header for Quinn, she could encourage her brother--another way to help the team.

Her heart tripped, temporarily caught in the euphoria, but with each beat, returning to reality and the certainty that calamity would soon upend her world. She hoped this time it wouldn't involve changing cities or names.

U

Chantz caught sight of Abelardo, the promising tie down recruit, slipping away from his chanting teammates. Maybe he could focus his mentoring on that particular freshman. Based on his sour face and the string of equally sour words leaving his mouth after today's short-go mistake, he might need some encouragement.

His attention shifted when the dark-haired roper pulled her hand free and sidled away from the knot of celebrating Bobcats, expression tight. Much harder to read than her twin, she was an intriguing enigma.

Chantz pushed off the wall still thinking about Yoani. He'd crossed to her out of instinct earlier when he'd recognized the grip of fear in her rigid muscles and pulsing throat. He'd been a senior teammate ready to share his experience, but mostly, the memory forever twisted around his motivation had sent him to her.

If he helped her succeed, did that lessen his failure?

Shaking away his morose thoughts, he prepared to return to his hotel room. One nice thing about being a bull rider––no horse to care for. He'd taken three steps when someone called his name. He pivoted to find Quinn hurrying toward him. Her boyfriend Tiago followed, toting Quinn's almost-three-year-old daughter on his shoulders, her favorite perch it seemed.

"Leaving the party so soon?" A smirk set the ebony-haired beauty's eyes dancing.

Not that she and Chantz had ever been anything but friends, but it was hard not to notice the inner light she'd regained since meeting Tiago and returning to the rodeo team. Chantz had heard the story of her assault and resulting pregnancy that had caused her to quit the team for two years until Tiago came looking for her. Their story was a modern-day fairytale.

He enjoyed this version of Quinn, raising a hand to shade his eyes and searching all around. "There's a party? All I see are some wound up Bobcats in what amounts to a back alley."

Quinn swatted his arm. Leaning into Tiago's side, she took Reina's hand. "See what I have to put up with, Tiger? My job is as tough as yours, so don't come home complaining about how easy I've had it."

Tiago––Tiger, Chantz bit back a retort about nicknames––produced a lazy smile. "I'll try to remember that." He tilted his head toward the girl above him. "Reina. Can you help me remember that Mommy's job is as hard as mine?"

The girl shook her adorable curls and laughed. "You're silly, Daddy!"

The title punched Chantz in the stomach. Reina returned his wave, then turned her attention to clapping as a pair of cowboys began a popular line dance.

"She's a smart one," Tiago said, then winked at Quinn, who blushed. "Takes after her mother."

Quinn wrapped an arm around his middle and gave a squeeze.

Chantz surveyed the remaining team members to give them a moment of semi-privacy. Both coaches had gone, leaving Blayden, Genevieve, and their crowd. Mostly the ones he tried to avoid so he wasn't goaded into being rude.

"Sorry!" Quinn smoothed hair off her face. "Could we talk? Maybe somewhere less public?"

"I've got some water and soda in my room. Are you going back to the hotel now?"

"After I check on Delilah."

"Great. I'll tag along if you don't mind, then we can go together."

They walked the five minutes to the stock barns and entered the dimly lit stall area. Reina chattered to herself while Tiago kept his arm firmly around Quinn's shoulders. They reminded Chantz of his parents. Even after nearly twenty-five years of marriage, they held hands and exchanged soft looks like the glances Tiago and Quinn shared.

Would he ever find a woman who looked at him with love? The only woman he'd dated seriously had been biding her time. If only he'd listened to his parents when they warned him about her? One more entry in his long list of failures.

Movement ahead caught Chantz's eye. Wearing the narrow-brimmed, low-profile, felt hat she preferred, Yoani emerged from a stall. Her dark hair had escaped the braid and hung loose around her shoulders. The style softened her profile. Made her seem more approachable.

"Hey, Yoani," Quinn called.

The cowgirl's head snapped up, and she retreated a step. Chantz frowned at the incongruity of her action, recognized the disaster looming. Lunging forward, he stretched toward her and caught her flailing arm before she fell into the muck tub she'd knocked from its place. Another reflex deflected the handle of the muck rake aiming for her head. Combined, the actions unbalanced him. His forward center of mass tangled with her momentum, pulling him after her.

At the last second, he twisted his pelvis to put himself on the bottom, his hip taking the initial jolt. Yoani's elbow shoved the air from his lungs and her body pinned him to the dirt, chest to chest. His Stetson popped off and spun once before settling onto his face.

Chantz lay in the relative darkness, mentally inventorying his limbs. Nothing seemed broken. Only when someone plucked the cowboy hat from his face, did he consider the inappropriateness of their position. He opened his eyes to find hers inches away. Deep, dark pools of shock, caution, and--was that fear?

A heady awareness of her curves, the ease of bearing her weight, of her long legs tangled with his, sent mixed signals to his addled brain. Toss her off or tighten his grip and linger. When her fruity scent mixed with the tang of horse and sweat invaded his nostrils, another thought sent his eyes searching for her lips.

The last time he'd kissed a woman, she'd been using him, and he'd encouraged her--even after he'd glimpsed her play-acting. A wave of self-disgust rolled over him. He couldn't trust himself to fall for anyone again. At least until he'd discovered who he wanted to be because until that point, how would he know if she loved him for himself?

He forced his lips to curve in a half grin. "How was it you didn't see us coming. Any other time you'd be scanning the shadows as if ninjas were about to invade our corner of Montana."

Pure terror lit her irises before they sparked with indignation and hurt. Without a word, she scrambled off him, yanking her arm from his grip.

What had that been about? He'd been riffing off a game he and his brothers used to play when they were kids—Cowboys and Ninjas. If he remembered correctly, his sister Paisley had always begged to be a Cowboy, but they'd always made her be a Ninja. Why had they done that?

A hand appeared before his face and he let Tiago help him up.

"That was some move you made there, twisting around like that." Tiago sounded impressed.

Chantz bent over and snagged his Stetson, slapped it against his leg to remove most of the dirt, then jammed it on his head. "Comes from rolling and twisting with the bulls. All in the hips." He sneaked a glance to where Quinn held Reina in one arm and a distraught and babbling Yoani in the other.

A strange yearning to be the one holding Yoani cinched his gut. His fingers twitched.

Tiago followed his sight line and cleared his throat to regain Chantz's attention. "Maybe we'd better post pone that talk until tomorrow."

"Yeah." He looked back once more. Hesitated. "You'll see the ladies to the hotel?"

"Trust me. I'll keep them safe." He cocked his head. "You okay?"

Touching his finger to the brim of his hat, Chantz downplayed the incident's impact, though his pulse and throbbing hip testified otherwise. "Yup. Goodnight."

Tiago gave a single nod, then moved closer to the women.

As Chantz walked away, an itching began inside his chest, and he wasn't sure he wanted to know what caused it. Best forget tonight ever happened. He had enough decisions to make without another distraction.